WHISPERS FROM THE WILL

The Mistwood Mysteries

Book 1

TINA VAN HOVEN

Cover by Elizabeth Mackey

Edited by Proof Perfect Editing

Formatting by Kalie Gerwig : Good Girl Author Services

ISBN: 978-1-951534-38-7

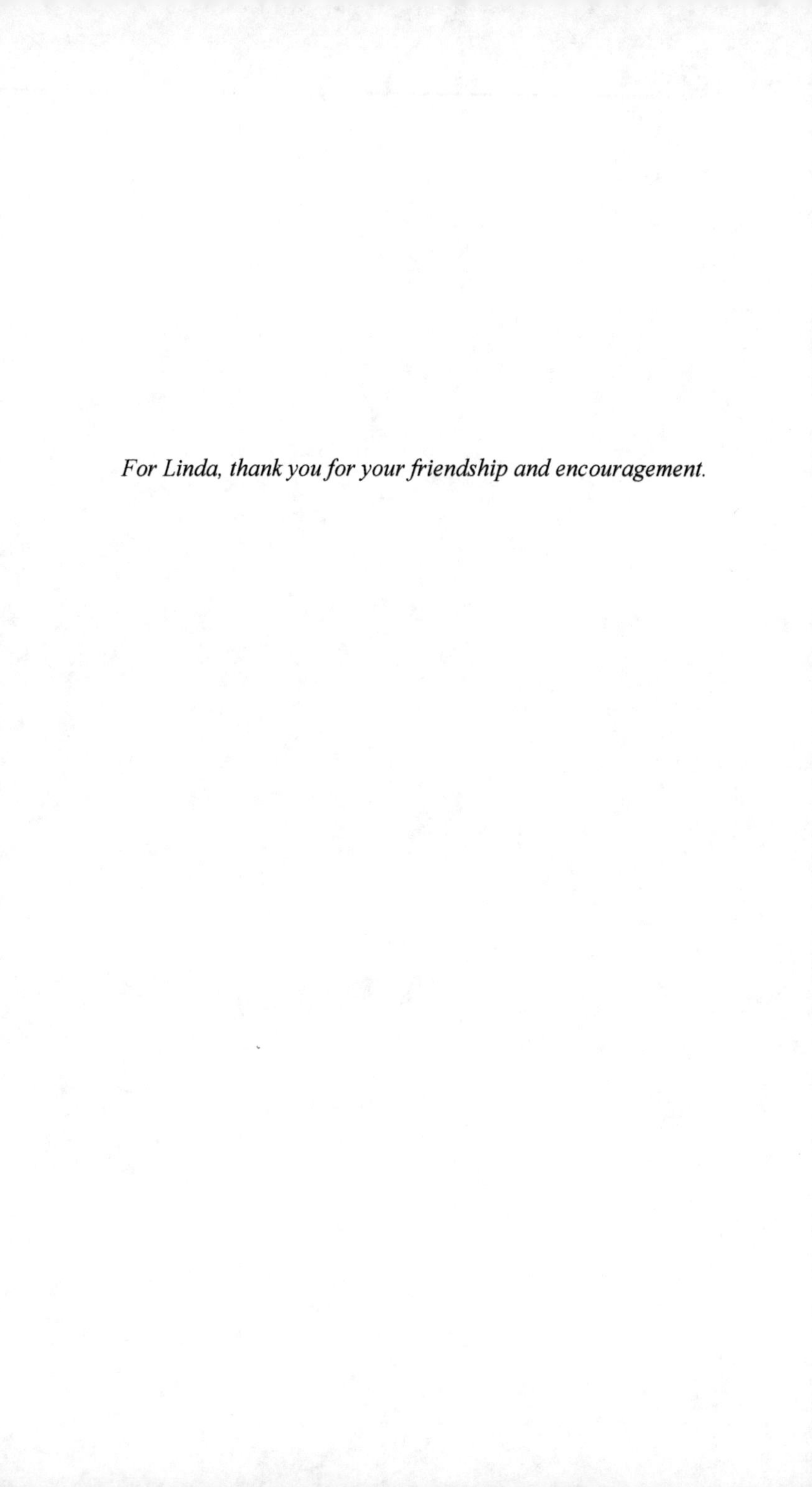

For Linda, thank you for your friendship and encouragement.

Contents

CHAPTER ONE

It Must Be Tuesday

Olivia March knew two things before she even turned off the ignition and stared at her family's ancestral home. First, she hadn't been back here for over twenty years. Second, her life was about to change.

March House stood on Main Street like a Victorian grande dame who had seen better decades and resented being reminded of it. Turrets rose against the slate-gray sky, all sharp angles and stained glass glinting with the last of the afternoon light. The porch wrapped around the north side, its white balustrades flaking like old lace. On the south side, a solarium curved outward in a wall of aging glass panes that reflected Mistwood Lake beyond, steel-blue, calm, and deceptively peaceful. The house seemed to still be the same, but it really wasn't. Aunt Izzy was gone.

Olivia rested her forehead against the steering wheel of her rented Subaru and exhaled slowly through her nose, the way her therapist had taught her after her third panic attack in the pastry kitchen at LeClair. In for four. Hold for four. Out for six.

Chicago felt like a different planet now. Michelin stars. Stainless steel counters. A head chef who smiled for critics and stole her work like it was mise en place. She'd left with one duffel bag, a box of knives, and the echo of her aunt's voice on the phone three weeks earlier.

You should come home, Livvy. Just for a bit.

Then Izzy had died. Not peacefully. Not neatly. Just suddenly. Found at the bottom of the main stairs by one of the high school girls who cleaned rooms on weekends. The coroner said it was an accident. The sheriff said it was unfortunate. The town said nothing at all, which Olivia had learned was far more suspicious.

She tucked her cell phone into the pocket of her sweater and left the rest of her possessions in the car before pushing the door open and stepping onto the gravel drive.

Mistwood smelled of pine, cold water, and wood smoke. A raven squawked from one of the pine trees on the property. The air had a bite to it, sharp enough to wake her up after the long drive from the Spokane airport.

The front door of March House opened before she reached it.

"Well, about time," said a woman with wild gray hair and an apron dusted in flour. "I was starting to think you'd taken a wrong turn and ended up in Montana."

Olivia blinked. "Lark?"

Lark Waverly beamed. "In the flesh, darling. And mostly caffeinated." She crossed the porch in two long strides and pulled Olivia into a hug that smelled like rosemary, lemon oil, and something vaguely herbal that might have been sage, or might have been weed. Olivia stiffened out of reflex, then melted into it before she could stop herself.

"I'm so sorry," Olivia said, her voice catching. "I should've come sooner. I just ... everything happened so fast."

Lark pulled back and cupped her face with flour-dusted hands. "No apologies. Izzy always said you'd arrive when you were meant to." She tilted her head, studying Olivia with unnerving clarity. "Though I will say, the house has been ... restless."

A familiar prickle crawled down Olivia's spine. "That's not ominous at all," she said lightly.

Lark grinned. "Oh, sweetheart. You have no idea."

Olivia stepped over the threshold. March House was exactly as she remembered and felt entirely wrong.

The parquet floors gleamed, but the air felt thick, charged. The setting sunlight slanted through stained-glass, scattering jewel tones across the foyer walls. The grand staircase curved upward, its banister smooth from generations of hands.

And someone cleared his throat behind her. "Must you let in drafts, Madam Waverly? The lady has only just arrived."

Olivia closed her eyes.

No.

Nope.

Absolutely not today. She turned slowly.

A tall man stood at the base of the stairs, dressed in late-Georgian attire: tailcoat, waistcoat, immaculate cravat. The top of a silver pocket watch glinted from his waistcoat pocket, its chain arching elegantly across his vest. He was a little overweight, dignified, and looking at her with mild disapproval. At his feet sat a whippet. The dog wagged its tail.

Olivia screamed.

It wasn't a delicate scream. It wasn't cinematic. It was a full-throated, pastry-chef-who-has-seen-some-things scream that echoed off the high ceilings and sent a flock of birds exploding from the trees outside.

The man winced. The dog barked.

Lark didn't flinch. "Oh, good," she said. "They finally stopped hiding."

Olivia's knees gave out. She grabbed the edge of the console table, breathing hard. "No," she said. "Nope. I quit. I'm leaving. I don't care what the will says. This house is haunted, and I am done with seeing dead people."

"Technically," the man said, peering at her, "we are seeing you."

"That is not helping," Olivia snapped.

The dog trotted forward, tail wagging enthusiastically. It sniffed her shoe and sneezed.

"Oh, for heaven's sake," Olivia muttered. "I'm seeing dead dogs now."

"Sir Alistair Pruitt," the man said, inclining his head. "Late of Bath. Deceased 1802. This is Bertrum. We usually call him Bertie. He's very excitable."

Bertie sat and looked pleased with himself.

Olivia turned to Lark. "You can see him too, right? Please tell me you can see him."

Lark shook her head. "Nope. But the temperature dropped three degrees, the floorboards are humming, and Snowball just puffed her tail like a bottlebrush. That usually means company."

As if summoned, a white cat padded into the foyer. She wore a collar with a tarnished Union service medal that swayed as she moved. Her blue eyes flicked past Olivia to the staircase and narrowed.

A young man in a faded Union uniform from the Civil War leaned against the banister, arms crossed. He tipped his head politely.

"Ma'am," he said. "Simon Talbot. Union Army. Died 1864."

Olivia laughed. It came out brittle and wrong. She stepped back until she was up against the wall.

"Seven," she whispered. "Izzy said there were seven. I thought they'd leave when she died."

"Eight, if you count Bertie properly," Sir Alistair said.

"Do not," Olivia said, pointing at him, "add a bonus ghost dog."

Bertie wagged harder.

The foyer filled slowly with figures. Some solid, some shimmering at the edges. A woman in a beaded flapper dress examined her lipstick in the reflection of a mirror that no longer reflected her. A stocky man in overalls leaned against a radiator that hissed approvingly. A young woman in a lace nightgown hovered near the stairs, smelling faintly of rosewater. A black man dressed in 1930's style brown slacks, a white shirt with suspenders, wearing a fedora and holding an old cornet, leaned in a doorway, light catching him like stage haze. An Asian woman with soil-smudged cheeks kneeled near a potted fern in the hallway, touching its leaves with reverence.

Olivia slid down the wall and sat on the floor. "Okay," she said faintly. "So I'm not cured."

Sir Alistair smiled gently. "Afraid not."

Lark came back into the room. She crouched beside Olivia, pressing a warm mug into her hands. "Tea," she said. "For grounding."

Olivia stared into the steam. "Izzy promised it would stop."

Lark's expression softened. "Izzy promised a lot of things."

"How did they all get here? I mean, these people never lived in this house, and surely they didn't die here?" Olivia took a tentative sip from the mug.

"Your aunt brought them here. You know how she loved antiques. Well, occasionally, when she went to estate sales or different antique stores, she'd run into an item that had a spirit attached to it. She didn't like the idea that they'd be stuck there alone. So she would buy the item and bring it home. Remember, Izzy didn't see this ability as a curse. She thought it a blessing." Lark stood up and walked back to the kitchen.

Olivia sat on the floor, looking at all the people staring back at her. "I don't know if I can do this."

The word *will* echoed, uninvited.

That night, after the ghosts retreated … well … most of them, anyway. Olivia lay awake in her childhood room, staring at the ceiling roses. She thought about the way Izzy's voice had sounded on that last call.

Urgent.

Almost afraid.

And about the whispers she'd heard while unpacking. Not voices. Not words.

Just … the sense of something unfinished.

Somewhere in the house, a cornet was playing "Sweet Georgia Brown."

Olivia closed her eyes. "It must be Tuesday," she muttered.

And March House listened.

CHAPTER TWO

What Really Happened on the Stairs

Morning arrived at March House the way guilt always did. Slowly. Relentlessly. And with a lot more light than Olivia was emotionally prepared to deal with.

The first thing she noticed when she woke was the quiet. Not the peaceful kind. The kind that settled over a place when it had learned how to hold its breath.

She lay still beneath unfamiliar sheets, staring at a ceiling trimmed with ornate plasterwork that belonged in a museum, not above her head. Pale morning light filtered through lace curtains, striping the walls in soft gold. The bed was comfortable in an old-fashioned, too-firm way, as if it had opinions about posture.

March House, she reminded herself. Aunt Izzy's house. Her house. The thought rested heavily on her chest.

Olivia swung her legs out of bed, toes brushing a braided rug that smelled faintly of lemon oil and something herbal—rosemary, maybe. The room creaked as she stood, not with complaint, but acknowledgment. The sound followed her as she crossed to the tall window overlooking Mistwood Lake.

Outside, mist hovered just above the water's surface and curled around the gazebo near the edge of the garden. The lake was perfectly still, reflecting the pale sky like glass. Somewhere in the distance, a loon called—lonely, haunting, beautiful.

She exhaled slowly.

Chicago felt like another life. Stainless steel counters. The bark of orders. The relentless heat and noise. The head chef's voice still lived in her bones, sharp as a blade: *Move faster, March. Do you want a star or a participation ribbon?*

Here, the loudest sound was the ticking of an old clock somewhere down the hall.

Olivia dressed quickly. Jeans, boots, a sweater she'd shoved into her duffel at the last minute, and headed for the door.

Sunlight leaked through the stained glass along the stairwell, breaking into fractured colors that drifted across the foyer like lazy ghosts of rainbows past. Dust motes floated in the beams, swirling gently.

"That," Lark announced from the doorway to the kitchen area with deep satisfaction, "is ancestral energy."

"That," Olivia lifted one eyebrow, "is dust."

Lark waved a hand as if brushing away negativity. Or possibly logic. "Same thing, different marketing."

Olivia followed Lark and sat at the long dining table. The older woman set a steaming, chipped mug of tea in front of her. The mug read *Good Vibes Only*, which felt like an act of aggression. The tea inside tasted like chamomile mixed with regret and maybe a hint of bark.

"What is in this?" Olivia asked.

"Grief and grounding tea."

"That is not a flavor profile."

"It is if you've lived long enough."

Olivia took another sip anyway because she was exhausted, jet-lagged, haunted, and her aunt was dead. Standards had slipped.

Lark settled across from her, folding herself into a chair like someone preparing to tell a story she had already told several times, but never to the right person. "All right." She pulled back a strand of gray hair and tucked it under a pin. "This is the official version."

Olivia lifted her eyes. "I'm listening."

"According to the town," Lark continued, "your Aunt Izzy was locking up for the night. Came down the main staircase. Slipped. Fell and broke her neck."

Olivia waited.

"And according to Sheriff Clay," Lark added, lowering her voice into a parody of authority and making air quotes, "Victorian staircases are tricky. Happens all the time."

Olivia snorted. "Did he actually say that?"

"He did. While checking his watch."

"Of course he was."

"Closed the case in under an hour," Lark said. "Said there was no sign of foul play, and he was already late for the Lions Club breakfast, and they were serving his favorite pancakes. Blueberry, I believe."

Olivia stared into her mug. Aunt Izzy had lived in this house for over sixty years. She had glided down those stairs in silk robes, wool socks, bare feet, carrying laundry baskets, stacks of books, and once a live turkey she refused to explain. She had never fallen.

"Izzy did not rush," Olivia murmured.

"No," Lark agreed. "She did not."

Olivia pushed back her chair and stood. Her legs felt steady now. Or at least steadier than they had twelve hours ago when a Georgian gentleman, his ghost dog, and the other unexpected residents had disturbed her return home.

She crossed the foyer to the base of the staircase.

The stairs were steep. Ornate. Polished to a sheen that caught the morning light and reflected it upward like a warning. The banister curved elegantly, dark mahogany worn smooth by generations of hands. Each step was shallow and narrow, built for decorum, not haste.

"This isn't a staircase you hurry down," Olivia observed. She placed a hand on the banister and looked up.

The ghosts were already there. They had gathered along the upstairs landing as if drawn by gravity, memory, or unfinished business. They watched her in silence, seven pairs of eyes trained downward. Well, eight if you count Bertie, who was lying on the floor and staring through the railings.

Something cold slid into Olivia's chest.

"All right," she said, swallowing. "You might as well say it."

Walt was the first to break formation. He hovered near the top step, wrench clutched in his hand like an accusation. "These stairs don't just throw people," he muttered. "Someone messed with something."

"That's comforting," Olivia said weakly.

Flossie appeared beside him, clutching her pearl-handled comb to her chest. Her voice was barely a whisper. "I heard a thud," she said. "But then I heard ... movement. Someone else was there."

Olivia's pulse quickened.

Simon stood halfway down the staircase, posture ramrod straight, hands clasped behind his back. His gaze was distant, alert. "The air that night," he said carefully, "felt like before an ambush."

"That is significantly less comforting," Olivia said.

Monique drifted lazily along the railing. "The energies are dissonant, darling," she said. "Like a Charleston played on a toy piano."

JJ leaned in the doorway, cornet tucked under his arm, expression solemn. Daisy hovered near the window, hands folded over her invisible flowers.

Sir Alistair stepped forward last, composed as ever. "Your aunt did not stumble," he said firmly. "Something or someone hastened her fall."

Fear hit Olivia fully then. Not the jump-scare kind. Not the scream and panic kind. This was colder. Heavier. It settled into her bones and stayed there.

She backed away from the stairs and turned, heart hammering.

"I need air," she said.

She fled through the dining room and into the solarium.

The glass walls caught the morning sun, flooding the space with light. Dusty tables sat abandoned beneath the windows. A sad little espresso machine crouched on a side counter, clearly purchased during a moment of optimism and poor budgeting.

Beyond the glass to the west, Mistwood Lake stretched out, calm and beautiful, the water reflecting the sky like polished steel.

Olivia stopped.

She could see it. All of it.

Tables cleaned and polished. Cups stacked neatly. Steam rising. Pastries displayed like jewels. Croissants filled with custard, fruits, and chocolate. Fruit tarts, glazed and shining. Eclairs, Napoleon desserts, and other delights. Morning light turning sugar into art.

"A coffee shop," she whispered.

The idea bloomed fully formed, bright and impossible and irresistible. Breakfast for guests. Coffee and pastries open to the public.

Afternoon tea. Evening dessert hours with lake views and soft lights.

"It might actually work," she murmured.

Daisy appeared beside her, smiling shyly, holding an invisible armful of pressed flowers as if offering approval.

Olivia exhaled a shaky laugh. "Of course, you like the idea."

Daisy only smiled.

Reality returned with a thud. The finances.

Izzy's office was dimmer than Olivia remembered, tucked away at the back of the house, lined with shelves crammed full of books, ledgers, and papers in no particular order. Olivia sat at the desk and opened the main ledger again.

This time, she paid attention.

The numbers didn't match. Expenses were higher than deposits. Transfers that went nowhere. Payments that should not exist. Her stomach tightened.

A half-written letter lay in the drawer, folded and refolded until the paper had softened.

If anything happens to me, look for the will near .... The sentence stopped there.

Snowball leaped onto the desk, sniffed, then jumped down and scratched insistently at a loose floorboard.

"What?" Olivia whispered. She got up and went to the cat. It took her a minute to pry the board up with shaking fingers.

Underneath lay a torn scrap of paper in Izzy's handwriting. *Don't trust ....* The rest was missing.

Olivia sat back on her heels, heart racing.

This was not an accident.

The ghosts gathered around her then, silent and watchful.

Sir Alistair spoke softly. "It appears, Miss March, that you have inherited more than a house."

Olivia looked around at the room, the house, the ghosts, the debt, the lake beyond the glass.

"Great," she said faintly. "Because I was worried things might be simple."

March House creaked in response.

And somewhere deep within its walls, something listened.

CHAPTER THREE

A House That Wants to Work and a Deputy Who Doesn't

Olivia woke up because her brain had apparently decided sleep was an optional lifestyle choice, like dairy or kindness.

At first, she thought it was the familiar, creeping edge of anxiety. The kind that came with a mental checklist of everything you had ruined, everything you might ruin, and everything you could ruin if you got out of bed wrong. Then she realized it was something else.

Someone was watching her.

Olivia did not open her eyes immediately.

She lay very still, holding her breath, letting the silence of March House settle around her. The air smelled faintly of old wood and lake water and whatever herbal scent Lark had diffused into the walls with the enthusiasm of a woman trying to fumigate reality itself.

A floorboard creaked somewhere far below. The plumbing gave a soft tick. The house was awake, even if it had the manners to pretend otherwise.

She opened her eyes slowly.

Flossie stood at the foot of the bed. She was pale and delicate and very, very dead. The lace nightgown she wore looked like it belonged in a museum or on a gothic romance cover, and her pearl-handled hair comb was clutched in both hands like a security blanket. Her head was tilted slightly, studying Olivia the way a cat studies a new piece of furniture.

Olivia stared back.

Flossie's eyes widened, realizing she had been caught doing something rude. A tiny whisper escaped her, barely audible. "Sorry." Then she flickered, her outline blurring as if the air itself was trying to edit her out, and she faded through the wall.

Olivia lay there for a long moment, staring at the empty space. She exhaled slowly. "Great," she muttered. "Even my insomnia has spectators."

Somewhere in the house, there was a light thump. Not a heavy sound, not violent, just a polite, inexplicable bump. March House had cleared its throat.

Olivia swung her legs out of bed and rubbed her eyes. The room was quiet, her childhood bedroom in name only. The wallpaper was the same delicate pattern of faded roses, but everything felt different now. The house had shifted its weight and was waiting to see what she would do.

One task at a time, she told herself. Reclaim normalcy. Or at least build a facsimile sturdy enough to stand upright. She got dressed quickly in jeans, a shirt, and a hoodie, hair pulled back into a messy ponytail. She brushed her teeth like a person who had not been haunted in her sleep. After glancing in the mirror, she washed her face and tried not to think about the fact that ghosts did not have to wash their faces and still looked fantastic.

When she stepped into the hallway, the air was slightly cooler. She hesitated, listening.

No voices. No cornet.

Good. Small mercies.

She headed downstairs.

The kitchen greeted her with sound first.

Janis Joplin, loud enough to suggest Lark believed the dead needed entertainment, too.

Olivia paused in the doorway and watched Lark move around the room as if she owned it, which she did in every way that mattered. Wild gray hair tied back with a scarf. Linen tunic. Flowing skirt. Strong arms stirring a pot with aggressive devotion.

"What are you making?" Olivia asked.

Lark didn't turn. "Breakfast."

"That is not a dish."

"It's an intention."

Olivia moved closer and peered into the pot.

Porridge bubbled thickly, slow and stubborn, with the texture of something used to patch holes in drywall.

"That could double as wallpaper paste," Olivia said.

Lark finally glanced over her shoulder, grinning. "Oats. Chia. A pinch of cinnamon. A whisper of honey."

"A whisper," Olivia repeated. "Because the honey is ashamed."

Lark laughed as if Olivia had said something adorable instead of accurate. She turned and thrust a mug into Olivia's hands before she could dodge.

"Tea," Lark declared. "This one is for new beginnings and digestive harmony."

Olivia looked at it suspiciously. The tea was a murky gold, flecked with bits of something that might have been chamomile or tree bark.

"What's in it?"

"Herbs."

"That narrows it down to all of nature."

Lark tapped the side of her nose. "It's blessed."

Olivia lifted the mug to her lips and took a careful sip.

It tasted as if someone had steeped optimism in hot water and then apologized for it.

"It's ... not horrible," Olivia conceded.

"See? New beginnings."

Olivia's stomach rumbled. Her body, traitor that it was, accepted the tea as nourishment. She sat at the small kitchen table and watched Lark ladle wallpaper paste into bowls.

"Sit," Lark said, and plunked a stack of papers on the table.

Olivia's chest tightened. "What is that?"

"Business reality," Lark said brightly, like it was some sort of spa menu.

Olivia stared at the papers.

Numbers. Notes. Overdue stamps. Handwritten reminders from Izzy in the margins. The faint scent of old ink and worry.

Lark sat across from her, her cheer dimming just a little. "I know you've barely gotten your feet under you," she said. "But you need to know what you're dealing with."

Olivia's spoon hovered over the porridge. "I'm dealing with ghosts."

"And debt," Lark said. "Don't forget the debt."

Olivia scanned the pages. Her eyes snagged on the mortgage. Behind.

Suppliers threatening to cut off deliveries.

Utilities. Delinquent. More than one.

Her throat went dry.

"Izzy," Olivia whispered.

Lark's expression softened. "Izzy was many things, honey. A collector. A caretaker. A magnet for the lost."

"Yes," Olivia said tightly. "And?"

Lark sighed. "She was not a good business manager."

Olivia let out a shaky laugh. "She ran a bed-and-breakfast for forty years."

"She ran it like she was hosting a never-ending tea party," Lark said. "Which, to be fair, she was. But she also occasionally hosted tea afternoons for locals. Made little sandwiches. Poured tea as if she were blessing the town. She had the marketing instincts of a turnip."

Olivia flipped another page and saw the booking numbers.

The fall business was going to be slow.

"Unless you create a reason for locals to come in," Lark said, as if reading her mind.

"Tourists are seasonal. Locals are constant. They have habits."

Olivia leaned back in her chair, eyes drifting toward the solarium doorway. Morning light spilled through the glass, turning the air golden, dust motes floating like glittering problems.

The espresso machine sat in the dining room like a depressed metal toad.

Olivia tapped the papers. "The coffee shop."

Lark perked up instantly. "Yes."

"That coffee shop isn't optional," Olivia murmured. The words came out low and steady, something she was admitting to herself. "It's survival."

Lark beamed. "I'll sage the cash register for prosperity."

Olivia narrowed her eyes. "Please do not set the solarium on fire."

Lark waved a hand. "It will be a controlled flame."

"Those are famous last words."

Olivia pushed away from the table, determination settling in. She could spiral. She could panic. She could sit on the kitchen floor and let the ghosts comfort her while the bank foreclosed and the town whispered.

Or she could do what she had always done. Work.

She grabbed her notepad and walked into the solarium.

The space was beautiful even in neglect. Glass walls. A stunning view of Mistwood Lake. Light so perfect it made her pastry chef soul ache. Dusty tables. Streaked panes. Fallen leaves gathered in corners like the house had been too tired to sweep them away.

Olivia started planning.

Counter space for pastries, she wrote, picturing a clean display case and trays of goodies lined up like soldiers.

A chalkboard menu.

Coffee seating. Airy, bright, scenic.

Possible afternoon tea service.

Her brain started to build it, piece by piece, a kitchen in her mind.

She circled the solarium slowly, measuring with her eyes, mapping where things could go. Where people could sit. Where a line could form. Where she could create an experience that wasn't just a bed-and-breakfast, wasn't just a haunted inheritance, but a place people wanted to come.

A house that wanted to work.

Daisy drifted in first, humming softly. She moved around the tables, brushing invisible pollen from them, hands delicate and purposeful. She smiled when Olivia paused at the window to admire the view of the lake.

"You like this?" Olivia asked quietly.

Daisy's smile deepened, shy and approving.

JJ appeared next, cornet lifting as he played a few low notes. Jazzy. Smooth. Atmospheric.

Olivia froze. "No."

JJ paused, expression innocent.

"This is a coffee shop," Olivia told him. "Breakfast service. Soft music. Quiet vibes."

He played a slightly more dramatic riff, as if offended.

"Absolutely not," Olivia said. "You are not turning my pastry display into a nightclub."

Monique drifted in on a sigh, the very concept of dust offending her. She lounged in midair above a dining chair, never actually sitting on it, and examined Olivia as if Olivia were a menu item.

"Pastries, yes, darling," Monique said. "But nothing with raisins."

Olivia blinked. "Excuse me?"

Monique lifted a hand, wrist limp with dramatic certainty. "Raisins are nature's regrets."

"I have never heard anything more accurate in my entire life," Olivia said, and felt a laugh tug at her mouth despite herself.

Walt wandered in and stared at the counter space. He muttered under his breath about what needed fixing, glancing up at the light fixture as if daring it to flicker incorrectly.

Simon took up his station near the front windows, watching the street outside with the intensity of a man guarding a perimeter.

Olivia paused in the center of the solarium, notepad pressed to her chest.

She was outnumbered.

She was haunted.

But she wasn't alone.

The realization hit her with an unexpected warmth.

The house creaked softly, in agreement.

Then the lights flickered.

Not like a short circuit. Not frantic. Just a slow blink.

A warm breeze moved through the solarium, though the windows were closed. Fallen leaves swirled across the floor in a lazy spiral, as the house itself stirred.

Olivia's skin prickled.

Sir Alistair materialized beside her, hands clasped behind his back, composed as ever. His scent of bergamot drifted faintly in the air.

He gazed around the solarium with a look of approval. "Your aunt wished for this as well," he said.

Olivia's throat tightened. "She never said."

"She did not need to," Sir Alistair replied. "A house is happiest when it is filled."

Goosebumps rose on Olivia's arms. Hope did too, bright and sudden and terrifying. Hope was dangerous. Hope got you attached.

She forced herself to keep moving, pencil scratching across paper, sketching a possible layout, trying to anchor herself in practical details.

That was when a deep voice spoke from behind her.

"You're Olivia March, right?"

Olivia startled hard enough that her pencil nearly snapped. She spun around.

A man stood in the doorway.

Tall. Tired. Rumpled in a way that suggested he had slept in his clothes or fought a bear or both. Buckskin jacket with fringe along the sleeves and back. A sheriff's shirt beneath it. Jeans. Boots that looked like they had actually touched dirt. His five o'clock shadow was not charming so much as it was a testament to a life with no patience for razors.

His eyes swept the solarium quickly, taking in the tables, the notepad, and the espresso machine visible through the doorway.

Unimpressed.

Olivia's stomach did a small, inconvenient flip anyway.

Oh, good, she thought. I'm attracted to the local buzzkill.

"Yes," Olivia said, forcing her voice steady. "That's me."

He stepped inside like a man entering a scene he already wanted to leave. "Luke Thatcher," he said. "Deputy."

"I know," Olivia said. "You're the real sheriff."

His jaw flexed. "Don't say that. My uncle is the sheriff."

"So it's true."

He sighed as if she were already a problem. "I'm just doing follow-up."

"On what?" Olivia asked, though she knew.

"Your aunt's death."

The air in the solarium shifted.

Monique's expression sharpened. Simon straightened. JJ lifted his cornet slightly, preparing to play a funeral dirge out of spite.

Olivia lifted her chin. "Go ahead."

Luke's gaze flicked to her notepad. "You settling in?"

"I'm trying," Olivia said.

Luke's eyes moved to the sketch on her paper, then back to her face. "You're the cook."

Olivia's eyebrows shot up. "Excuse me?"

Luke didn't blink. "Clay said you were the cook from Chicago. Michelin star place."

"I'm a pastry chef," Olivia corrected, bristling.

He shrugged. A gesture that suggested pastries were not a valid category of human skill. "Still cooking."

Olivia forced a smile that showed absolutely no warmth. "And you're the deputy who thinks women fall down stairs for fun."

Luke's gaze narrowed. "Accidents happen."

Monique rolled her eyes so hard the chandelier in the dining room flickered faintly.

JJ played a soft, sarcastic wah-wah note.

Luke glanced toward the dining room, frowning. "You got wiring issues?"

Olivia smiled sweetly. "You have no idea."

Luke cleared his throat. "Look. I'm here because your aunt's death was recent. Clay wanted me to check in. See if you had any questions."

"I do," Olivia said immediately. "Plenty."

Luke's posture became more guarded, as if he regretted offering.

Olivia stepped closer, notepad forgotten. "There's a ledger that doesn't match the bank statements. There's a half-written letter from my aunt that ends mid-sentence. There's a loose floorboard in her office and a torn scrap that says, 'Don't trust' and then nothing. She was trying to warn me."

Luke's expression remained skeptical, but something in his eyes sharpened at the mention of the letter. "People write a lot of things," he said carefully.

"Accidents don't write halfway finished warnings," Olivia snapped.

Luke paused.

For a half second, something shifted. A flicker of attention. A hint that she had landed a point.

Then he shut down again, shoulders tightening. "That's Clay's department," he said. "I'm just following up."

"And Clay closed the case in under an hour because he wanted pancakes," Olivia said, unable to stop herself.

Luke's mouth twitched, like he was fighting a smile or a headache. "Yeah," he said. "That sounds like him."

Olivia leaned in, voice low. "Do you really think my aunt fell down those stairs by accident?"

Luke met her eyes.

For a moment, he looked tired in a way that wasn't about sleep. Like he carried Mistwood on his back and didn't want more weight added.

Then he broke eye contact. "I think accidents happen," he said again, more firmly, as if repeating it could make it true.

Olivia's frustration flared. "Fine," she said. "So you're not going to listen."

Luke's gaze returned to her, and his voice went flat. "I'm going to do my job."

"And what is that?" Olivia asked. "Ignore evidence and call me the cook?"

His jaw flexed again. "Don't go digging around," he said. "This town doesn't like outsiders stirring things up."

Olivia's pulse kicked. "I'm not an outsider. This is my family's house."

Luke's expression didn't soften. "You left."

The words hit harder than she expected.

Luke seemed to realize it a beat too late, because his eyes shifted with a hint of regret.

Then he stepped back, already retreating. "I'll let Clay know you have concerns," he said.

"That's not listening," Olivia called after him.

Luke didn't turn. "It's follow-up."

He left before she could argue more.

Snowball trotted after him, tail high like she was escorting him out, then paused in the doorway and looked back at Olivia with a disapproving meow.

Olivia stared at the cat. "Oh, sorry," she muttered. "Next time I'll hypnotize him into competence."

Snowball blinked slowly, unimpressed, and padded away.

Olivia turned back to the solarium.

The ghosts had gathered, orbiting her in a loose circle of eccentric, spectral satellites.

Monique sighed dramatically. "Well," she said. "He's handsome in a 'government-issued headache' sort of way."

Olivia's cheeks warmed. "I did not say that."

Monique's smile was wicked.

JJ played a tiny, smug note.

Simon looked like he wanted to stand guard at the door until Luke returned and apologized properly.

Olivia exhaled and stepped into the center of the room, looking at her sketches, the light, the lake beyond the glass. The dust. The hope.

"All right," she said softly, but firmly. The words settled into the space like a vow. "I'm staying."

The house creaked, a long, warm sound that felt almost like relief.

"We fix the finances," Olivia continued. "We find that will. And we find out what happened to Izzy."

The chandelier brightened, not blinding, just a gentle lift in glow.

The floorboards creaked again, friendlier this time. Less complaint, more approval.

JJ played a triumphant little riff.

Daisy smiled as if she were offering flowers to a grave and a garden at the same time.

And for the first time since Olivia had arrived in Mistwood, she felt it.

March House might actually want her here.

She only hoped the living residents of Mistwood would eventually get on board. Because the dead already had opinions, and they were not shy about sharing them.

CHAPTER FOUR

The Sheriff, the Staircase, and the First Warning

Olivia drank Lark's "clarity and courage" tea, standing at the kitchen counter, bracing herself like a boxer before a match.

It tasted like mint and stubbornness, with a faint aftertaste of something that might have been fennel or might have been defiance distilled into leaf form.

"This is aggressive," Olivia said.

Lark smiled serenely. "It's proactive."

"I feel like it wants me to argue with authority."

"Good," Lark said. "Authority needs the exercise."

Olivia was halfway through the mug when voices drifted in from the parlor. One of them was loud, confident, and carried the unmistakable cadence of someone who enjoyed being listened to.

She sighed. "That'll be him."

"The sheriff?" Lark asked.

"The parade float with a badge," Olivia muttered and headed for the front of the house.

Sheriff Clayton Dawes stood in the parlor as if he were attending a ribbon-cutting instead of revisiting the scene of a suspicious death. He wore a spotless uniform, his smile bright enough to power a small town fundraiser, and his hands carefully avoided touching anything at all.

He caught sight of Olivia and immediately stepped forward,

arms opening in a gesture meant to convey empathy without requiring effort.

"Miss March!" he boomed. "My condolences. Such a tragedy. Your aunt was beloved by … most."

Olivia blinked. "… Most?"

Clay chuckled like he had made a charming joke instead of an accidental confession. "Well, you know how these things are. Strong personalities. But no one ever deserved such an unfortunate end."

He glanced at the antique mirror above the mantel, adjusted his smile by a fraction, then turned back to her.

"I wanted to stop by personally," he continued. "Make sure you're settling in. Answer any questions. Reassure you."

Olivia folded her arms. "Reassure me about what?"

Clay waved a hand, the gesture broad and polished. "The accident."

There it was.

He launched into the official story with the ease of a man who had rehearsed it in front of a bathroom mirror.

"No signs of struggle," he said. "No forced entry. No sign of foul play. Old houses are tricky things, Miss March. Staircases, especially."

He gestured vaguely toward the foyer, as if the stairs might overhear and feel defensive.

"Very tragic," he went on. "But these things do happen."

Olivia felt her jaw tighten.

She tried anyway.

"The finances don't line up," she said. "There's a ledger that doesn't match the bank statements. There's a note fragment from my aunt warning me. She was scared."

Clay nodded sympathetically, already preparing his dismissal. "Grief does strange things to people. Makes patterns where there aren't any."

"And the staircase?" Olivia pressed. "She didn't run down those stairs. Ever."

Clay smiled again. It was the kind of smile that suggested he believed deeply in his own reassurances.

"Accidents happen on old staircases," he said. "Very tragic, but case closed."

Olivia felt heat flare behind her ribs.

"So that's it?" she asked. "You don't even want to look at the stairs?"

Clay's tone softened into something patronizing. "Miss March, I understand you're upset. New town, loss in the family, big changes. But my advice is to focus on healing and hospitality."

The words landed like a slap.

"Let the professionals handle the rest," he added smoothly. "Digging into painful memories won't bring anyone peace."

Olivia opened her mouth to argue.

Before she could, someone shifted behind Clay.

Deputy Luke Thatcher lingered near the staircase, his posture awkward, hands shoved into his jacket pockets. He looked deeply uncomfortable, like a man trapped between duty and embarrassment.

He said nothing.

But he looked.

His eyes moved over the staircase with quiet intensity. He crouched slightly, fingers brushing a spindle before he stopped himself. His gaze snagged on the banister, then on the middle stair.

Olivia followed his line of sight.

A scuff mark. Darker than the rest. Too focused. Too sharp.

Luke straightened quickly when he realized she was watching him as he looked.

Their eyes met.

For half a second, something passed between them. Recognition. Not agreement, but awareness.

Luke cleared his throat. "Just … be careful," he said gruffly. "Old houses have a way of shifting."

Then he stepped back, retreating like a man who had already said too much.

Clay clapped his hands together. "Well then! I'll let you get back to settling in."

He reached into his pocket and produced a glossy pamphlet, handing it to Olivia with a flourish. "Fundraiser breakfast this Sunday. Pancakes, raffle, community spirit. You're welcome to attend."

Olivia stared at it. "I'll pencil it in between grief and homicide."

Clay laughed, not hearing the words. "Take care now."

The front door closed behind them.

The house inhaled.

The temperature shifted. The air thickened. The quiet deepened.

And then the ghosts arrived.

Walt appeared first, hovering near the banister, wrench clenched in his hand. "He's blind as a rusty nail," he muttered. "That railing didn't loosen itself."

Simon stood halfway up the stairs, posture rigid, eyes distant. "Something happened here," he said. "A wrongness." His voice echoed faintly, layered with something older and darker, like memory bleeding through.

Monique swept in, waving a hand dramatically toward the staircase. "Darling, this wasn't a stumble. This was sabotage." She leaned closer to Olivia and whispered, "Also, the sheriff's aftershave could kill a canary."

Daisy knelt beside the loose spindle, touching it gently, as if listening for sorrow embedded in wood.

Sir Alistair joined them last, dignified and grave. "Your aunt knew danger was coming," he said. "She tried to warn you."

Olivia swallowed hard.

Before she could respond, Snowball padded down the stairs, Simon's medal chiming softly against her collar. The cat stopped in front of Olivia and dropped something at her feet.

A scrap of paper.

Olivia's breath caught as she kneeled and picked it up.

Izzy's handwriting. Clearer than the fragment she had found before.

You must be cautious. Not everyone is who they seem.

The bottom dropped out of Olivia's stomach.

Lark appeared behind her, voice gentle. "The house is talking to you, dear."

"Yeah," Olivia said hoarsely. "And I need it to start using complete sentences."

Later that afternoon, Olivia stepped outside with the compost bucket, needing air and movement and something that did not involve warnings from beyond the grave.

The back veranda was quiet. Too quiet.

She noticed the footprints first, pressed into the soft dirt near the door. Not old. Not random.

Then the cigarette butt.

Her pulse jumped.

Pinned to the back door with a nail was a folded scrap of paper.

Her hands shook as she reached for her phone. She took a picture. Clear. Close. Proof.

Only then did she pull the note free. LET THE DEAD REST.

The temperature plummeted.

Simon materialized beside her, hand hovering near where his rifle used to be. "We're with you," he whispered.

Behind her, the rest of the ghosts appeared, an oddly assembled honor guard.

JJ played a low, ominous note.

Olivia pocketed the note, heart pounding. "Okay," she whispered. "Then we ask louder."

She locked the door behind her and stood in the dining room, staring at the future cafe space.

"Someone hurt Izzy," she murmured. "And someone's afraid I'll figure out why."

Outside, the wind rattled the solarium glass.

Inside, March House listened.

CHAPTER FIVE

The Ghost Council Convenes

The first thing Olivia did after waking up was check her phone. Not because she was addicted to social media. She did not follow social media anymore, unless you counted the group chat with her former pastry team that existed solely to complain about laminated dough and men who called themselves "visionaries" while stealing other people's work.

No, she checked her phone because yesterday someone had nailed a threat to her back door. And because she had been smart enough, for once, to take a picture before touching anything.

She lay on her back in bed, the old quilt bunched at her waist, morning light creeping around the edges of the curtains. She opened her photo gallery and found it immediately.

The back door. The nail. The folded paper, pinned in place like a warning label on a product called *Welcome to Mistwood: Now Including Murder.*

LET THE DEAD REST.

The letters were blocky, harsh, and deliberate. Not rushed. Not sloppy. Whoever wrote it had taken the time to press down hard. The timestamp sat cleanly at the bottom of the image like a smug little witness.

Clear. Time-stamped. Irrefutable.

A relief washed through her so quickly her eyes stung. "Okay," she whispered, exhaling. "Proof. Actual proof."

Then she saw something she had not noticed last night, because last night her brain had been busy screaming internally and wondering if she could accidentally set a bed-and-breakfast on fire.

Behind the note, in the glass pane of the back door, was a reflection. Not her reflection. Not the kitchen light. Not the vague blur of the veranda. A shape.

Tall. Narrow. Long coat, with the hem hanging past the knees. The head and shoulders were indistinct, the outline smudged by the curve of the glass, but it was there. It did not look like a trick of light. It looked like a presence.

Human?

Or a ghost?

Olivia zoomed in until the pixels turned into modern art. The shape stayed stubbornly vague, as if it were hiding on purpose.

Her stomach tightened.

"You have got to be kidding me," she muttered.

She sat up and immediately texted the photo to herself. Then she opened her email and sent it to a backup account she barely used, the one she kept for important things like receipts, passwords, and proof that people were trying to intimidate her.

March women were no fools. Olivia might be late to the lesson, but she could learn.

She stared at the image again. The coat. The height. The blur. "Human or ghost," she murmured, "either way, it is not comforting."

A floorboard creaked somewhere in the hall. Olivia froze. "Do not," she shouted to the ceiling, "start watching me before coffee."

No one answered. But the house felt, for a moment, like it had leaned in.

Olivia dressed quickly and headed downstairs, phone clutched in one hand, a talisman. Her nerves felt stretched thin, but beneath them, there was something else now. A thread of determination, tight and sharp, like a sugar ribbon pulled to the edge of snapping.

She stepped into the dining room and stopped dead.

The long dining table was full.

Not full in the normal way. There were no plates, no mugs, no breakfast spread, no Lark humming in the background. But a presence claimed every chair.

Sir Alistair sat at the head of the table, posture immaculate, hands folded, gaze calm and expectant. Monique lounged halfway sideways in her chair as if the dining room had been converted into a private club and she had the membership card. JJ stood on one side of the table, polishing his cornet with exaggerated seriousness, preparing for a performance that the dead would review.

Simon stood at parade rest, chin lifted, eyes forward. Daisy floated near the center of the table, arranging phantom wildflowers into a vase that was very much empty but somehow still looked prettier in her hands. Walt scowled at the chandelier overhead. He and the light fixture must have unresolved issues. Flossie hovered near Olivia's chair, fingers tight around her pearl-handled comb, flickering nervously like a candle in a draft.

The dining room looked like the world's strangest séance. Except Olivia was the one being summoned.

She stared at them. They stared back.

Sir Alistair cleared his throat. Dramatically. Of course, he did.

"Miss March," he said with grave formality, "the household requests your presence for an internal conference."

Olivia blinked once. Twice. "Is this a ghost meeting?"

Monique lifted a finger. "Darling, it is a council. A meeting sounds like we are discussing paint colors."

JJ played a bright little ta-da flourish, the notes ringing through the room like a trumpet announcing royal nonsense.

Olivia looked at the empty chair, clearly meant for her. "You set places."

"We did." Sir Alistair pointed to her chair. "As you have noticed."

Walt muttered, "Took long enough. We've been waiting."

Olivia lowered herself into the chair slowly, having learned in the last forty-eight hours that sudden movements tended to lead to additional haunting.

"All right," she said, setting her phone down on the table. "Fine. Let's do this. What is the agenda?"

Monique smiled like a cat that had just found a sunbeam. "The murder, darling."

"That is not an agenda item," Olivia said. "That is an entire criminal case."

Simon's expression did not change. "We are prepared."

JJ lifted his cornet as if saluting the concept of preparedness, then played a suspicious little two-note riff.

Olivia grabbed a pen and her notepad. "Okay. One at a time. I am begging you. I have worked in a Michelin-starred kitchen. I have survived dinner service with three people calling 'behind' at the same time. I can handle chaos. But if you all talk at once, I will start throwing objects, and we will all have a bad day."

Flossie gasped softly, clutching her comb tighter.

Alistair nodded. "Agreed. We will proceed in order."

Monique tilted her head. "Order is such a harsh word. Let's call it choreography."

"No," Olivia said. "Order. Simon, start."

Simon stepped forward slightly, still stiff as a soldier. "On the night your aunt died," he said, "I heard footsteps."

Olivia's pen paused. "Footsteps on the stairs?"

"Not only the stairs," Simon replied. "In the hall. In the foyer. Heavy. Deliberate. Not your aunt's pace."

Olivia underlined heavy.

"Are you sure it wasn't Lark?" she asked.

Simon's jaw tightened. "Madam Waverly moves like a woman who has learned to avoid squeaky boards. This was not that. This was someone who did not care who heard them."

Walt grunted, satisfied. "Told ya."

Olivia wrote:

Heavier footsteps. Someone didn't care about noise.

"Flossie," Olivia said, "you said Izzy said something earlier that day."

Flossie's eyes darted nervously around the table, as if she expected someone to yell at her for speaking. Her voice came out tiny. "She was in the parlor," she whispered. "She looked ... tired. Like she had been holding her breath for days. And she said, 'Not again.'"

Olivia's hand tightened around her pen. "Not again," she repeated. "Like this has happened before."

Flossie nodded barely. "She sounded frightened."

Monique waved her hand dismissively. "Frightened, yes, but also angry. Your aunt had spark, darling."

Olivia wrote:

Izzy said: Not again. Fear + anger.

"Walt," Olivia said, "you said something about tinkering."

Walt leaned forward, scowl deepening. "Two nights before the fall. I heard metal. Tools. Someone messing near the staircase. Not fixing it. Messing."

Olivia's pen scratched quickly. "Where exactly?"

"Base. Side. By the molding," Walt said. "Like they were working the railing loose."

Flossie shivered. "Izzy always held the banister when she walked," she said, voice trembling. "Even during the day. She trusted it."

Olivia swallowed hard. She wrote:

Tool noises near staircase. Two nights before. Railing.

Daisy lifted her hand slightly. Olivia turned to her, softer. "Daisy?"

Daisy's voice was quiet but clear, like a breeze through leaves. "She hid something in the garden."

Olivia's pen paused mid-word. "In the garden," she repeated. "What?"

Daisy shook her head slowly, expression sad. "I only know she did. I felt it. Like a secret pressed into soil."

Monique sighed. "Always with the dramatic hiding places. If I had a secret, I would put it in a hatbox."

Olivia stared at Daisy. "Can you show me where?"

Daisy's gaze dropped. Her hands twisted together. "I am not sure. The garden is large. The feeling was ... near. Close to the house."

Olivia wrote:

Something hidden garden. Near house.

"Monique," Olivia said, "you mentioned shadows."

Monique's eyes glittered. "Midnight," she said. "Parlor. Shadows moving. Not like the house settling, darling. Like someone slipping. And I know a shadow with a guilty conscience. They move differently."

JJ played a soft, dramatic riff like a movie soundtrack.

Olivia pointed her pen at him. "Do not score this."

JJ grinned and played the first few notes of "Suspicious Minds" completely off key, like he was mocking both the song and the concept of subtlety.

Olivia wrote anyway, because information was information, even when delivered with the musical finesse of a haunted kazoo.

Patterns began to form in her notes. Not a perfect picture. Not a clean story. But something. A timeline.

Fear building. Someone in the house. Someone returning. Someone messing with the staircase. A threat nailed to the door. A reflection in the glass.

Olivia lifted her eyes slowly, looking around the table at seven faces that ranged from solemn to smug to mildly offended by raisins. "You all agree on one thing."

They waited.

"Someone was inside this house before Izzy died." She continued. "And whoever it was came back on the night she fell."

Silence.

Even JJ stopped playing.

"That's not an accident," Olivia said, voice low. "That's stalking."

Walt nodded once, grim. Simon's gaze hardened. Flossie's eyes filled with tears she could not shed. Daisy clasped her hands tighter.

Monique leaned in. "Finally," she whispered. "A little drama worthy of this house."

Olivia ignored that. She tapped her pen on the notepad. "Did any of you see the person clearly?"

They all shifted.

Daisy lowered her eyes. Simon's shoulders moved slightly,

carrying the weight of not being able to protect someone. JJ raised his cornet and played a single mournful note that felt like fog.

Alistair stepped forward, voice calm but heavy with truth. "None of us actually saw the person. We could sense. We could hear. We could feel wrongness, but we didn't see them."

Olivia's frustration flared, hot and sharp, then cooled into something steadier.

"All right," she said. "So you can't hand me the killer. That would be too easy, and this is my life now, so of course it can't be easy."

Monique smirked. "Darling, if it were easy, you would not be involved."

Olivia narrowed her eyes. "Watch it."

Walt stood abruptly. "Come on. I got somethin' real. Not vibes. Not feelings. Real." He headed for the staircase, and Olivia followed, pen still in hand.

Walt motioned sharply. "Look down."

Olivia crouched near the baseboard at the bottom of the stairs, her knees protesting. She leaned close, squinting at the wooden molding.

At first, she saw nothing but varnish and age. Then she spotted it.

A faint scrape along the molding. Thin, pale exposed wood was revealed beneath the finish, as if someone had dragged metal against it. Fresh enough that the color had not darkened.

Her breath caught.

"A tool," she whispered. "Something metal struck it. Hard."

Walt nodded, satisfaction flickering across his gruff face. "Told ya. Somebody used a tool here. Loosened that railing."

Olivia stared at the scrape, her throat tightening.

Flossie hovered behind her, voice trembling. "Izzy always held the banister," she whispered again. "She trusted it."

Olivia swallowed. Her chest ached.

"This wasn't an accident," she said, voice rough. "This was deliberate sabotage."

Walt crossed his arms, pleased. "Finally."

They returned to the dining room, and Olivia sat again, her notepad now filled with scribbles and underlines and increasingly aggressive punctuation. She reached into her pocket and pulled out her phone.

"I'm taking this to Luke today," she said, holding it up. "The photo, the note, and what I found. The sheriff too, but mostly Luke."

Monique's eyes lit up. "Ah, yes. The handsome man with the permanent scowl."

JJ played a slow, sultry riff.

Olivia stared at him. "No."

JJ played it again, louder.

Olivia pointed a finger at the entire table. "No. Not like that. He's just competent. Sort of."

Monique fanned herself theatrically. "Competence is terribly attractive, darling. Especially in a town where the sheriff carries pamphlets instead of evidence."

Olivia's cheeks warmed. "I did not say attractive."

The ghosts collectively smirked.

Even Alistair's mouth twitched, the traitor.

Olivia glared at them because she was not going to discuss her inconvenient response to Luke Thatcher's jawline with a panel of dead people who had nothing better to do than judge her choices.

She gathered her notes carefully, folding them once, then again, and tucked the threatening paper into a folder as if it were a legal document. Because it was.

Evidence.

Proof.

She stood.

The ghosts hovered close, watching her with something that felt like investment.

Alistair stepped forward and gave her a solemn bow. "Take care, Miss March. The living are often more dangerous than the dead."

"That is not reassuring," Olivia muttered, but she nodded.

Snowball appeared at her feet and trotted toward the door with purpose, Simon's medal jingling softly on her collar like a tiny bell of courage.

Olivia followed, the folder under her arm, her phone in her hand, her spine straighter than it had been yesterday.

She paused at the threshold and looked back at the dining room. The ghosts were still there. Waiting. Watching.

Alliance was a strange word for a haunting, but it fit. Olivia exhaled.

"Okay," she whispered to herself. "Today I tell the authorities everything."

She opened the front door.

Cold air rushed in. Mistwood waited.

Today, she stopped being passive.

Today, she became a sleuth.

And if Luke Thatcher called her "the cook" again, she was going to make him eat that title with a side of evidence.

CHAPTER SIX

A Will, a Warning, and a Wall of Resistance

The Mistwood County Sheriff's Office smelled like burned coffee, floor cleaner, and a vague sense of misplaced authority.

Olivia paused just inside the doorway, adjusted her grip on the folder tucked under her arm, and squared her shoulders.

Inside the folder were printouts of Izzy's financial discrepancies, neatly highlighted. The threatening note was sealed in an envelope and had been since she'd photographed it. Her phone was already unlocked, with the image of the nail and the message ready to display. On the front of the folder, written in thick black marker, were the words: **NOT AN ACCIDENT. PLEASE READ.**

She had debated softening it and had decided against it.

Tucked into the pocket of her coat was Sir Alistair's silver pocket watch, its familiar weight steadying. The faintest scent of bergamot hovered near her shoulder.

"You're doing well, Miss March." Alistair appeared beside her.

Olivia exhaled. "Let's hope they agree."

She crossed the room toward Luke's desk.

Luke Thatcher looked up from a stack of paperwork, his expression shifting from tired to wary in the space of a heartbeat.

"Miss March." He frowned. "Why are you here?"

"Because I have evidence, actual evidence."

His eyebrows lifted just a fraction at the word evidence. Not skepticism. Interest.

She sat in the chair across from his desk, clutching the folder like a shield.

That was when she heard it. Tiny ghost footsteps.

Olivia's eyes flicked sideways just in time to see Bertie materialize beside Sir Alistair's boots.

The whippet blinked, tail wagging furiously, and immediately darted under the nearest desk.

Luke frowned. "Do you hear something?"

"Nope," Olivia said too quickly.

Bertie popped out from under the desk, sniffed a filing cabinet, then bolted into a perfect figure eight around Luke's chair.

Luke stiffened. "Okay, there's definitely a draft or something."

Olivia slapped a hand over her mouth and pretended to cough.

Bertie, clearly delighted with himself, ran to the nearest trash can and stuck his head in it.

"Oh no," Olivia whispered. She coughed again.

Luke stared at her. "Are you alright?"

"I'm fine," she wheezed. "Just ... allergies."

Sir Alistair's voice drifted softly to her ear. "Terribly sorry, Miss March. Bertie hasn't been away from the house much since Miss Izzy's passing. He likes to explore."

Sheriff Clay chose that exact moment to enter the station.

"Miss March!" Clay boomed, smiling like he was unveiling a plaque. "Good to see you engaging with the community."

He glanced at Olivia's hunched posture. "Oh dear. Emotional moment?"

"Yes," Olivia croaked. "Very moving."

Luke looked between them, deeply confused.

Olivia straightened, regained control, and opened her folder. "I brought evidence," she said again, more firmly. "That my aunt was threatened. That someone was on the property. And that the staircase—"

Luke held up a hand slightly. "Let's start with the photo."

Grateful, Olivia pulled out her phone and turned the screen toward him.

Luke leaned in.

The note was clear. The nail is unmistakable. The timestamp placed Olivia inside the house when the threat was left.

Then Luke's eyes narrowed.

He leaned closer, tilting the phone.

"You were inside," he intoned. "And someone was behind your house."

He didn't say, someone threatening you, but Olivia heard it anyway.

Her pulse kicked.

"Yes."

Luke straightened. "I'll need a copy of this."

She airdropped it to him. His phone pinged. He stared at the image again, longer this time.

Something shifted.

Belief, at least partial, settled into his expression.

That was when Sheriff Clay clapped his hands.

"Well now! What's all this?"

Clay swept forward, uniform starched, smile gleaming. He glanced at the phone, then at the folder, then back at Olivia.

"Miss March! You are certainly keeping busy."

Bertie ran past the sheriff to another trashcan. He seemed to be exploring the contents of every trash receptacle in the building.

"I brought evidence that my aunt was threatened," Olivia said. "That someone was on the property. And that the stairs were sabotaged."

Clay waved a dismissive hand. "Old houses creak. Floors shift. Shadows spook people. You've had a frightful week. Stress can make things seem ... sinister."

Luke's shoulders tightened. He looked mortified.

Clay plucked the envelope from the desk.

"Well now," he said cheerfully. "This is probably a prank by local kids. Happens every spring."

"It's September," Olivia said flatly.

Clay froze for half a second. Then he laughed. "Well! Precocious kids. We'll look into it."

He slipped the envelope into his pocket.

Olivia's stomach dropped.

"Wait," she said. "That's evidence."

Clay smiled. "And I have it."

Bertie ran in a circle around the sheriff and stopped. He sniffed at the man's trousers and lifted his leg.

Olivia made a strangled sound, bent forward, shoulders shaking, and started coughing again.

Sir Alistair chuckled. "I'm sorry, Miss March. Bertie has strong opinions about incompetent authority."

Bertie finished and trotted away proudly.

Olivia straightened her shoulders. Enough with the distractions; it was time to show them what she had. She laid out everything then. The finances. The ledger. The loose floorboard. The partial warning. The scrape along the molding.

Clay listened with exaggerated patience.

Then he said the words she had dreaded.

"The case is closed."

Olivia's hands curled into fists.

"We simply don't have the resources to chase ghosts," Clay added, laughing at his own joke.

"I'm not asking you to chase ghosts," Olivia said calmly. "I'm asking you to do your job."

Clay gave her a polite, condescending smile. "Sometimes a fall is just a fall."

"In this case, it isn't." Olivia got up from her chair.

"One more thing." Clay smiled. "If no will is found, March House defaults to the next eligible claimant."

She froze.

"Mister Theodore Bramble," Clay continued. "Extended family. Also, one of the primary creditors."

Olivia's blood went ice cold.

Bramble. The developer. The condo dreamer.

Not a chance.

She grabbed her folder and stormed out.

Luke followed her into the crisp air.

"Olivia. Wait."

She stopped.

"I didn't say your aunt's death was an accident," Luke said. "I said we don't have enough yet. And I believe someone left that note."

"Then why let Clay dismiss me?"

Luke's jaw worked. "I'll look into it. Quietly. Off the record."

She finally looked at him.

"Fine," she said. "But I'm investigating too."

Luke almost smiled. Almost.

"Yeah," he said. "I figured."

Back at March House, Snowball trotted out to meet her. Simon appeared beside the porch. JJ announced her arrival with a jazz riff.

Olivia touched Alistair's watch.

"I'm finding that will," she said.

Sir Alistair and Bertie appeared beside her.

Alistair smiled. "Very well, Miss March. Then let us begin."

CHAPTER SEVEN

A Town Full of Secrets and Suspects

The smell hit first. Cinnamon, warm and sweet, curled through the kitchen like a spell. Cardamom underneath it, darker and sharper, the kind of scent that suggested someone in this house had standards and would be enforcing them aggressively.

Olivia stood at the counter with flour on her sweater, hair pulled into a messy ponytail, and a tray of scones in front of her like a challenge. She was not baking because she felt domestic. She was baking because she needed a test recipe for the future coffee shop, and she refused to be the kind of person who opened a business on hope and vibes alone.

Also, she needed something to do with her hands besides wringing them.

She cut cold butter into the flour with practiced precision, working quickly before the kitchen heat could sabotage the texture. She stirred in cinnamon and cardamom, then added cream, folding gently, careful not to overmix. She shaped the dough, pressed it into a circle, and sliced it into wedges.

The oven was preheating, humming in approval.

"All right," Olivia murmured, sliding the tray into the heat. "Let's see if you're worthy of becoming a local addiction."

The scent intensified within minutes. Which, apparently, was the equivalent of ringing a dinner bell for the dead.

JJ drifted into the kitchen first, shoulders loose, humming a jazz tune that sounded pleased with itself. The faint shimmer around his form caught the light like the warm haze of a nightclub. He tilted his head, inhaled, and gave a small approving nod.

"Oh, good," Olivia said. "You can smell."

JJ winked and hummed a little louder.

Monique appeared next, conjured by the idea of anything remotely fashionable. She leaned against the counter in a way that suggested she was both judging Olivia and helping her.

Monique's gaze traveled over the bowls, the measuring cups, the flour dusting Olivia's sleeve. "Cinnamon cardamom," she said. "Very sophisticated. But, darling."

Olivia didn't like that tone. "But darling, what?"

Monique tapped a finger against one of Olivia's measuring cups. "Why do you insist on using these American measurements?"

"They work," Olivia said.

Monique sighed dramatically. "Cups are such a vulgar unit. Like measuring diamonds with a shovel."

"I am not baking diamonds," Olivia said. "I am baking scones."

"Still," Monique replied, as if Olivia had missed the point, and the point was Monique.

Walt materialized near the oven with the air of a man who had been summoned by the sound of machinery. He squinted at the temperature dial as if it were lying.

"Too low," he muttered.

"It's set exactly where it should be," Olivia said.

Walt grunted. "Five degrees hotter. Trust me."

Olivia narrowed her eyes. "You are a rusty wrench ghost. Why would I trust you on pastry science?"

Walt looked offended. "Because I know heat."

JJ hummed something that sounded like laughter.

Flossie drifted in, slower than the others, hovering near the doorway with her comb clutched in both hands. She looked toward the staircase, then away, then back again as if the stairs might suddenly confess.

Olivia's chest tightened.

Simon was next, pacing near the entryway like a sentry, his gaze fixed on the front of the house. He moved with contained intensity, boots silent, posture rigid.

Daisy appeared near the window, her gentle smile brightened by sunlight. She stood with her hands loosely clasped, looking toward Mistwood Lake as if the morning light itself was a comfort.

Olivia looked around her kitchen.

A jazz musician humming approvingly. A flapper ghost complaining about cups. A mechanic muttering about oven temperature. A nervous woman haunted by stairs. A Civil War soldier guarding her doorway. A gardener admiring the sun.

"Okay," Olivia muttered. "This is normal now."

The oven timer ticked. The house creaked. Somewhere in the walls, a pipe made a sound like it was eavesdropping.

Olivia turned to face them all, wiping her hands on a towel.

"All right," she said. "While we wait for my scones to become the next great reason for Mistwood to forgive my existence, I have a question."

Monique's eyes lit. "A question. How thrilling."

Olivia ignored that. "Who would have wanted to hurt Izzy?"

The kitchen erupted.

Walt spoke first, like he had been waiting for permission to accuse the human race. "Anyone with a wrench."

"That is not a suspect list," Olivia said. "That's a hardware store."

Walt crossed his arms. "Tools don't lie."

Monique tossed her hair, which moved even though it was not made of anything. "Clearly, the culprit is anyone with poor fashion sense."

Olivia blinked. "That is also not a suspect list."

Monique sniffed. "It is a very accurate one."

JJ lifted his chin and hummed a single, offended note. "Someone who hates jazz."

Olivia stared at him. "You think Izzy was killed by an anti-jazz murderer?"

JJ played a quick riff that sounded like a yes.

Simon stopped pacing. His eyes narrowed. "Someone who knew the house well," he said. "A tactical ambush requires familiarity. Timing. Terrain."

Monique rolled her eyes. “Terrain. Darling, it’s a staircase.”

Simon’s gaze sharpened. “Staircases can be weaponized.”

Olivia’s stomach turned. “Yes,” she whispered. “Apparently, they can.”

Daisy spoke last, her voice soft as a breeze. “Hazel Finch.”

Silence fell.

Walt’s scowl shifted to suspicion. Monique’s expression sharpened. Simon went still. JJ’s humming faded into a low note.

Olivia’s pulse quickened. “Hazel Finch,” she repeated, tasting the name.

Daisy nodded once. “Yes.”

Olivia grabbed her notebook and scribbled the name down.

Walt grunted. “Who’s Hazel Finch?”

“Probably someone with terrible hats,” Monique said.

Olivia underlined the name anyway. It wasn’t helpful that the ghosts had wildly different theories, but one thing was clear.

They were invested.

And she was, apparently, the only living person in the room who could translate their chaos into something actionable.

The oven timer beeped.

Olivia opened the oven and pulled out the tray. The scones were golden, edges crisp, the tops cracked slightly where steam had forced its way out. The scent was rich and tempting, the kind of smell that made a house feel like a home even when it was haunted and broken.

She set them on the counter to cool.

JJ hummed appreciatively.

Monique leaned in and inspected them as if she were judging a contest. “No raisins,” she said, approving.

“Raisins are nature’s regrets,” Olivia said automatically.

Monique smiled as if they had bonded.

At that moment, Lark swept into the kitchen with a teapot and an expression that said she had been listening from the hallway because she absolutely had.

“Tea,” Lark announced, pouring into mismatched mugs. “This one protects from enemies and bad vibes.”

Olivia took one. “Does it taste like enemies?”

“Only if you deserve it.”

Olivia sipped cautiously. It tasted of herbs and resolve, with a faint citrus note that made her feel marginally less like she might set someone on fire.

Lark leaned against the counter and nodded toward Olivia's notebook. "So," she said, "you're making a list."

"Apparently," Olivia said. "The ghosts have theories."

Lark's eyes twinkled. "Oh, I'm sure they do."

Olivia hesitated. "You have theories too?"

Lark sipped her tea. "Darling, Mistwood is prettier than it is honest."

Olivia's pen hovered. "Okay," she said. "Who?"

Lark held up a finger. "Theodore Bramble."

Olivia's jaw tightened. "The developer."

"The same," Lark said. "He pressured Izzy to sell. Offered money. Promised improvements. Said it would be good for the town. Izzy told him where to shove his 'vision.' Politely, of course. With a smile."

Olivia wrote:

Theodore Bramble.

Lark held up a second finger. "Hazel Finch from the historical society."

Olivia's eyes narrowed. "Historical society?"

Lark nodded. "Hazel thought Izzy was too whimsical with her antiques. Wanted everything cataloged and controlled. Izzy didn't appreciate being told how to live in her own house."

Olivia wrote:

Hazel Finch.

A third finger. "Marvin Pike."

Olivia paused. "Who?"

"Former handyman," Lark said. "Fired last year for 'borrowing things permanently.'"

Olivia stared. "Borrowing. Permanently."

Lark shrugged. "Izzy had a way of phrasing things."

Olivia wrote:

Marvin Pike.

"Where is he now?"

Lark's mouth tightened. "Currently working out of town on a construction project. That's what I've heard."

Olivia wrote it down and circled it. "I haven't seen him."

"You won't," Lark said. "Not yet."

Olivia didn't like the way she had said that.

Fourth finger. "Carla Dawes."

Olivia's pen froze. "The sheriff's wife."

Lark nodded slowly. "Carla fought with Izzy over lake access rights. That little path along the edge of the property. Carla wanted it opened. Izzy refused."

Olivia's stomach twisted. "Why?"

"Because people don't ask nicely," Lark said. "They take."

Olivia wrote:

Carla Dawes.

She looked down at her list and added a heading at the top in large letters.

SUSPECTS

- *Theodore Bramble*
- *Hazel Finch*
- *Marvin Pike*
- *Carla Dawes*

Underneath, she had written: People who hate jazz, then crossed it out so hard it tore the paper.

JJ played an offended note.

Olivia stared at him. "It's not personal."

JJ played another note that said it absolutely was.

Olivia shut her notebook.

"All right," she said. "I'm going into town."

Lark nodded; she had been waiting for that. "Errands."

"Errands," Olivia agreed, because it sounded more normal than quietly interrogating half the town. She grabbed her purse. Her notebook. Her courage, which she found wedged behind her ribs. And Sir Alistair's pocket watch, because having a Georgian ghost escort was apparently her new version of pepper spray.

Snowball followed her to the door, tail up, eyes half-lidded. The cat looked at Olivia with mild interest, then yawned hugely.

"You're not coming," Olivia said.

Snowball blinked, then flopped dramatically onto the hallway rug.

"Right," Olivia muttered. "Midday naps are your priority. Must be nice."

Outside, Mistwood was crisp and bright, the air cold enough to sharpen thoughts. The street was quiet, storefronts neat, holiday lights still strung along awnings from last winter, because Mistwood struck her as the kind of town that believed seasonal cheer could be permanent if you just refused to take it down.

Sir Alistair materialized beside her as she walked, hands clasped behind his back, the very picture of a Georgian escort who would absolutely judge modern shoes.

"Do proceed with caution, Miss March," he said. "The truth rarely greets visitors politely."

Olivia snorted. "Neither do most of the living, apparently."

Her first stop was the coffee kiosk downtown. Not because she wanted to support the competition. But because she wanted to see what Mistwood considered acceptable coffee.

The kiosk was polished, charming, and smelled of burned espresso and syrup. A man stood near the counter, speaking smoothly to the barista as if he owned both the kiosk and the surrounding air.

Theodore Bramble turned as Olivia approached.

He was polished. Opportunistic. Smiling. His coat was expensive. His hair was perfect. He smelled faintly of expensive cologne and entitlement.

"Miss March," he said warmly, like they were old friends who had never tried to buy each other's houses out from under them. "My condolences. Izzy's death was tragic."

He paused just long enough for the word tragic to land, then continued seamlessly.

"If you ever want to sell March House," he said, "I'll make the process painless. Merciful, even."

Olivia's smile tightened. "Merciful."

Bramble beamed. "Yes. You're grieving. It's an enormous responsibility. Property upkeep. The stress of running a business. I would hate to see you overwhelmed."

Sir Alistair's voice, low and sharp, drifted into Olivia's ear. "Vulture."

Olivia kept her expression polite. "When was the last time you saw Izzy?"

Bramble's eyes flickered for a fraction of a second, then smoothed again. "Oh, you know. Town events. The occasional meeting. I always tried to maintain a friendly relationship."

"Friendly," Olivia repeated. "Did she feel that way?"

Bramble chuckled. "Izzy was ... stubborn. She had strong opinions about her house. But that's what I admired about her."

Sir Alistair made a sound that was not quite a growl, but close.

Olivia nodded, filed the smoothness away like a knife. "Thank you," she said, and stepped away before she said something that would get her banned from local businesses.

As they walked away, Alistair leaned in. "He lies beautifully," he murmured. "I despise him."

Olivia made a minor note in her notebook and put a star beside Theodore Bramble's name.

Next stop: the historical society.

The building smelled of old paper and disapproval. Shelves of pamphlets lined the walls. Photos of Mistwood's "founding families" stared down from frames.

Hazel Finch looked as if she had been carved out of old cedar. Sharp. Upright. Permanently disappointed. Her hair was pinned back so tightly that Olivia suspected it could cut glass. She wore a cardigan that looked like it had never known joy.

Hazel's eyes traveled over Olivia as if appraising her for pests.

"I'm Olivia March," Olivia said.

"I know who you are," Hazel replied, her tone implying that knowledge was unfortunate.

Olivia forced a smile. "I have a few questions about Izzy. Any recent conflicts?"

Hazel's mouth tightened. "Isadora was ... eccentric."

"People keep using that word," Olivia said. "It's starting to feel like code for something."

Hazel's gaze sharpened. "She did not approve of proper historic property management."

Olivia blinked. "She lived in her own house."

"Yes," Hazel said, "and she treated it like a stage for whimsy."

Olivia's spine stiffened. "She treated it like her home."

Hazel sniffed. "I loved the house. The March House is a heritage home. A treasure. And now I hear you are considering a cafe?"

Olivia held her ground. "A coffee shop. Yes."

Hazel's eyes narrowed. "Turning a historic property into a commercial novelty is irresponsible."

Olivia's temper sparked, but she kept her voice even. "The house is behind on payments. It needs income."

Hazel's eyes flickered. Not guilt. Not sympathy. Something else.

Hazel's voice dropped slightly. "Some people don't value tradition," she said. "And some learn too late."

Olivia's skin prickled. "What does that mean?"

Hazel's mouth became a thin line. "It means what it means." She refused to elaborate, turning away to fuss with a stack of brochures as if they needed rescuing.

Sir Alistair leaned close to Olivia's ear. "I'd search her attic."

Olivia wrote Hazel Finch's name again and drew two stars beside it.

Her third stop was the general store.

Running into Sheriff Clay's wife in a place full of canned soup and yarn was exactly the kind of small-town irony the universe seemed to enjoy.

Carla Dawes was chatty, polished, and entirely too curious. Her smile was warm, her hair perfectly done, her outfit chosen with care.

She greeted Olivia like a friend, which immediately made Olivia suspicious.

"Oh, honey," Carla said, clasping Olivia's arm lightly. "I'm so sorry about Izzy. We were all just heartbroken."

Olivia nodded. "Thank you."

Carla leaned in as if sharing a secret. "Of course, Izzy was stubborn about that lake access path."

Olivia's stomach tightened. "The path."

"Yes," Carla said sweetly. "Some people just can't compromise. You'll be more reasonable, won't you?"

It wasn't phrased as a question, not really. It was a gentle demand wrapped in sympathy.

A chill slid down Olivia's spine.

"I'm still settling in," Olivia said carefully.

Carla's smile never wavered. "Of course. Take your time. But the town needs cooperation."

She patted Olivia's arm and drifted away, leaving Olivia standing beside a display of jarred pickles with the distinct feeling she had just been sized up.

Outside the store, Alistair reappeared, his expression grave. "That woman negotiates like a general preparing for invasion," he said.

Olivia exhaled. "Good. I've always wanted to go to war over a footpath."

On her way back toward March House, the old sheriff department SUV rolled up beside her like an accusation. Luke leaned across the passenger seat to lower the window. "I heard you were making the rounds," he said.

Olivia stopped walking. "I'm investigating."

Luke's jaw worked, the universal sign of a man both impressed and irritated. "Just don't stir up more trouble than you can handle."

Olivia lifted her notebook. "I'm not stirring anything. I'm sorting truth from noise."

Luke's eyes narrowed. "You're the cook," he said, as if it explained everything.

Olivia's eyebrows shot up. "That is not my name."

"It's how Clay described you," Luke said, and his tone made it very clear he did not approve of his uncle's descriptions.

Olivia stepped closer and held out a fresh copy of her suspect list.

Luke hesitated, then took it. He read it. His expression shifted as he scanned the names.

He looked up at her. "Bramble."

"Yes," Olivia said. "Smooth. Too smooth."

Luke's mouth tightened. "Hazel Finch."

Olivia nodded. "She hates joy."

Luke's gaze flicked back down. "Carla."

Olivia's voice went flat. "She wants my lake access and thinks sympathy is a crowbar."

Luke exhaled slowly, then tapped the last name. "Marvin Pike. You haven't talked to him."

"Lark says he's out of town," Olivia said. "Working construction."

Luke's eyes darkened slightly. "Convenient."

Olivia watched him.

"I'm not saying stop," Luke said finally. "I'm saying, be careful who you trust."

In Olivia's pocket, Alistair's watch ticked once. She wasn't sure if it was approving or ominous. Possibly both.

Luke looked at her for a long moment, then sighed. "You're going to do this no matter what I say."

"Yes," Olivia said simply.

Luke rubbed his jaw again. "Yeah. I figured." He rolled the window up and drove off, leaving Olivia standing in the road with her notebook and her bruising sense of purpose.

Back at March House, she spread her notes across the dining table like she was preparing for war.

The ghosts clustered around her.

"We have four strong suspects," Olivia announced. "Tomorrow we start digging deeper."

JJ played a suspenseful note.

Monique clapped as if this were opening night.

Simon saluted, crisp and solemn.

Daisy smiled softly.

Walt muttered, “People who break staircases are cowards.”

Olivia’s gaze slid toward the staircase. The polished wood. The ornate railing. The place where Izzy had fallen. The weight of what she was doing pressed down hard. She lifted her chin anyway. “We’re going to find out who did this.”

The house hummed in agreement, low and steady, like a heartbeat beneath the floorboards.

And for the first time, Olivia believed it.

CHAPTER EIGHT

The Garden Clue and the Near Miss

Late afternoon turned the solarium into a honey-colored greenhouse, all warm light and deceptive peace. Sunlight poured through the tall glass panes on the left side of March House and pooled across the tiled floor like molten gold. Dust motes floated in the beams like tiny, lazy ghosts of their own, drifting and spinning as if they had nowhere important to be. The lake beyond the property glinted steel-blue through the glass, calm and quiet, secrets in its depths and patiently watching a woman come home to inherit a haunted bed-and-breakfast and a murder-shaped problem.

Olivia had learned a long time ago not to trust pretty things. Not plated desserts. Not charming people. Not sunny afternoons. Still, she tried.

She stood at the solarium counter with her sleeves pushed up, forearms dusted in flour, elbows deep in pastry dough. The butter she had cut in earlier had finally surrendered, softening into the flour so the dough felt like damp sand under her fingertips.

She was testing recipes. Again.

Because apparently she had become the sort of person who did that now. The sort of person who baked as a coping mechanism while living in a Victorian mansion that creaked like it was gossiping behind her back, and played host to seven opinionated spirits with the manners of a dinner party where everyone hated each other but had nowhere else to go.

Olivia folded the dough over itself, trying to keep her movements calm and steady. In Chicago, she would have been plating, piping, torching, timing a dozen things at once. Here, in Mistwood, she was making pastries to convince future guests that March House was a charming place to stay, not a crumbling haunted money pit run by a woman who screamed the first time she saw a ghost as a child and still had not emotionally recovered.

She pressed her palms into the dough. The scent made her stomach settle, just a little.

"Okay," she murmured to herself. "You can do this. You can bake. You can run a B & B. You can survive in a town where everyone looks like they have been here forever, and you are the strange new thing they are poking with a stick."

The house creaked.

Olivia glared over her shoulder at the solarium door. "Do not creak at me. I am doing my best."

Silence.

Then the air shifted.

It was not dramatic. There was no gust of wind. No flickering candle flames. Just a subtle drop in temperature, as if someone had cracked open the door to a freezer two rooms away. Olivia's hands stilled in the dough. Her shoulders tightened.

"Oh no," she mumbled. "No, thank you. I am busy. I am butter-deep in dough. Whatever ghostly need this is, it can wait until I have at least one tray in the oven."

A faint movement caught her eye.

Daisy Chen appeared near the solarium shelf, right where her pressed-flower journal sat, safe and still, as if it had always belonged there.

Daisy looked different.

Not in the way the ghosts sometimes did, shimmering at the edges or growing slightly more solid when they were worked up. Daisy looked different because her expression was not soft. Not dreamy. Not gently curious.

She looked grave.

She held her journal close, an anchor keeping her from drifting away.

Olivia straightened slowly, keeping her palms on the counter like she might need it to hold her upright.

"What?" Olivia frowned. "Is that face?"

Daisy lifted an invisible journal, the way she sometimes did, reading something only she could see. Then she pointed sharply toward the back of the property.

Toward the garden.

Olivia looked at the oven. It was preheated. The tray was ready. The dough was technically behaving.

She looked back at Daisy. "You are not asking me to go outside."

Daisy pointed again.

Olivia narrowed her eyes. "No."

Daisy's brows drew together, not angry, but intent. Urgent.

It was the urgency that hit Olivia hardest.

Daisy had been the gentle one. The calm one. The one who drifted like a breeze through March House, trailing the scent of soil and crushed leaves, and occasionally appearing at inopportune times to stare at Olivia as if she were judging her life choices.

This was not Daisy in casual garden mode. This was Daisy in warning mode.

Olivia wiped her hands on her apron, leaving pale streaks across the fabric. "You want me to follow you," she said, already irritated at the answer forming in her own mouth.

Daisy nodded once.

"Right now."

Daisy nodded again.

Olivia exhaled through her nose, the way she did when she was trying very hard not to scream at the universe. "Fine. But if my scones burn, I am blaming you in a way that is both petty and spiritually creative."

Daisy did not smile.

That made Olivia's stomach tighten.

She turned, shoved the tray into the oven, and muttered, "Do not burn. Do not betray me. I have had enough betrayal in my life."

Then she followed Daisy.

Daisy moved through the solarium doors as if she belonged to the air itself, which, unfortunately, she did. Olivia stepped out behind her onto the back steps, and the late afternoon sunlight hit her face, warm and golden.

The garden spread out behind March House like a living, breathing creature. It was overgrown. Wild. Izzy's pride and joy and proof that her aunt had never believed in the concept of "manageable." Herbs ran rampant in thick green waves. Lavender bushes leaned into the path as if they were trying to hug her ankles. Rosemary had grown into a woody, defiant shrub. Thyme crept in sneaky little tendrils across the stones.

It was beautiful.

It was a mess.

It had thousands of hiding places.

Olivia's gaze slid automatically to the tree line beyond the property fence. The boundary was clear, the fence line marking the edge of March House territory.

Inside the fence line, Daisy could go anywhere. That had become an odd comfort in a life where comfort was now defined by supernatural property boundaries.

Daisy walked ahead of her, leading her along the herb beds. Olivia's boots sank slightly into the soft earth. The scent here was stronger than near the house, thick with crushed lavender and damp soil. It reminded Olivia too much of childhood visits, of Izzy's hands smelling like rosemary and lemon and something faintly smoky, like incense.

Daisy stopped near a patch of lavender that had grown tall and thick, the purple spikes bending in the breeze.

She kneeled.

Olivia waited, heart thudding, irritation draining away into something sharper. "Okay," She whispered, as if loudness might scare away whatever Daisy had sensed. "Show me."

Daisy pressed her hand to the soil.

Then she flickered.

Her form wavered like heat haze over asphalt.

"Hey," Olivia said, suddenly alarmed. "No, no. Don't do that. Don't do the mysterious disappearing act when I am standing in a garden full of hiding places and potential murderers."

Daisy faded completely.

Olivia stared at the spot where she had been. The lavender swayed gently, innocent as any plant could be, while probably hiding spiders.

"Not helpful," Olivia muttered, dropping into a crouch. She brushed her fingers through the dirt. It was loose. Recently disturbed. That made her pause. Her pulse quickened. Then she saw something. A corner of rusted metal, half-buried in the soil.

Olivia's breath caught. She dug carefully, fingers working around the edges. The metal was cold and rough against her skin.

A small tin. Rusted. Decades old. The thing looked like it had been hidden in the ground on purpose and left there until someone brave or stupid enough found it.

Olivia swallowed hard and lifted it out. Her hands shook. "Okay," she whispered. "Okay. This is either a clue ... or Izzy's extremely old emergency cookie stash."

She pried at the lid. It resisted. Rust had glued it shut with time. Olivia braced it against her knee and worked her nails under the edge, wincing as grit scraped against her skin. The lid popped open with a soft crack.

Inside was a folded slip of paper, yellowed at the edges. A key. And a photograph.

Olivia stared at the photo first, because her brain had decided it would rather process visuals than whatever emotional freight the paper might contain.

Izzy. Young. Not young-young, but younger than Olivia had ever known her. Her hair was darker, pulled back, and she wore that same sharp expression she had always carried, the one that said she had seen a thousand things and was unimpressed by most of them.

Beside her stood Hazel Finch.

Hazel looked younger, too, though even in the photo she had that same poised, tight-lipped air, as if she were holding a secret behind her teeth.

They stood in front of the historical society building. They were smiling. But it was stiff. Forced. The sort of smile people wore when the photographer said, "Say cheese," and what they really wanted to say was, "I will destroy you if you ever speak of this again."

Olivia's stomach flipped.

Hazel Finch.

She unfolded the slip of paper with fingers that felt too clumsy for something this fragile.

The handwriting was unmistakable. Izzy's.

If something happens, tell her the truth about Hazel. Signed: I.M. Isadora March.

Olivia's throat tightened so fast it hurt.

"If something happens," she whispered, eyes burning. "Izzy, something did happen."

Her gaze snapped up instinctively, searching for Daisy.

Nothing.

The garden felt ... different. Not just quiet. Eerily still. Even the breeze seemed to hold its breath.

Olivia's skin prickled.

Snowball appeared at the edge of the garden path. Her fur bristled. Her tail puffed out. She stared toward the treeline beyond the fence.

Olivia's heart thudded again, harder.

Snowball growled.

It was tiny. Fierce. A sound Olivia had never heard from her cat, who normally expressed displeasure by walking away with theatrical disappointment.

The medal on Snowball's collar clinked softly as she shifted her stance.

Olivia's stomach sank.

"Simon," she whispered.

As if summoned by her voice, Simon Talbot manifested beside the cat. His expression was serious. His posture rigid. The sunlight made him look more transparent, as if the day itself resisted the idea of his existing.

His gaze was fixed on the trees.

His hand hovered near where his rifle would have been.

Olivia's mouth went dry. "Is someone out there?"

A branch snapped.

The sound was sharp. Too close.

Olivia froze so hard her muscles ached.

Snowball's ears pinned back. Her fur stood even higher.

Simon took a step forward, protective. Something or someone was watching them.

Olivia's breath came shallow. "Okay," she whispered, voice thin. "I got the message. I am leaving now. I am leaving so politely."

Sir Alistair suddenly appeared behind her.

Olivia jerked. A sharp gasp ripped out of her. The tin almost slipped from her hands.

Alistair's expression was not mild disapproval today. It was anger, controlled but intense. Like an Englishman who had reached the limit of his emotional range and was now prepared to be extremely stern about it.

Bertie stood at his side.

The ghost dog's hackles were raised. His nose lifted, sniffing the air. A low growl rumbled from him, the first time Olivia had ever seen him anything but be delighted to exist.

Alistair's voice was clipped. "Miss March. We must go. Now."

Olivia clutched the tin tighter. "What did Daisy lead me to? And why is everyone suddenly acting like we are in the last act of a thriller?"

Alistair's gaze never left the treeline. "Now."

Bertie growled again.

That did it.

Olivia backed away from the lavender patch, slowly at first, eyes flicking between the trees and the path back to the solarium. Snowball moved with her, close to her legs like a furry white bodyguard. Simon followed, his presence a steady weight of protection.

They moved as a unit, like a feline-infantry squad escorting a very nervous pastry chef with a rusted tin box. Olivia reached the solarium steps. Relief surged in her chest. She was steps away from glass and locks and walls that, while not actually keeping ghosts out, at least kept most humans at bay.

Then something hit the ground behind her.

Hard.

The impact was heavy enough that Olivia felt it through the soles of her boots.

She whirled.

A rock lay in the dirt where she had been standing seconds earlier.

It was not a pebble. It was not a small garden stone. It was a solid, heavy rock, the kind that belonged in landscaping, not flying through the air.

Someone had thrown it. From the treeline. At her. Olivia's blood turned to ice. She bolted.

She tore up the solarium steps, shoved the door open, and stumbled inside, slamming it shut behind her with both hands. Her fingers fumbled at the lock, shaking so badly she almost missed.

Click.

Locked.

She leaned against the glass, chest heaving, tin box clutched like a lifeline.

Outside, the garden sat in calm, golden stillness, as if nothing had happened.

As if someone had not just tried to put a rock through her skull.

The ghosts flickered into full alert.

Monique appeared first, materializing with a gasp, one hand flying to her chest. "Someone threw a rock? At *you*?"

JJ's cornet blared a sharp note from the parlor, sudden and piercing, like an alarm.

Walt manifested with a scowl so deep it could have cracked concrete. "Who's messing with my garden?"

Flossie hovered near the staircase banister, half-hidden, eyes wide with fear.

Simon took his place near the solarium door, shoulders squared, gaze hard.

Alistair straightened his coat with furious dignity, as if preparing for battle in a drawing room.

Olivia pressed her forehead to the glass, breath shaking. Her vision blurred for a moment, adrenaline making everything too bright.

"That," she rasped, "was not an accident."

She slid into the nearest chair, knees weak, the tin still clutched in her hands.

Her first real clue. And it had almost gotten her killed.

She stared down at the contents again, forcing herself to breathe.

A tin box. A cryptic note. A photograph of Izzy and Hazel Finch. A key that felt suddenly heavy, as if it belonged to something bigger than a lock. And the unmistakable sense that Hazel Finch was hiding something enormous.

Olivia swallowed hard. She had not caught the person watching her.

She had not seen a face. Had not heard a voice. Had not even gotten a glimpse of movement, just the sound of the branch snapping and the rock hitting the earth like a promise.

Try and fail.

Olivia slumped deeper into the chair. Her hands trembled as she folded the tin shut, the rust scraping faintly.

"Okay," she whispered, more to steady herself than to speak to anyone else. "Hazel Finch has just moved to the top of the list."

Alistair stood behind her, his voice lower now, solemn. "Miss March ... someone is escalating."

JJ played a low, ominous note that seemed to settle into the bones of the house.

Olivia stared at the locked door, then at the garden beyond the glass.

The sunlight still looked warm. The lavender still swayed gently. Everything outside still looked peaceful. But she knew better now.

Someone had been out there, watching her, waiting. Someone had thrown a rock big enough to kill her if it had hit. And they had done it without hesitation.

Olivia's fingers tightened around the tin until her knuckles ached.

Her voice came out soft, shaking, but firm. "I'm not backing down."

The house creaked softly. Not a threatening creak. Something closer to an agreement. March House itself had heard her and decided, yes. That is the correct level of stubborn for this family.

Olivia swallowed, lifting her chin. She looked at the tin, at Izzy's handwriting, at the key that promised answers. If someone thought they could scare her off with a rock and silence, they were about to learn something.

Olivia folded the tin shut one more time, as if sealing her decision.

Her fingers trembled. Her voice did not.

"I'm not backing down," she repeated, half to herself and half to the ghosts who stood guard around her.

The oven timer buzzed, and she nearly jumped out of her skin.

Somewhere in the quiet, danger shifted, patient and unseen.

CHAPTER NINE

The Developer's Threat

Morning at March House arrived quietly, which Olivia had learned was suspicious in its own way. Sunlight filtered through the solarium glass in clean, pale sheets, turning the tiled floor into a grid of soft reflections. The lake beyond the property was calm, mist lifting slowly from its surface as if the world was taking a careful breath. For the first time since the incident in the garden, Olivia allowed herself to believe she might get a few uninterrupted hours of normalcy.

She clung to that belief with both hands.

The solarium table was buried under papers. Not chaotic papers, she told herself. Purposeful papers. Organized papers. Papers that meant she was building something rather than just reacting to threats and ghostly warnings.

There were spreadsheets printed out and annotated in pen. She had catalog pages torn from restaurant supply magazines. And graph paper covered in careful pencil sketches of seating arrangements. Her coffee shop's layout.

She leaned over the table, coffee mug cooling beside her, tapping her pen against the page while she compared espresso machine models.

"This one pulls faster," she muttered, scanning a column of specs. "But it costs enough to qualify as a second mortgage."

She circled a number, then crossed it out again. Pricing out espresso machines was humbling in a way that culinary school had not prepared her for. In Chicago, equipment costs had been someone else's problem. Here, every dollar felt personal because it was.

She slid the espresso pages aside and pulled her pastry menu draft closer. Scones were a given. Cardamom, cranberry-orange, maybe lemon rosemary if Daisy insisted. She jotted down ideas, then frowned thoughtfully.

"Savory options," she murmured. "You can't run a cafe on sugar alone." She made a note about breakfast sandwiches, then paused, pen hovering.

"Weekend jazz brunch," she said aloud, squinting at the ceiling. "That could work. Assuming JJ behaves."

JJ, who had been leaning in the doorway pretending not to listen, lifted his cornet and played a flirtatious little riff.

"That," Olivia said flatly, "was not an answer."

Sir Alistair stood near the corner of the room, hands folded behind his back, posture impeccable as ever. He surveyed the papers with an air of deep approval, as if Olivia were not planning a cafe but restoring an ancestral estate to its proper glory.

"You demonstrate admirable diligence, Miss March. Your aunt would have approved."

Olivia smiled. "She would have argued with my pricing and told me to charge more."

"A wise woman."

Daisy appeared near the window, half-transparent, smiling softly. She drifted closer to the table, peering down at Olivia's seating sketch, then pointed to a corner of the drawing and gestured enthusiastically.

"You think herbs there," Olivia said. "Decorative planters?"

Daisy nodded, delighted.

"I am not growing basil indoors," Olivia said firmly. "That is how things spiral."

Daisy laughed silently and drifted away, trailing a faint scent of earth.

It was a good morning. Quiet. Productive. Almost peaceful.

Bertie growled.

Olivia froze, pen still mid-note.

"Bertie," she said carefully, "if this is about the mail carrier again, I am not taking your side."

Bertie stood at the solarium window, small body rigid, hackles raised. A low, warning growl rolled from his chest, far more serious than his usual enthusiastic indignation.

Sir Alistair turned sharply. "That is not his usual objection bark."

Olivia straightened and followed Bertie's line of sight.

A black SUV rolled to a stop along the street directly in front of March House.

Not the driveway. The curb.

Her stomach dropped.

The vehicle sat there, engine idling, glossy and expensive and entirely out of place among Mistwood's collection of aging trucks and practical SUVs.

Theodore Bramble stepped out.

Olivia's fingers tightened around the edge of the table. "Oh," she whispered. "You have got to be kidding me."

Bramble adjusted his coat, glanced up at the house, and then deliberately approached the front porch via the walkway, every movement calculated to ensure she saw him coming.

And she did.

As Olivia plated her test pastries, arranging them with unnecessary precision, her gaze flicked back to the solarium glass again and again, tracking his progress.

Her pulse thudded.

Theodore Bramble. Developer. Investor. A professional shark in a tailored suit. The man who smiled like he was doing you a favor while pushing you off a cliff.

Olivia set the plate down and wiped her hands on her apron, already rehearsing polite refusals in her head.

"Do not," she told herself quietly, "throw a pastry at him."

Bramble knocked. Once. Firm. Confident.

Olivia took a breath and opened the door.

"Miss March!" Bramble said, flashing an apologetic smile that never reached his eyes. "Sorry to drop by unannounced. Only a moment of your time."

He stepped inside without waiting for an invitation.

Olivia's jaw tightened.

Sir Alistair appeared instantly behind her, spine stiff, expression offended on a deeply personal level.

Bertie circled Bramble's legs, growling softly, ghostly teeth snapping inches from expensive leather shoes.

Bramble did not notice.

"What do you want, Mr. Bramble?" Olivia asked, her voice cool.

He held out a folder. "A simple business matter."

She took it reluctantly and flipped it open.

A buyout offer.

The number stared back at her. Low. Offensively low.

Olivia laughed once, sharp and humorless.

"With your aunt gone, and no will located," Bramble said smoothly, "the property is in a transitional state. It would spare you considerable trouble if you sold before things get complicated."

Olivia snapped the folder shut. "I'm not selling."

Bramble's smile hardened. "You haven't even heard the number."

"I've seen enough."

He leaned in slightly, lowering his voice. "Izzy made things difficult for a lot of people. If you follow in her footsteps, you may find yourself in similar difficulties."

Bertie lunged.

Ghost teeth snapped inches from Bramble's calf.

Olivia flinched despite herself.

Bramble mistook it for fear.

Good.

A car door slammed outside.

Boots crunched on gravel.

Bramble turned just as Luke Thatcher stepped onto the porch, his SUV parked behind the black one on the street.

Luke took in the scene at a single glance.

Bramble. Olivia. The folder.

His eyes narrowed.

"Problem here?"

Bramble straightened. "Just a business discussion. Miss March knows what's best for her."

Luke stepped between them.

He was not smiling.

"You need to leave."

Bramble hesitated, then backed up one step. Then another.

Before turning away, he gave Olivia a final, cold stare.

"You're making a mistake, Miss March," he said. "The house will swallow you the way it swallowed your aunt."

Then he left.

Luke waited until the SUV drove away before turning back to Olivia.

"What did he say to you?"

She handed him the folder.

Luke scanned it and snorted. "He's been after March House for years. Showing up at your door is new."

"He threatened me."

Luke rubbed his jaw. "Don't be alone outside. Especially near the property line."

"I'm not hiding in the house like a frightened cat."

"I didn't say that." He was silent for a moment. "But be careful. People like Bramble don't like being told no."

"Thank you."

Luke nodded and left.

Sir Alistair watched him go. "A gentleman of few words. Refreshing. Though he needs a tailor."

Olivia laughed.

Then she looked back at the folder.

A photocopy slipped free. Old. Signed by Hazel Finch.

Her stomach tightened.

Alistair leaned closer. "Miss March … things are converging."

Olivia exhaled slowly.

"Hazel Finch is definitely at the top of the list."

CHAPTER TEN

Hazel's Secrets and a Closed Door

Morning sunlight flooded the solarium as if it had somewhere important to be. It came in fast and bright through the glass wall, warming the tiles beneath Olivia's feet and turning the air into something golden and deceptively cheerful. Outside, Mistwood Lake glittered through the property like polished steel. The mist rising off the water moved slowly, curling and thinning as the day woke up. The town itself took a long, careful breath. March House looked peaceful from the outside.

Inside, Olivia knew better.

She sat at the solarium table with her coffee mug cradled in both hands, staring at the photograph she had pulled out of the rusted tin box, hoping it might rearrange itself into an explanation if she glared hard enough.

Izzy and Hazel Finch. Standing together in front of the historical society building. Their smiles were stiff. Too controlled. The smiles people offered when they were being photographed with someone they had to tolerate, not someone they loved.

It was the minor details that bothered Olivia most. Izzy's shoulders were drawn just a fraction too tight. Hazel's chin was lifted, daring the camera to question her. Their bodies were angled slightly away from each other, a gap between them that said, without words, that their connection was not warmth. It was an obligation. It was history. It was something that held them close without letting them actually touch.

Olivia tilted the photo toward the light, then away again, studying the way the sun caught the glossy surface.

"Okay," she mumbled. "So either my aunt and Hazel Finch had the most awkward friendship in the history of human relationships, or Hazel Finch is lying."

Behind her, JJ leaned in the doorway, cornet tucked loosely under his arm. He played a soft little riff, the notes suspicious and curling, like they were sneaking around corners.

"I know," Olivia murmured. "It doesn't scream best friends."

JJ shifted the melody into something that sounded like skepticism dressed up as jazz.

"Izzy hid it," Olivia said, tapping the photo with one finger. "Buried it. In the garden. In a tin box that looks like it survived a century and three emotional breakdowns. You don't do that with a casual acquaintance."

JJ played a slow, questioning note.

"I'm not talking to you because you are helpful," she told him. "I'm talking to you because you're here and because if I talk to myself I sound like a documentary narrator, and I refuse to become that person."

JJ grinned and played something that sounded dangerously like amusement.

At the solarium threshold, Snowball sat like a tiny statue, white fur immaculate, tail wrapped around her front paws. Her blue eyes were fixed on the street. She looked peaceful, but Olivia had learned that Snowball's version of peaceful was basically a high-level military readiness, just with better grooming.

Simon stood near her, his presence faint in the bright light but unmistakable. He wasn't lounging. He wasn't drifting. He was watchful. Guarded. Ghost-cat patrol, the world's strangest neighborhood watch.

Every so often, Simon's gaze flicked toward the property line, then back to the street, as if he expected danger to stroll by wearing a smile and carrying a rock.

Daisy materialized near the table, a gentle smile and soil-smudged cheeks faintly visible through the sunlight. She leaned in and tapped the photo, too.

Not Izzy. Hazel.

Olivia looked at her. "Yes. I understand."

Daisy's expression softened, but there was still something intent behind her eyes. Not urgency, exactly. More like quiet insistence. Pointing toward a truth Olivia did not want.

Olivia exhaled slowly.

"I'm going," she said.

Daisy nodded and faded.

Olivia pushed back her chair. The legs scraped against the tile with a small, sharp sound that echoed through the solarium.

The scrape felt too loud. Everything felt too loud lately.

She picked up the photograph and held it in both hands for a moment, as if bracing herself. Then she slid it into her pocket carefully, flattening it so it would not bend. The pocket watch was next.

Sir Alistair's silver pocket watch sat where Olivia had left it earlier, on the small side table by the solarium shelf. It looked innocent there, like an heirloom, like something that belonged in a glass case with a little label beneath it.

Olivia knew better.

She slipped it into her coat pocket and felt the weight settle against her hip.

"Okay," she said quietly. "If I am doing this, I want backup."

Sir Alistair appeared immediately, the way he always did when his watch moved. Tall. Immaculate. Slightly offended by everything modern. He glanced around the solarium with the air of a man assessing whether sunlight itself had permission to shine in this room.

"You are leaving the house," he observed.

"Yes," Olivia said. "To go interrogate Hazel Finch."

Sir Alistair's eyebrows rose. "Bold."

"That's one word for it."

Bertie appeared beside him, tail wagging once, then stopping abruptly, sensing the seriousness emanating from his master and Olivia. He sniffed the air and gave a low rumble that made Olivia's stomach tighten.

"Great," Olivia muttered. "Even the ghost dog thinks this is a bad idea."

Sir Alistair straightened his cuffs. "Nevertheless, it is your decision."

Olivia looked at him. "Are you worried about me?"

Sir Alistair's expression remained dignified, but his tone softened just slightly. "I am concerned that your town has thrown projectiles at your head."

"That's fair."

She turned toward the hallway. And nearly collided with Lark.

Lark Waverly emerged from the kitchen carrying an armful of cleaning supplies that looked like they had been gathered for battle. A dust cloth hung from her shoulder like a sash. A spray bottle was tucked under her arm. She held the vacuum cleaner with the vacuum hose trailing behind her like a stubborn snake.

Her wild, gray hair was tied up in a loose scarf. Her jangly necklace of polished stones clinked with each step. She smelled faintly of patchouli, rosemary, and lemon oil, which was now Olivia's primary scent association for both comfort and impending chaos.

"Well," Lark announced, "I have declared war on the upstairs hall runner. It has been holding on to dust like it's a family heirloom."

Olivia blinked. "Good morning to you, too."

"It's not good yet," Lark said, eyes narrowing as she looked past Olivia toward the solarium. "It's just morning. Good is a state of mind."

Then her gaze flicked to Olivia's coat pocket.

Lark's smile sharpened. "You've got the fancy watch. That means you're leaving."

Olivia paused. "How do you always know that?"

Lark's eyes twinkled. "The air shifts. The house hums differently. Also, Snowball gets that look on her face like she's about to file a police report."

Snowball, as if offended, flicked her tail once without looking away from the street.

Olivia took a breath. "I'm going to Hazel Finch's house."

Lark froze. Not dramatically. Not dropping the supplies. Just a moment where she went still, and her humor dimmed, replaced by something steadier and heavier.

"Hazel," she repeated quietly.

Olivia nodded. "I need answers."

Lark's gaze drifted to the photograph's outline in Olivia's coat pocket, as if she could see it through the fabric.

"The energy in this room is shifting, dear," Lark said softly.

Olivia gave her a look. "Because you disapprove of my plan or because you have a mystical premonition?"

"Yes," Lark said promptly.

Olivia exhaled. "Lark."

Lark stepped closer, lowering her voice as if she were sharing a secret with the walls themselves. "Hazel Finch runs half the town's history. She knows everyone's grandmothers, everyone's scandals, and where all the bodies are buried. And I don't just mean metaphorically."

Olivia's stomach tightened. "Did Izzy ever talk about her?"

Lark's expression softened. "Rarely. When she did, it was never casual." Her fingers tightened around the vacuum cleaner handle. "She cared about Hazel once, in her own way. And Hazel cared about Mistwood in a way that can turn sharp when someone challenges it."

Olivia swallowed. "I'm not challenging Mistwood. I'm trying to figure out why Izzy wrote a note about Hazel and buried it like a confession."

Lark's eyes went distant for a heartbeat. "Izzy loved people fiercely," she said. "Even the ones who didn't deserve it. She believed the past should be faced. Hazel believes the past should be locked in a box and buried under the floorboards."

Olivia's throat tightened at Izzy's name. "I miss her."

Lark's smile trembled, then steadied. She reached out and squeezed Olivia's arm, firm and grounding. "I do too," she whispered. "Every day."

For a moment, the house felt still in the way a home goes quiet when it is listening. Then Lark cleared her throat briskly, humor snapping back like a rubber band. "All right. Before you go poking the town dragon, let me give you something."

Olivia blinked. "A sword?"

"A tea," Lark corrected, already turning toward the kitchen. "For courage. And grounding. And because you have a face that says you have eaten nothing except anxiety and coffee."

Olivia followed her to the kitchen doorway. "Lark, I can't stop for tea."

"You can," Lark said. "Because I am the heartbeat of this house, and the heartbeat says you are drinking the tea."

Olivia opened her mouth to argue. Then she shut it. Lark was already pouring steaming liquid into a travel mug, moving with the brisk confidence of a woman who had decided long ago that emotions were best handled with herbs and stubbornness.

Lark handed the mug to Olivia. "Drink. And remember, if Hazel says something that makes your stomach twist, that's your intuition. Or indigestion. But likely intuition."

Olivia took it. "Thank you."

Lark's gaze turned serious again. "Be careful," she said. "This town is small. The secrets feel bigger because there's nowhere for them to go."

Olivia nodded once. "I'll be fine."

Lark snorted. "You're an amateur sleuth with a haunted pocket watch and an attitude problem. You're absolutely not fine. That's why you're interesting."

Olivia couldn't help it. She smiled. "I'll be back soon."

Lark lifted her dust cloth like a blessing. "Go with good energy. And if you get murdered, I am haunting everyone."

Olivia stepped out the front door before she could respond to that.

The air outside was crisp, a cold that smelled like pine and lake water. Mistwood's main street was quiet, the morning slow to fully wake. A few cars passed. A dog barked somewhere in the distance.

Hazel Finch's house was only a few blocks away. Close enough that Olivia could walk. Which was good because walking kept her from overthinking. It kept her moving.

Sir Alistair walked beside her, his boots making no sound on the sidewalk. Bertie paced ahead and then back again, restless, sniffing at invisible currents like he could smell trouble.

The Finch residence appeared around the corner like a judgment.

It was tidy, old-fashioned, and intimidating in the way only houses owned by stern elderly women could be. The yard was neat. The steps were swept. The porch railings looked freshly painted. Curtains hung in the windows as if they had been measured for exact moral correctness.

Olivia stopped at the base of the steps. Her gut tightened. Something was off. Not supernatural, exactly. More like the air around the house held itself too still, like it was waiting.

Bertie started sniffing again, pacing in tight circles.

Sir Alistair manifested more solidly, frowning. "There is a certain rigidity to this place," he murmured.

"Like the entire house is holding its breath," Olivia whispered.

The curtains twitched. Hazel was watching. Deciding whether to answer.

Olivia lifted her hand to knock.

The door opened just before her knuckles made contact.

Hazel Finch stood there like a sentry. Gray hair pinned into a practical knot. Cardigan buttoned up. Spine straight. Eyes sharp as a spelling bee judge who enjoyed failure. Her gaze swept over Olivia in one quick assessment and landed on Olivia's face with cool recognition.

"Miss March," Hazel said. "I assume you're here about your aunt."

Olivia swallowed. "Yes."

Hazel's eyes narrowed. "People have been talking."

Olivia forced a polite smile. "Small towns are famous for their discretion."

Hazel did not smile back. "What do you want?"

Olivia pulled the photograph from her pocket and held it up. "You knew her well. Why didn't you tell me?"

Hazel's gaze flicked to the photo for a fraction of a second. Just long enough for Olivia to see the tightening in her jaw.

"I wouldn't say well," Hazel said crisply. "We were acquaintances. On certain committees. That's all."

Sir Alistair leaned toward Olivia's ear. "She lies as easily as she breathes."

Olivia kept her expression calm, even as irritation flared. "Izzy hid this photo," she said, voice gentle but firm. "Why?"

Hazel's eyes sharpened. Something flashed there, quick and dangerous. Anger, yes. But fear too.

"I don't appreciate being interrogated on my porch," Hazel said sharply. "Isadora was impulsive, reckless, and unwise. Her choices were her own."

Olivia bristled. "Are you talking about her antiques? Or the will she never told me about?"

Hazel froze. For a beat, the world went silent.

Even Bertie stopped pacing.

Hazel's expression became rigid, like a door locking. Then she said calmly, "I think you should leave." She stepped back inside. The door began to close.

Bertie growled.

Alistair muttered something that sounded like it belonged in an old duel and was a worse insult.

Olivia moved without thinking, sliding her foot between the door and the frame. Not aggressive. Not reckless. Just firm.

"Hazel," Olivia said, keeping her voice low. "Someone tried to scare me off. I'm not going away. If you know something, if you know why Izzy wrote about you, if you know who wanted her gone—"

Hazel's eyes flashed with cold fury. And then she slammed the door.

The impact jolted Olivia backward. Her foot slipped free, and she stumbled down one step, catching herself on the porch rail. For a heartbeat, she just stood there, stunned. Try and fail again.

Then something fluttered at her feet. A scrap of paper, pushed out by the force of the door closing.

Bertie sniffed it immediately, nose pressed close, confirming it was real.

Olivia bent and picked it up. It was a torn corner of an old photograph.

The edges were scalloped, vintage. The paper was thick, slightly yellowed. The image showed the corner of March House, the wrap-around porch visible, the angle familiar enough that Olivia's chest tightened.

She flipped it over. A handwritten date.

1989. The night she confessed.

Olivia's breath caught hard enough that she tasted cold air. "She confessed," Olivia whispered. "What did you confess, Izzy?"

Hazel's voice came from behind the closed door, low and vicious. "Don't dig where you don't belong."

Olivia's fingers tightened around the photo fragment. She slipped it into her pocket. Her pulse was racing now, not just with fear, but with certainty. Hazel knew something. And Hazel was terrified Olivia would uncover it.

Olivia stepped off the porch slowly and started walking back toward March House. The town felt smaller now. The street felt narrower. The houses on either side seemed to lean in, watching her pass. Halfway down the block, an SUV rolled up beside her. Luke's ancient department vehicle.

Of course it was.

It coasted along at walking speed, then stopped beside her. Luke leaned out the window, eyes narrowed. "Did you just get thrown off Hazel Finch's porch?"

Olivia stared at him. "Maybe."

Luke exhaled slowly, then rubbed his jaw, the familiar gesture that made it clear he was thinking too hard and resenting it. "Hazel doesn't slam doors unless she's scared," he said.

Olivia kept walking, forcing him to either keep up or give up.

He drove alongside her.

"You know her pretty well?" Olivia asked, glancing at him.

Luke nodded once. "She's on every committee in Mistwood. Runs half of them. Won awards for community service. She's protective of the town in her own way."

Olivia's mouth tightened. "Protective enough to lie to me?"

Luke's gaze shifted forward. His jaw flexed. "Protective enough to keep old secrets buried."

Olivia pulled the photo fragment from her pocket and held it up. "This fell out when she slammed the door."

Luke parked and got out, walking beside her now. He took the fragment carefully, studied the image and the writing on the back. His expression darkened. "I don't like this," he mumbled.

Olivia watched him, noticing the tension in his shoulders, the way his eyes scanned the street as if he expected someone else to appear.

"Find anything else," Luke said, "and you call me."

Olivia arched a brow. "I thought I wasn't supposed to stir up trouble."

Luke glanced at her, unimpressed. "You seem incapable of that."

Olivia blinked. "Thank you?"

Luke's mouth twitched, almost a smirk, but it vanished before it could fully form. "That wasn't a compliment."

Olivia smiled anyway.

Luke handed the fragment back. "Be careful," he said again, softer this time. Then he nodded once, awkwardly, having said more than he intended, and returned to his SUV.

Olivia watched him drive away, heart doing a small, annoying flutter that had nothing to do with fear.

She hated that. She hated even more that she did not hate it enough.

Back at March House, the solarium felt like a shelter.

Lark was in the hallway, fighting with the vacuum like it had insulted her ancestors.

"I told you," Lark said to the vacuum, "you are not the boss of me."

The vacuum whined.

Lark looked up as Olivia entered. Her eyes flicked over Olivia's face, her posture, the tension she carried.

"Oh," Lark said softly. "You went."

Olivia nodded, stepping into the solarium. "Hazel slammed the door in my face."

Lark clicked her tongue. "That's not good."

"No," Olivia agreed. "It's very not good."

She spread her clues across the solarium table, one by one, laying them out like a puzzle she refused to let defeat her. The photo from the tin. The torn fragment Hazel had inadvertently given her. The note about the confession. Bramble's threat. The attempted assault in the garden.

The staircase sabotage evidence that still hovered in the back of Olivia's mind like a shadow.

The ghosts gathered around her, drawn as if by gravity.

JJ leaned in and played a low, suspenseful riff that made the air feel heavier.

Daisy twisted her hands anxiously, her gaze fixed on the torn fragment.

Simon stood at attention, rigid and protective.

Walt appeared and muttered, "People who hide things are guilty."

Flossie nodded sadly, eyes soft with worry.

Alistair looked grave. His posture proud, but his expression was shadowed.

Olivia picked up a pen and wrote Hazel Finch's name at the top of her suspect list.

Then she circled it. Once. Twice. Three times.

Her voice was quiet but steady. "Hazel Finch knows something she shouldn't. And I'm going to find out what."

The house creaked softly. Not in complaint. In agreement. March House was settling around her, bracing for what came next. And Olivia, for the first time since she arrived, felt something solid beneath the fear. Resolve.

CHAPTER ELEVEN

Sabotage in the Solarium

Olivia was halfway through grinding coffee beans when the scream hit. It was not a normal scream. Not a startled yelp, nor a surprised shriek. It was a high, warbled sound that started at human panic and veered into banshee territory, echoing through March House as if the walls were amplifying it out of sheer enthusiasm.

Olivia froze, hand still on the grinder.

A scoop of beans slipped from her fingers and clattered onto the counter. A few escaped and bounced to the floor as if they were trying to flee the house before she could make them into anything useful.

Her heart slammed against her ribs.

"No," she yelled, already moving. "Nope. Absolutely not. I am not doing this today."

Sir Alistair flickered into existence beside her so fast the air seemed to snap. His expression was sharp, his posture instantly rigid, the ghostly equivalent of a man reaching for a weapon that did not exist.

"Miss March," he said, voice low. "Danger."

Olivia did not waste time asking what kind.

She sprinted.

Her socks slid slightly on the parquet floor as she tore through the dining room, nearly knocking a chair sideways. The smell of coffee followed her, suddenly useless, the comforting ritual destroyed before it even began.

She rounded the corner and almost collided with Lark.

Lark Waverly came rushing toward her, hair flying, eyes wide, clutching a feather duster in one hand and a sage bundle in the other. She armed herself with the first two things she could grab. Her apron was crooked. One of her earrings was missing. Her whole body radiated indignation so powerful that Olivia could practically taste it.

"Someone vandalized the solarium!" Lark cried. "And I just saged it yesterday!"

Olivia skidded to a stop, breath catching. "What?"

Lark waved the sage bundle like a warning wand. "I am telling you, the universe is rude. I cleansed that room with love and rosemary and good intentions, and someone had the audacity to come in and mess with it, anyway!"

Behind Lark, Daisy appeared in the hallway, wringing her spectral hands, her gentle face pulled tight with anxiety.

From somewhere deeper in the house, JJ's cornet gave a low, foreboding note that slid under Olivia's skin like cold water.

Olivia's mouth went dry. "Lark. What do you mean, vandalized?"

Lark turned sharply, motioning with the feather duster. "Come look."

Olivia followed her into the solarium.

And stopped dead in the doorway. The solarium was a disaster. Several of the potted herbs Olivia had been experimenting with were smashed across the tile floor. Ceramic shards glittered in the sunlight like broken teeth. Soil was scattered everywhere, dark and damp, smeared in wide, violent arcs. Someone had kicked the pots hard enough to make a point. A plant stand lay on its side, splintered, one leg snapped clean.

Olivia's stomach lurched. Her cafe dream, laid out in sketches and menus and hopeful delusion, looked like someone who did not believe in pastries or ambition had stomped on it. Her gaze snapped to the window. One of the solarium windows was slightly ajar. The latch had been forced. From the outside. And sitting in the middle of the floor, like a taunt, was a garden stone. Not a little pebble. Not something that a bored squirrel could have thrown. A stone far larger than a hand, heavy enough that Olivia's mind immediately and unwillingly replayed the image of the rock that had hit the ground behind her in the garden. The one that could have killed her.

The sunlight struck the stone, making it look almost ordinary. It was not ordinary. And then Olivia saw the glass. The words were scrawled across it in dirt, big and ugly and unmistakable. STAY OUT.

Olivia's breath left her in a thin sound.

"They got inside," she whispered.

Lark clutched her sage bundle tighter, knuckles white. "I felt something last night," she said, voice trembling with anger and fear. "A bad shift in the energy. I should have saged twice."

JJ blew a sharp, offended note, as if he, too, took personal issue with strangers breaking into his house.

Walt flickered in near the window frame and immediately dropped to one knee, inspecting the latch. "Modern tool marks," he grumbled, running ghostly fingers close to the damage without quite touching it. "Someone pried it open, all right."

Snowball stood in the solarium doorway, fur bristling, tail puffed as if pure outrage had electrocuted her. Simon manifested beside her, posture rigid, gaze sweeping the room and then the outside grounds. He was mapping a battlefield perimeter.

Monique materialized with a gasp so dramatic it could have been rehearsed. "How gauche!" she exclaimed, eyes wide as she took in the wreckage. "They didn't even wipe their feet."

Olivia swallowed hard. Her pulse was loud in her ears. Someone had been here. In her house. While she slept. While Lark slept.

While the ghosts watched, helpless in the way they sometimes were, bound to objects and rules and invisible lines that did not stop human malice.

Her hands shook. She forced herself to move forward, careful with her steps so she did not cut her feet on pottery shards. The tile felt colder than it should have in the morning sun.

She crouched near the toppled plant stand, lifting one broken piece, then setting it down again when she realized it was beyond saving.

"Okay," she whispered, more to herself than anyone else. "Okay. Breathe. Breathe like you are not about to lose your mind."

She reached out to gather the shredded remains of one knocked-down herb pot, scooping soil back into a rough pile. Her fingers brushed something beneath the broken ceramic.

Paper. Her stomach tightened. She slid her hand under the pot shards and pulled out a scrap of newspaper folded into a crude square.

For a moment, she just stared at it, heart pounding. Then she unfolded it. Inside was a handwritten message. Block letters. Thick black marker. Aggressive. Unmistakable.

YOU'RE NEXT.

The words seemed to vibrate in the bright light. The threat had weight.

Olivia's throat went dry so fast it hurt. For a moment, she could not breathe at all.

Lark stepped close behind her, peering over her shoulder. Her face went pale.

"Oh, honey." Lark looked frightened. "That's not a good vibe at all."

Olivia stared at the message, her vision narrowing. You're next. Not stay away. Not stop asking questions. Not go home. You're next.

It was not a warning anymore. It was a promise.

The room seemed to tighten around her. The sunlight was suddenly too bright. The air too thin.

The ghosts rallied.

Sir Alistair stepped behind Olivia, tall and imposing, his expression turning cold enough to frost glass. "This is unforgivable," he said, voice clipped like a blade.

Bertie ran in frantic circles, nails making no sound on tile, then charged straight at the broken window and barked furiously at the outside world.

Olivia jerked upright and turned her head toward the window as if she were watching something real outside.

"Uh," she muttered, because Lark was watching and she could

not very well explain that the ghost dog was attempting to fight the universe. "Probably a stray squirrel."

Lark blinked at her. "A squirrel vandalized the solarium?"

"No," Olivia said quickly. "A different squirrel. A rude one."

Lark narrowed her eyes. "You've got that look again."

Olivia hesitated.

Lark sighed, resigned. "The I'm talking to invisible people look."

Olivia swallowed, still holding the newspaper scrap. "Lark ... someone broke in."

"I know," Lark said fiercely, squaring her shoulders. "And I'm not letting fear freeze us."

Walt grumbled near the window, still inspecting the latch. "Should've installed motion lights. Or barbed wire. Or both."

Daisy kneeled near a smashed pot, her ghostly hands moving through the shards as if trying to re-form it by will alone. Her face was stricken.

Flossie materialized beside Olivia, clutching her pearl-handled comb to her chest, whispering over and over, "Danger ... danger ..."

JJ played a riff so sharp it rattled the windowpanes, the ghostly equivalent of bad vibes shouted through a trumpet.

Simon took a post by the window, gaze scanning the grounds beyond the glass, posture locked into soldier-ready stillness.

Snowball sat in the doorway like a tiny white sentinel, eyes wide and furious.

Olivia's fingers tightened around the paper. She forced herself to look up again at the dirt-scrawled words on the glass.

STAY OUT.

A handprint smeared on the inside of the frame caught her eye. It was not random.

It was too defined, too deliberate. Fingers. Palm. The pressure marks of someone who had braced themselves while climbing in.

Olivia stepped closer, heart hammering. The dirt smudges formed an almost perfect handprint. Someone had pried the latch and climbed inside. From the garden side. Under cover of darkness. While she slept.

Her pulse spiked. If they got this close. If they were inside. If they were willing to throw stones and leave threats. Whoever killed Izzy was escalating.

The thought hit like a shove.

This was not some vague small-town drama. This was not gossip, suspicious glances, or committees arguing about bake sale funds. This was violence. This was intent.

Lark's hand landed gently on Olivia's shoulder. Warm. Solid. Grounding.

Olivia's breath hitched, and she realized she had been holding it.

"Sweetheart," Lark said softly. "Izzy once said the house protects its own. And I believe it."

Olivia swallowed, eyes stinging.

Lark squeezed her shoulder. "But protection doesn't mean inaction. You can't let fear freeze you."

Olivia turned her head slightly, looking at Lark. "I'm not frozen."

Lark lifted a brow. "You are vibrating, Olivia."

That almost made Olivia laugh, but the sound caught in her throat.

Lark's eyes softened. "Someone is scared," she continued, quieter now. "That means you're close."

The words slid into Olivia's chest like a match lighting. Close. Hazel's fear. Bramble's threat. The garden attack. This break-in. Someone was unraveling. Someone was losing control.

Olivia forced her shaking hands to still. Then she did the smart thing. She stopped moving. She stopped touching anything. She backed away from the broken glass and the dirt-scrawled threat, and the smashed herbs, and she pulled out her phone. Her fingers trembled as she dialed the sheriff's office.

Clay's voicemail answered.

Olivia stared at the screen for half a second, listening to the cheerful recorded greeting that sounded like it belonged to a man hosting a pancake breakfast, not running a law enforcement department.

She hung up. Immediately redialed. This time, she didn't waste time.

"This is Olivia March at March House," she said, voice tight. "I need Deputy Thatcher. Right now."

She ended the call before anyone could offer her a suggestion involving patience or calming tea.

Lark watched her with approval, sage bundle still clutched like a weapon. "That's my girl."

Olivia swallowed, forcing steadiness into her breathing. "I'm done pretending this is nothing."

The house creaked softly.

The ghosts shimmered brighter, as if drawn by her resolve.

Luke arrived in minutes. His SUV pulled up to the street curb in front of March House, not into the driveway, recognizing the need for speed and proximity. He jogged up the porch steps, jaw clenched, eyes scanning the house like he expected to catch someone mid-crime.

Olivia met him at the door and led him through the dining room into the solarium.

Luke's face hardened the moment he stepped inside. His gaze swept over the scene. The forced window latch. The smashed pottery. The thrown stone. The dirt-scrawled words. The newspaper scrap in Olivia's hand. The block-letter threat. YOU'RE NEXT.

Luke exhaled slowly. The kind of breath that said this just went from annoyance to real danger.

He pulled on gloves without hesitation. "Good," he said, voice clipped. "You didn't touch anything."

Olivia lifted her chin. "Of course not."

Sir Alistair, unseen beside her, murmured approvingly, "Smart woman."

Luke moved methodically, the way only someone deeply competent could. His presence changed the air in the solarium, turning chaos into a scene he could control. He photographed the damage first, moving around the room with careful steps, the camera snapping quietly. He bagged the threatening note, sliding it into the evidence bag as if it were radioactive. He swabbed the windowsill. Checked the tool marks. Measured the forced latch gap with a practiced eye. Examined the stone's position and angle, reconstructing the trajectory in his mind.

Lark stood nearby, hugging her sage bundle, whispering prayers under her breath, her lips moving with quiet determination.

Snowball sat like a tiny crime-scene sentry, eyes fixed on Luke.

Simon stood guard behind her, posture unwavering.

Luke stopped in front of the dirt-scrawled STAY OUT and frowned deeply.

"This isn't a prank," he said. "This is escalation."

Olivia swallowed hard. "I know."

Luke turned to her, eyes sharp. "From now on, you don't go outside alone. Not even into the garden."

Olivia opened her mouth, instinctive defiance rising. Then she saw his expression.

He was not ordering her as if she were a reckless child. He was worried.

The realization landed with a strange warmth in her chest that she did not have time to process.

Olivia closed her mouth slowly. "Fine," she said, voice tight. "I won't go alone."

Luke nodded once; it mattered more than he wanted it to. He stepped aside and lifted his radio.

"Thatcher to Dispatch," he said. "I need a CSI kit and evidence pickup at March House."

Clay's voice crackled through a moment later, loud enough that Olivia heard it clearly.

"Probably just wind damage," Clay said, tone breezy. "You know how those old houses are."

Luke did not even blink.

"It's a break-in," he said, voice flat. "With threats." His tone left no room for argument.

There was a pause on the line. Then Clay muttered something useless that Luke ignored.

Olivia met Luke's eyes. This was the first time he had fully believed her. Not just tolerated her. Not dismissed her as an outsider with opinions. Believed her.

An hour later, after prints were dusted and evidence collected, Luke stood in the solarium doorway and gave Olivia a final look.

"Lock your doors," he said. "All of them. I'll be checking in."

Olivia nodded. "I will."

Luke held her gaze for a beat longer than necessary, then turned and left, boots crunching on the gravel shoulder as he headed back to his SUV.

The front door shut. The house seemed to exhale.

Sir Alistair materialized beside Olivia, adjusting his cuff with deliberate calm. "He is a good man," Alistair said. "Somewhat disheveled ... but good."

Bertie barked once in agreement, tail wagging furiously.

Only after the deputies left did Olivia finally let herself move again.

She and Lark began cleaning. Lark rolled in the shop vac like a proud commander, patting it affectionately. "Come on, Mabel," she murmured. "We have trauma to vacuum."

Olivia swept glass into evidence-safe bins Luke had left behind for disposal, hands steady now, anger replacing the shaking.

Daisy hovered near a shattered herb pot, trying to reassemble it. Her hands passed through shards again and again, frustration written across her gentle face.

Walt muttered about reinforcing the latch.

JJ played a low, simmering note that felt like determination in sound form.

Flossie floated around them, tidying dust motes as if cleanliness could ward off evil.

Simon remained planted by the window, watchful.

Snowball sat beside him, eyes narrowed.

Olivia straightened at last, dust on her cheeks, breath still a little shaky but steady. She looked at the ruined solarium. The heart of her cafe dream. She looked at the ghosts behind her.

She looked at Lark, solid and unshakeable at her side. And she said, voice firm, "I'm not backing down. Whoever did this thinks they can scare me. They're wrong."

March House creaked softly. Not ominously. It was a vow.

The ghosts shimmered brighter.

Lark patted Olivia's shoulder. "That's my girl."

And the sunlight kept pouring in, bright and merciless, the house itself refusing to go dark.

CHAPTER TWELVE

Luke Takes Her Seriously

The dining room of March House had become what Olivia could only describe as a bureaucratic war room. It was not, strictly speaking, built for this. It had been built for polite breakfasts served on china, for evening conversations under soft lamplight, for the guests who wrote glowing reviews about "historic charm" while ignoring the floorboards that creaked like they were holding grudges.

Now it was covered in paperwork. Not normal paperwork, either. Not harmless receipts and schedules and reservation logs. This was the paperwork that carried threats in its margins and secrets at its edges.

Olivia sat at the long dining table with an enormous cup of coffee in front of her. There were faint smudges of dust on her fingers because, no matter how hard she tried, March House had a way of making her look like she had wrestled an attic.

She had arranged everything neatly in piles because chaos on paper was the one kind she could control.

Pile one: the buyout offer Theodore Bramble had shoved at her, the number still insulting every time she looked at it.

Pile two: the torn photograph corner Hazel Finch had dropped when she slammed the door in Olivia's face. The scalloped edge sat like a little jagged grin. The date on the back, 1989, seemed to stare up at her every time she moved it.

Pile three: the threats. The newspaper scrap that said YOU'RE NEXT in thick, aggressive block letters. The memory of STAY OUT scrawled in dirt across the solarium glass.

Pile four: the permit application to turn the solarium into a cafe. Forms. Requirements. Boxes to check. A line that asked for "intended business use" like she could write "coffee shop that will probably be haunted" without someone calling a therapist.

Olivia stared at the permit application for several long seconds, then rubbed her temples. "I don't even know what I'm looking for anymore," she muttered.

Across the table, Monique lounged in a dining chair as if it were a chaise in a Paris salon. She looked immaculate as always, black beaded flapper dress catching the light, lipstick perfect, eyes sharp. She flicked her gaze over Olivia's outfit with open disdain. "That sweater is fine for casual sleuthing, darling, but not for bureaucratic warfare."

Olivia didn't look up. "It's a sweater. Not a sword."

"It is a very ... earnest sweater."

"That is the nicest insult you've ever given me."

Monique waved a hand. "Wear something that says you are competent and unafraid. Bureaucrats can smell weakness. It's like perfume to them."

Walt appeared near the doorway, half-faded, scowling as he glanced toward the hall. "Need sturdier door locks," he muttered, as if he had been thinking about it for hours and resented that no one else had prioritized it the way he did.

Daisy drifted in and out near the dining-room windows, her gaze repeatedly flicking toward the solarium, anxious. She kept peeking in that direction as if expecting another intruder to crawl through the glass at any second.

Simon stood in the doorway like a sentinel, posture rigid. Snowball was curled against his shin, white fur bright against the darker wood floor, her eyes half-lidded but alert in that way cats managed to be while pretending they were napping. The medal on her collar glinted faintly when she breathed.

The entire room seemed to be holding its breath.

Then Lark bustled through the hall with a basket of clean linens balanced on her hip, humming Fleetwood Mac under her breath.

She moved as if she could hold March House together with nothing but determination, patchouli, and a healthy disrespect for negative energy. She tossed a glance toward the dining table. "You look like you're preparing to fight an octopus."

Olivia sighed. "Feels about right."

Lark's humming didn't stop. "Octopuses are smart. Bureaucrats are worse."

"That is deeply comforting."

Lark set the basket down on a sideboard, smoothed a sheet with a practiced hand, then studied Olivia's face.

"The energy in here is crunchy," she observed.

Olivia blinked. "Crunchy."

Lark nodded solemnly. "Like stepping on dry leaves that you didn't know were there. You're thinking too hard. Your brain is making that noise."

Olivia exhaled. "How do you always know when I'm spiraling?"

Lark tapped her own chest. "Heartbeat of the house, sweetheart."

Monique sniffed. "She's right. Your aura is practically clenching."

Olivia finally looked up. "Please do not say aura with that much confidence. You are dead."

Monique smiled. "And yet, I still have taste."

Olivia dropped her gaze back to the papers, trying to focus. Permit meeting. Cafe dream. Threats. Hazel. Bramble. Izzy. Her stomach tightened. She took a sip of coffee. It was strong enough to qualify as emotional support.

A knock hit the front door.

Olivia jolted so hard the coffee sloshed.

Snowball's ears perked. Simon's posture tightened. Daisy drifted toward the hallway, wanting to see but also wanting to hide.

Lark lifted her head, eyes narrowing in that intuitive way that suggested she was reading the world like tea leaves.

"Oh," she mumbled. "That boy's energy signature is a storm cloud wrapped in flannel."

Olivia's pulse spiked. "Luke?"

Lark didn't answer. She just headed toward the door, linens

forgotten, sage bundle somehow already in her hand like she had been waiting for an excuse.

Olivia stayed seated because she had learned that if she stood up too fast in moments like this, she tended to do something dramatic, like fling papers or accidentally confess to crimes she hadn't committed.

Sir Alistair materialized near the dining table, straightening his coat with measured approval. "Ah," he said. "The deputy."

Bertie popped into existence and trotted in a circle around the table, tail wagging.

"Please," Olivia murmured, "do not bark at him."

Bertie barked once, softly, promising nothing.

Luke stepped inside.

He didn't enter as a casual visitor. He entered like an officer. His eyes scanned automatically: doorways, corners, hallways, windows. The way someone looked when they were checking a perimeter, not stepping into a home. His buckskin jacket hung open. His jaw was shadowed with five o'clock stubble. His eyes looked tired but sharp.

Lark stepped aside, sage bundle still in hand. "Morning," she said cheerfully, as if she hadn't just described his aura as weather.

Luke gave her a polite nod and kept moving toward the dining room.

Alistair straightened more. Luke's presence demanded dignity from the entire room.

Bertie circled Luke's boots, sniffing and rumbling low in his throat.

Luke didn't react to the ghost dog, of course, but he paused slightly as if he sensed ... something. A shift. A pressure. His gaze flicked downward for a fraction of a second, then back up.

Olivia watched him, her chest doing that annoying little flutter it had started doing in his vicinity.

She blamed adrenaline.

Luke's gaze landed on her and held.

"I need to talk to you," he said.

Olivia swallowed. "About the break-in?"

Luke stepped closer to the table, eyes flicking to the stacks of evidence. His brain was already sorting it into categories.

"About everything," he said.

That should not have sounded intimate. It did.

Luke reached up and pulled his hat off, setting it on the table.

It was the first time Olivia had seen him remove it indoors. Something about it felt strangely personal, like he had just stepped out of his role as Deputy Thatcher and into something quieter and more real.

Olivia's throat tightened.

Luke's voice was low and serious. "Between the attempted assault in the garden, the break-in, the threats ... someone's targeting you. And they're not stopping."

Olivia nodded, because pretending otherwise would be insulting to both of them. "I know."

Luke met her eyes, steady and fully present. His jaw flexed, a familiar sign he was thinking hard. Then he said quietly, "I should've taken you seriously sooner."

Olivia stared at him.

It wasn't a grand apology. Luke Thatcher didn't do grand. But it was the closest thing to an admission she had heard from him since she'd arrived in Mistwood, and it lifted a weight.

Monique leaned toward JJ and whispered loudly enough that Olivia heard it, "Oh, he likes you."

JJ played a swoony jazz note that had no business existing in a tense conversation.

Olivia's cheeks warmed. She did not look at either of them. She did not react. She absolutely did not acknowledge that her heart had just done an annoying little hop.

Luke looked down at the table. "Show me what you've got."

Olivia slid the piles toward him, careful and organized, as if she were presenting evidence to a judge instead of a grumpy deputy who looked as though he had never enjoyed a meeting in his life.

Luke studied the tin from the garden first. The key. The photograph of Hazel and Izzy. The torn corner dated 1989. His expression darkened. Then he said something Olivia did not expect.

"Izzy and Hazel used to be close."

Olivia's breath caught. "You knew that?"

Luke nodded once. "Everyone in town knew. Or suspected. They were on committees together, always together. Then something happened in the late '80s. A big falling-out. Hazel won't talk about it. Izzy never did either."

Olivia's fingers tightened on the edge of the table. She slid the torn photo fragment toward him. "Hazel dropped this. It says the night she confessed. Confessed what?"

Luke's hand went still for a beat. He gripped the table edge, jaw tight. "I don't know," he said. "But whatever it was ... it broke them."

Sir Alistair stepped closer, murmuring softly near Olivia's shoulder. "Whatever truth lies there, Miss March ... it frightened her."

Olivia leaned forward. "She's lying about something. And she's scared I'll dig it up."

Luke did not argue. He looked up at Olivia, eyes narrowed. "Hazel Finch isn't physically dangerous," he said. "But she's powerful. She knows everyone in this town. She controls every historical record."

Olivia felt her pulse quicken. "If Izzy hid something in those archives ..."

Luke nodded grimly. "Hazel could destroy it."

The words hit like cold water.

"And if someone else found out about that secret," Luke continued, voice lower now, "they might kill to keep it buried."

Olivia's heart thudded.

It was the first time Luke had said it. Not implied. Not hinted. Acknowledged. Murder.

This was no longer an unfortunate accident. Not to Luke. Not anymore.

The dining room felt suddenly smaller, the walls closer.

Lark slipped into the room quietly, sensing the heaviness and refusing to let it settle unchecked. She set down a tray of chamomile-lavender tea on the table with purposeful gentleness.

"You two look like you're planning a coup," she said briskly. "Drink something."

Olivia managed a small, grateful smile.

Luke picked up the mug as if it might bite him. He sniffed it cautiously.

Olivia watched, equal parts amused and touched by his obvious distrust of anything herbal.

Luke took a sip. His shoulders lowered, just a fraction. It was subtle. Barely there.

But Olivia saw it.

The ghosts leaned in like spectators at a sporting event.

Monique whispered, "He likes it."

Walt muttered, "No, he's pretending."

JJ played a little flourish that sounded like encouragement.

Olivia pressed her lips together, fighting a laugh.

Luke set the mug down, gaze flicking to Olivia's face again as if noticing her expression.

"What?" he asked warily.

Olivia cleared her throat. "Nothing."

Lark smiled sweetly. "That tea fixes a lot of things, Luke."

Luke's mouth tightened. "I don't need fixing."

"Everyone needs fixing," Lark said cheerfully. "That's what living is."

Luke exhaled through his nose and turned back to the evidence, but he looked calmer. Slightly less like a storm cloud wrapped in flannel. He stood up, setting the mug down with care.

"I'm officially reopening the investigation," he said.

Olivia blinked. "Can you do that? Without Clay?"

Luke's expression did something very close to a smirk, except it stayed mostly trapped behind professionalism.

"No," he said. "That's why I'm doing it without telling Clay."

Olivia stared at him. A secret investigation. With her. Her breath caught. "Luke?"

He stepped closer, voice lower, steady. "You're not alone in this, Olivia."

Her cheeks warmed again, annoying and undeniable. Olivia swallowed. "Good," she said, forcing her voice to stay firm. "Because I'm not backing down."

Luke's mouth curved, not much, but enough. "I didn't think you would," he said.

The words settled a warmth in her chest.

Luke headed toward the porch. At the door, he paused and

looked back. “I’ll check on Hazel,” he said. “Quietly. You focus on the house. And don’t wander alone.”

Olivia opened her mouth to argue automatically, then closed it. “Fine.”

Luke nodded once and left.

Snowball trotted after him to the end of the porch, tail flicking. Simon glowed faintly behind her, posture straight, like he was saluting.

Inside, Olivia turned back to her ghostly household. Her voice came out soft, surprised, determined. “Okay,” she said. “We’re really doing this.”

JJ played a rising jazz riff.

Monique snapped her fingers.

Daisy beamed.

Walt grunted approval.

Flossie peeked out with nervous determination.

Alistair stood tall, dignified, ready.

And March House seemed to settle warmly around them, not creaking in warning, but bracing itself. A home that had decided it would protect its own.

CHAPTER THIRTEEN

The Empty Hiding Place

Olivia was in the kitchen doing the one thing that usually made her feel like a functional human being. She was making dough. Not the complicated, dramatic sort of dough that required the precision of a surgeon and the patience of a saint. Just another solid test batch for pastries, the kind she could tweak and adjust until it behaved. Flour dusted her fingertips. Butter was cold and obedient. The mixing bowl sat steady in her hands like an anchor.

For a few minutes, it almost felt normal. Then the air changed.

Olivia paused mid-stir, spoon hovering. Not because she heard something, but because she felt it in her skin first, a shift in pressure as if the house had leaned closer to listen.

Daisy flickered into view near the pantry door.

Olivia immediately knew something was wrong.

Daisy did not drift in with her usual gentle calm, smiling like a woman who carried sunshine and garden dirt in her pockets. Daisy was pacing.

Pacing.

A ghost who normally floated like a breeze was moving back and forth in quick, anxious steps, wringing her spectral hands trying to twist the worry out of them.

It was unsettling in a way Olivia couldn't fully explain. Seeing a ghost panicked was like watching a lighthouse start screaming.

"Daisy?" She set the spoon down. "What's wrong?"

Daisy turned sharply. Her eyes were wide, intent, almost frantic. She pointed toward the back lawn. Then, toward the lake. Then toward the old gazebo at the back of the property near the fence line, with a spectacular view of the lake.

Olivia's stomach tightened.

Snowball, who had been loafing on the kitchen mat with the regal laziness of a cat who believed the world existed to provide her warmth, lifted her head. Her ears twitched. Then she stood and trotted toward the back door with purpose.

Simon appeared behind her instantly, rigid and alert, as if he had been waiting for a reason to manifest fully.

Sir Alistair materialized beside Olivia, expression composed but watchful. "Miss March," he said, voice low, "I believe Daisy wishes to show you something important."

Olivia stared at Daisy, then at the back door. A rock had almost brained her the last time Daisy had led her somewhere.

"This is becoming a pattern," Olivia muttered.

Daisy pointed again, more urgently.

Olivia exhaled. "All right. Fine. But if this ends with me being murdered in a gazebo, I am haunting everyone in this town out of spite." She wiped flour off her hands, grabbed a hoodie from the hook by the kitchen door, and tugged it on.Just outside, she told herself. Just a minute.

The second she reached for the back door handle, Lark poked her head into the kitchen from the hallway, wild gray hair half-tied up, apron already smudged with something that looked suspiciously like dust and determination.

"Going somewhere, honey?" Lark asked, eyes narrowing in that way that said she was about to be both supportive and extremely unimpressed.

Olivia forced a casual tone. "Just outside. I'll be back in a minute."

Lark gave her a long-suffering, mom-of-grown-kids look that made Olivia feel twelve and guilty even though she was thirty-one and paying bills.

"Mm-hm." Lark didn't sound impressed.

From the parlor, JJ's cornet drifted in with a warning riff, low and uneasy. The ghost equivalent of be careful, but with jazz.

Olivia paused with her hand on the door. "Thank you for the ominous soundtrack," she called in the direction of the parlor. "Very subtle."

JJ answered with a note that sounded like, you're welcome, but also you're doomed.

Olivia opened the back door and stepped outside. The air hit her immediately, crisp and sharp with a September chill. Mistwood had that particular kind of cold that didn't feel like winter yet. Instead, it seemed the season was turning its head and watching you.

Leaves skittered across the lawn in little bursts, dry and restless. The lake glimmered steel-blue, calm but uninviting, its surface so smooth it seemed to hide something beneath it.

Daisy glided ahead, motioning for Olivia to keep up.

Sir Alistair stayed at Olivia's back; a formal bodyguard who also happened to be dead.

Bertie darted around the yard, nose to the ground, sniffing aggressively at bushes. Could he smell danger hiding behind the hydrangeas?

Snowball followed behind Olivia, tail flicking. Simon's presence hovered close to her, his aura a shimmering, invisible armor around the cat. It made Snowball look somehow even more like a small general leading troops into battle.

Olivia's boots crunched softly on the lawn as she crossed toward the gazebo. It was made of weathered wood and peeling paint. The type of structure that had probably been romantic once and now mostly served as a place for spiders and secrets.

As she got closer, Olivia felt it. A wrongness. Not a ghost, exactly. Not the chill that came with spirits or the charged hum of the house when the ghosts were active. This was different. This was the sensation of something having happened here. A disturbance, similar to finding footprints in fresh snow, except the snow was invisible, and the footprints were in her gut. A presence that had already come and gone.

Olivia slowed, eyes scanning the area. The gazebo itself was still. The lake lapped gently nearby, innocent as ever. But she no longer trusted innocence.

Daisy floated inside the gazebo and pointed toward the bench that ran along one side.

Olivia stepped up onto the gazebo floor. The boards creaked under her weight, the sound loud in the quiet morning. The smell of lake water and old wood rose around her.

Daisy pointed again, more specifically.

A plank on the bench. A loose one.

Olivia kneeled, moving carefully, controlled. Not disturbing anything unnecessarily. Luke had drilled at least one good habit into her during the break-in: do not touch things like an amateur who wanted to ruin evidence.

She slid her fingers under the edge of the plank. It lifted more easily than it should have.

Olivia held her breath.

Underneath was a small compartment, tucked neatly into the bench structure. It was shallow but wide enough to hold something important. Something flat. Something folded.

It was a perfect hiding place. The sort of hiding place someone used when they didn't trust the world to leave their secrets alone.

Olivia's pulse spiked hard. A will. A document. Something Izzy didn't want anyone to find until the right moment.

Olivia leaned closer. And froze. The compartment was empty. Not old-empty. Not abandoned-empty. Recently disturbed empty.

Dust smudges marked the wood where something had been slid out. The dust wasn't settled evenly. It was streaked, as if fingers or paper had dragged through it. On the gazebo floorboards nearby, faint but visible if you were looking, was a boot print.

Olivia's throat tightened. And caught on the edge of the compartment, a tiny flag of loss, was a scrap of parchment-like paper. Torn. As if someone had pulled a document out too fast and ripped it.

Olivia stared for a long moment, heart sinking. "Someone beat us here," she whispered.

Daisy's expression crumpled. Her hands twisted anxiously. Her eyes looked almost apologetic; she had led Olivia to hope and then watched it vanish.

Sir Alistair crouched beside Olivia, peering into the empty

compartment, frowning deeply. "Someone opened this in a hurry," he said, voice tight. "And recently."

Bertie gave a low, whining growl, the sound of a dog who wanted to bite someone but could only exist in frustration.

Snowball hissed suddenly, staring out toward the lake as if she sensed something moving where it shouldn't.

Simon's posture snapped even more rigidly. He shifted slightly, gaze scanning the tree line beyond the gazebo like a lookout watching for enemy movement.

Olivia forced herself to focus. The scrap. The only thing left. She pulled out her phone first and took photos. One of the compartment. Another from a different angle. Then another close-up of the dust smudges. Another of the boot print on the floorboards. Evidence. Proof. She had learned the hard way that her memory was not enough.

She set the phone down and carefully lifted the torn scrap of parchment-like paper. It was thicker than modern printer paper. Smoother. Slightly textured, elegant in a way that suggested old documents and important signatures. Her fingers trembled. She turned it slightly. One word was visible on it. Just a fragment of a line.

"... March."

Olivia's breath caught. "The will was here," she whispered. And now it was gone. A sound exploded from the water. A splash, sudden and sharp, loud enough that Olivia jerked so hard she nearly toppled backward.

Daisy recoiled, hands flying up, her form flickering.

Sir Alistair straightened sharply, gaze snapping toward the shoreline.

Bertie barked, ghost-barking furiously at the lake, paws scrabbling uselessly on the gazebo boards.

Snowball arched, fur puffing, eyes wide.

Simon manifested fully, stance widening, his presence suddenly heavier, protective.

Olivia whipped her head toward the water. Ripples spread outward in widening rings.

As if someone, or something, had just slipped beneath the surface. The lake looked calm again within seconds, but Olivia's skin had gone cold. A chill crawled down her spine. Someone had been here. Not hours ago. Not yesterday. Now. Watching. Waiting. Knowing exactly when she would come.

Olivia's heart pounded so hard she felt it would climb out of her throat. She backed away from the gazebo slowly, eyes fixed on the water, then on the tree line, then on the path back toward the house. She did not run. Running would have made her panic worse. But she moved fast.

Then Luke's SUV pulled up in front of March House.

Olivia saw it through the trees and felt a jolt of relief that was immediately followed by irritation, because of course, he had arrived at the exact moment she needed him, which meant he was going to say something infuriatingly correct.

Luke jogged down the path toward her, expression hard, eyes scanning her like he was checking for injuries.

"What happened?" he demanded as he reached her. "Lark said you went outside alone …"

"I wasn't alone," Olivia snapped automatically.

She gestured vaguely, because explaining, "I had a ghost entourage" was not something she was ready to say in the open air with the lake watching.

Luke's gaze flicked around. Quick visual sweep. Tree line. Gazebo. Shore. His jaw tightened.

"Olivia," he said, voice low, "you need to stop running off without telling me."

"I wasn't running off," Olivia shot back. "I needed to check something."

Luke paused.

His expression shifted into something between confusion and resignation. He shook his head once. "I'm not dealing with this right now."

Olivia pulled the torn parchment scrap from her pocket and held it out to him. "Look."

Luke took it carefully, studying it with a frown. He rubbed his thumb lightly over the paper, brows knitting.

"This looks old," he said. "Really old."

"It was in the hiding place," Olivia said, voice tight. "Someone got here first."

Luke crouched, moving toward the gazebo bench without hesitation. He inspected the loose plank, the compartment, and the dust smudges. His jaw flexed, the telltale sign he was deeply troubled.

"They knew exactly where to look," Luke muttered. "This wasn't random."

Olivia's hands curled into fists. "No."

Luke stood, gaze sharpening. "Who else knew Izzy hid things out here?"

Olivia swallowed. "Hazel. Maybe Bramble. Maybe both."

Luke stared toward the gazebo for a long beat, then toward the lake where the ripples had faded.

His posture stiffened. "We're dealing with someone who isn't just threatening you," he said. "They're moving ahead of you."

Olivia looked back at the empty compartment. The failure hit like a punch. Try and fail.

Again. Always one step behind. Always chasing. Always watched. Her voice came out smaller than she wanted. "We're running out of time."

Luke met her gaze, steady and fierce. "No," he said. "They're running out of places to hide."

The words landed like a reset. A rope thrown to her.

Behind Olivia, Simon stood at Snowball's side, posture straight, the faint glow of his presence steady and loyal. Daisy drifted closer and touched Olivia's shoulder with a soft, cool glow that felt like reassurance more than cold. You're not alone, it seemed to say. Scared, yes.

But not alone.

Back inside March House, Lark was waiting in the kitchen as though she had been holding her breath the entire time Olivia was gone. She had a mug in her hands already, steam curling up, the scent sharp and comforting.

Fear-fighting tea, if Olivia had to guess. Lemon balm and courage, with a dash of I told you so.

"You look like you need this," Lark said, pressing it into Olivia's hands. "And also maybe a nap."

Olivia accepted the tea, fingers shaking just slightly. She inhaled the scent, grounding herself.

Sir Alistair stood tall behind her, composed as ever.

JJ drifted in and played a low, determined jazz note that felt like a promise.

Walt muttered from the doorway, "We'll find the rest of that paper."

Flossie hovered nearby, whispering encouragement like a nervous prayer.

Olivia took a sip of the tea. Warmth spread through her chest, calming just enough that she could feel the anger beneath her fear again. She squared her shoulders. "If they want to chase me," she said, voice steady now, "they should be worried about what happens when I start chasing back."

March House creaked in agreement. Not ominously. It was a vow.

And Olivia held the mug tighter, staring toward the back door, knowing the lake was still out there, calm and watching, and whoever was stealing Izzy's secrets was going to learn that Olivia March did not back down just because the world told her to.

CHAPTER FOURTEEN

The Fake Will

Early evening settled over Mistwood with that calm, picture-perfect softness the town specialized in. The sky outside the windows faded from pale blue to bruised lavender. The lake beyond the trees turned steel-dark, catching the last light in narrow, gleaming strips as if someone had dragged a blade across its surface. A chilly breeze moved through the pines and nudged the porch wind chimes into a lazy, tinkling rhythm. March House looked almost cozy from the outside.

From the inside, Olivia knew better. She stepped onto the wrap-around porch to bring in the day's packages, tugging her hoodie tighter around herself as the air nipped at her cheeks. The porch boards creaked under her feet, familiar now, the house speaking in its own odd language.

Snowball padded beside her, tail held high, a silent white escort with the attitude of a queen inspecting her territory.

Olivia bent to scoop up the stack of parcels left near the door. There were two small boxes, a padded mailer, and one lopsided package wrapped in too much tape. And then she saw it. A plain, unmarked envelope nestled among the packages as if it had always belonged there. No postage. No return address. No helpful little barcode. Just her name, written in block letters across the front: Olivia March. Her stomach tightened.

Snowball stiffened instantly, arching her back, fur puffing, making her look like she'd had been struck by a static charge made entirely of bad intentions. The medal on her collar clinked softly.

Simon manifested at the edge of the porch, posture rigid and alert, eyes scanning the yard and the walkway as if he expected someone to step out of the shadows.

The air cooled another degree.

Sir Alistair flickered into existence at Olivia's shoulder the moment her fingers brushed the envelope. His voice was low and precise. "Miss March," he said. "I feel ill intent."

Olivia swallowed. Of course, he did. Of course, the first unmarked envelope of her entire adult life had to come with a ghostly advisory warning.

"Thank you," she muttered, gathering the packages with one arm while she held the envelope in the other. "That's exactly what I wanted from my mail. Ill intent."

She stepped back inside, shutting the door firmly behind her. The lock clicked, loud in the quiet.

Snowball followed her through the house, still bristling.

Simon came through the doorway, a shadow guarding her flank.

Olivia carried everything into the dining room and set the packages down on the sideboard, but she did not put the envelope down. She could feel it in her hand like a weight. A dare.

By the time she reached the dining room table, the ghosts were assembling. It was always like that, as if March House had a signal that went off whenever trouble arrived.

JJ drifted in first, cornet in hand, humming a low, uneasy jazz line that made the room feel tense with no one saying a word.

Monique appeared near the fireplace, tapping one ghostly high heel against the floor in an impatient rhythm. She expected the world to hurry up with the drama.

Daisy materialized by the window, clutching her pressed-flower journal to her chest, her personal armor.

Walt flickered near the doorway, arms crossed, scowl already locked into place.

Flossie hovered near the staircase, smoothing the front of her nightgown, nervous fingers fluttering.

Simon took his position by the dining room entrance; a guard for a war council.

Sir Alistair stood near Olivia's shoulder, solemn and still.

Bertie appeared at his feet, hackles raised, ears perked, the very picture of a small dog ready to charge into battle against anything, including a piece of paper.

Olivia stared at the envelope. Her hands trembled.

Lark, who had been dusting the bookshelves with fierce focus "for energetic balance," paused mid-swipe. She stared at Olivia's face, then at the envelope.

Lark slowly turned off her feather duster like it was a power tool. "You look like you found a snake in your mailbox," she said.

Olivia let out a shaky breath. "It might be a snake."

Lark's eyes narrowed. "No return address?"

"No postage," Olivia said.

Lark clicked her tongue. "That is never good."

Olivia sat at the table. Carefully. As if sitting down might keep her from bolting. She set the envelope in front of her.

The ghosts leaned in, because, of course, they did.

Olivia slid a finger under the flap and opened it. The paper inside was crisp. Neatly folded. Too clean. Olivia pulled it out. It was a will. A neatly typed, legal-looking will, printed on official-looking paper that tried very hard to appear legitimate. She read the first line, and the room tilted. The will named Theodore Bramble as the sole beneficiary of March House and all attached assets. Date: six months ago. Signature line: Isadora M. March. Witness lines: blank.

Olivia stared at the page until the words blurred.

JJ blasted a sour note, sharp enough to make the glass in the cabinet vibrate.

Monique recoiled from the paper. "Oh, absolutely not."

Walt gasped. It was an actual gasp, a startled inhale that made Olivia turn her head, because she had not known ghosts could do that.

Flossie vanished behind the banister from something she was not emotionally prepared for.

Daisy's face crumpled. Heartbroken.

Olivia's throat tightened. Her voice came out thin. "This is … this is ridiculous."

Sir Alistair leaned over her shoulder, gaze narrowing as he

scanned the page. His expression turned cold. "This," he said with absolute certainty, "is a forgery."

Olivia barely breathed. "Yes," she whispered. "Izzy never typed anything. She handwrote everything."

Monique flicked the paper with a ghostly finger, lips curling. "And she certainly wouldn't sign a will with a plain ballpoint pen. How déclassé."

Olivia stared at the signature line.

It looked like Izzy's name. It did not feel like Izzy. Izzy would have ranted for an hour about the font alone.

The dining-room windows suddenly brightened as headlights washed across them. Olivia's head snapped up.

Luke's SUV pulled up along the street.

A moment later, there was a light knock at the front door. Not the aggressive pounding of someone demanding entry. Just a knock, polite but firm. Luke stepped inside without waiting long, as if the house itself had already told him something was wrong. "I was in the area," he started. Then he stopped when he saw Olivia's face. His gaze flicked to the table. "What happened?" he asked, voice low.

Olivia pushed the will toward him.

Luke picked it up, scanning quickly. His expression darkened by the second. "This is fake," he said flatly.

Olivia swallowed. "Bramble?"

Luke's jaw flexed. "Maybe. He benefits." He held the paper up slightly, eyes narrowing.

"But Hazel has access to every historical document in town," he added. "She could make a fake will believable." He sat down abruptly, elbows on his knees, the posture of a man who had just realized the situation was worse than he wanted it to be. "Whoever made this," Luke said, voice tight, "wants to end the investigation. They want you to think Izzy left everything to Bramble. They want you to stop looking."

Olivia met his eyes. The fear in her chest shifted, sharpened, and became something else.

"They don't know me very well," she said.

Luke's mouth twitched, a hint of grim approval.

Lark, who had been pretending not to eavesdrop but absolutely had been eavesdropping, stepped closer with her sage bundle tucked under one arm.

"Honey," Lark said, voice thoughtful, "Izzy broke her wrist about … what … ten, twelve years ago?"

Olivia froze.

The memory hit fast. Izzy in a sling. Izzy furious about physical therapy. Izzy complaining endlessly about her handwriting changing.

"Yes," Olivia said slowly. "She had physical therapy for months afterward. Her handwriting changed a lot. She complained about it constantly."

Luke's gaze snapped to the date on the forged will. "This document is dated six months ago," he said.

Olivia grabbed a folder and flipped through Izzy's records, fingers moving fast and focused. She pulled out an older document ... a property insurance form which Izzy had updated five years ago, well after the wrist injury, and held it up.

She held them side by side. The difference was unmistakable.

The insurance form showed Izzy's post-injury signature. Shakier curves. Shorter loops. A distinctive change in the way she wrote the M in March. The forger used her old signature. Long, sweeping, elegant. The way she wrote before the wrist break.

"This," she said, "is her actual signature." She set the insurance form next to the will, aligning the signature lines. The difference was immediate. Even to someone who had never studied handwriting.

Luke stared. "Okay," he intoned. "That settles it."

He leaned back, jaw flexing in that *Deputy Thatcher is extremely irritated* way. "This was planted to mislead you," he said. "Or the courts." He tapped the will lightly. "Which means whoever forged it knows what's in the real one."

Alistair murmured softly near Olivia's shoulder. "A dangerous certainty, Miss March."

Olivia's breath caught.

Luke nodded grimly. "Whoever made this didn't know her well enough to fake the new signature."

Lark beamed at Olivia, as if she had just watched her child ace an exam.

"Well, look at that," Lark said brightly. "The universe sent us a smoking gun."

JJ launched into a triumphant jazz victory riff that made the air feel lighter, if only for a heartbeat.

Olivia sat back slowly, breathing harder now. The pieces clicked together in her mind like locks turning. The garden attack. The solarium break-in. The empty hiding place. The watchful presence at the lake. Now, there's a forged will on her porch. Someone was losing control. Someone was afraid she was getting close.

Sir Alistair nodded once, grim. "They're desperate," he said. "And desperation makes the living dangerous."

Olivia stared at the forged will, and the fear in her chest burned down into something clean and hot. Resolve. She stood abruptly, chair scraping back. "I'm done reacting," Olivia said. "If they want a fight over the will, they'll get one. But I'm not stopping."

Luke rose too, standing across from her like a wall she could lean on. "Then we work together," he said. "Quietly. Carefully. On my terms and yours."

Olivia nodded once. "Deal."

Lark crossed her arms, sage bundle raised like a wand. "And spiritually supervised," she added.

Walt snorted in approval.

Daisy's smile returned, soft but steady.

Flossie fluttered in near the staircase again, nervous but nodding.

Simon stayed by the door, guarding.

Bertie barked toward the porch, ready for battle against any enemy.

Alistair's expression softened, pride flickering through his usual sternness.

The air in the house shifted. Not ominous. Intent. March House itself leaned in, listening.

Olivia looked at Luke, then at Lark, then at the ghosts gathered like a strange, loyal family around her.

"Let's find the real will," she said. And in that moment, she stopped being a frightened inheritor clutching clues like lifelines. She became a hunter. March House creaked softly in agreement.

CHAPTER FIFTEEN

The Investigation Board

Olivia woke up to the smell of smoke and rosemary and the deeply unsettling realization that, at some point, her life had become a folklore warning told to children who refused to go to bed. The smoke was not coming from a kitchen disaster, which honestly would have been more comforting. This was a deliberate, ceremonial kind of smoke. The "I read one crystal blog, and now I'm an expert on your aura" kind of smoke. She lay there for a moment in her childhood bed at March House, staring at the ceiling, listening.

The house was awake. Not the normal creaks and groans of an old Victorian settling into the day. This was different. Charged. Restless. Like the building itself had decided it would take part in the investigation, whether Olivia wanted it to or not.

A muffled shuffle rose from downstairs.

Then the unmistakable sound of someone humming. Not a normal person, hum. A jazzy, playful hum that had absolutely no business existing inside a murder investigation.

Olivia swung her legs out of bed and muttered, "I swear, if someone is doing interpretive spiritual cleansing at seven in the morning, I'm selling this house to the first vampire who walks by."

She tugged on a sweater, shoved her feet into socks, and trudged toward the stairs.

At the landing, she paused. The dining room looked like a crime scene and a bakery had gotten into a bar fight, and neither one of them had cleaned up afterward.

Flour dusted the counter in a soft white layer. Evidence papers were scattered across the dining room table like someone had tried to do a puzzle and then rage-quit halfway through. A ribbon spool lay on its side. There were pushpins, notecards, and what looked suspiciously like a highlighter cap on the floor.

In the middle of the chaos stood Lark Waverly, barefoot, hair wild, waving a burning sage bundle in slow circles as if trying to smoke out a demon, a bad vibe, or possibly a raccoon.

"Sweetheart," Lark said brightly without looking up, "the house is thick with stress. I'm doing a cleanse."

Olivia blinked. "Is that sage?"

Lark smiled like someone who had been waiting her whole life to say the word with authority. "It is."

Olivia stared at the smoke curling toward the chandelier. "And what exactly are we cleansing?"

"The energy," Lark said, as if that clarified everything.

Walt drifted by the doorway, his stocky form half-faded at the edges, a permanent expression of irritation carved into his face. He eyed the sage as if it had personally offended him. "I'd rather cleanse the guy who broke the window," he muttered.

From the corner, JJ let out a playful little jazz "whoooo" in perfect imitation of Lark's slow sweeping motions, like he was providing a soundtrack for the exorcism.

Olivia closed her eyes and inhaled.

Rosemary. Smoke. Patchouli. A hint of lemon oil. And faintly, the scent of flour that made her stomach grumble despite everything.

"I'm too young for this," she said. "I'm thirty-one. I should be stressed about taxes or aging or whether I own enough socks. Not sage smoke and murder notes and being haunted by a cornet."

JJ held the cornet up like an innocent baby angel.

Lark stepped closer, still wafting smoke. "You're stressed, sweetheart. The entire house is stressed. We all feel it."

Olivia opened one eye. "You cannot possibly feel the house being stressed."

Lark gave her a look. “Oh, honey. I can feel stress like other people feel weather. This place has storm clouds hanging over it.”

Walt muttered, “The only storm cloud is the idiot who thinks breaking windows is subtle.”

JJ “whooooed” again, this time with a little flourish.

Olivia pinched the bridge of her nose. She could already feel a headache forming. Or maybe that was just the sage trying to burrow into her sinuses and set up residency.

“Okay,” she said, lowering her hands. “Okay. Today, we get organized.”

The effect was immediate.

The ghosts, who had been drifting and muttering and watching Lark’s ritual as if it were a cable drama, gathered closer. Like children who had just heard the word cookies.

Sir Alistair Pruitt manifested near the doorway, tall and elegant, dressed in his usual late-Georgian attire that would have made him a menace at a modern wedding. His silver pocket watch glinted faintly, the chain arching neatly across his waistcoat. His expression was composed, but Olivia had learned that his version of composed included a wide range of silent judgment.

At his feet, Bertie trotted into the dining room, tail raised, tongue slightly out, vibrating with excitement. The dog had the energy of a creature who had never once heard the words calm down in his entire life or afterlife.

Simon appeared near the entryway, posture straight, gaze sweeping the room.

Flossie hovered near the staircase, hands clasped together so tightly Olivia expected her fingers to fuse.

Monique leaned against the wall with the casual confidence of someone who believed she could intimidate a suspect just by blinking slowly.

Daisy lingered at the edge of the room, quiet, watchful, eyes flicking toward the solarium and beyond as if she could see the garden through the walls.

Lark lowered the sage bundle, satisfied. “See? The house likes that. It’s responding.”

Olivia stared at her. “The house is a building.”

Lark smiled. “The house is a personality.”

Walt snorted. "The house is expensive."

Olivia ignored him and rolled her shoulders. "First step. I need a board."

Lark's eyes lit up. "A vision board?"

"A murder board," Olivia said flatly.

Lark clapped once. "Even better."

Olivia went to the storage closet and yanked the door open, sending a faint waft of old cedar and forgotten linens into the hall. She dragged out a large corkboard that looked like it had been waiting for this moment for decades.

Behind her, Lark appeared carrying a cardboard box with bold handwriting scrawled across the side.

OFFICE SUPPLIES-DO NOT OPEN (IZZY)

Olivia stopped. Slowly, she turned her head. "That is absolutely a trap," she said.

"Oh, it's totally a trap," Lark agreed cheerfully. "We're opening it."

Olivia stared at the box. "My aunt is dead, and she's still bossing me around."

Sir Alistair inclined his head. "The mark of an excellent matriarch."

Olivia dragged the corkboard into the dining room while Lark set the box down like an offering. They opened it. Inside, arranged with suspicious precision, were color-coded note cards, pushpins, highlighters, ribbon, and three identical unused journals stamped with black block letters:

TOP SECRET.

Olivia stared. "She bought matching journals."

Lark laughed. "Your aunt had a sense of humor. And also a sense of dramatic occasion."

Olivia picked up one of the journals and flipped it open. The first page was blank. Waiting. Like the universe was mocking her. She set it down and focused.

They propped the corkboard on a dining room chair, where the solarium light spilled in, bright and clear. Olivia adjusted it until it stood straight. Perfect. Controlled. Something in her life needed to change. She divided the board into three columns and pinned the headings at the top: SUSPECTS/MOTIVES/CLUES.

The ghosts gathered like curious children around a new toy. Bertie trotted in a circle, tail whipping. A small flag of enthusiasm.

"All right," Olivia said, taking a deep breath. "We do this like professionals. Or like … whatever I am now."

"Haunted," Walt supplied.

"Tired," Monique added.

"Overdue for coffee," JJ murmured.

Olivia shot JJ a look. "Everyone, hush." She took a deep breath and began.

Under suspects, she pinned the first card: Theodore Bramble

Monique leaned close, tapping the pushpin lightly with one perfectly manicured ghost nail. "He smells like greed."

Olivia exhaled. "Yes. Greed is a scent now. Great. Fantastic." Next, she pinned Hazel Finch.

Daisy hesitated. Her gaze locked on Hazel's name, and something shifted in her expression. Fear. Not dramatic, not performative. Real.

Olivia's stomach tightened.

Daisy lifted her hand and pointed slowly, as if the name itself was dangerous.

Olivia swallowed. "Noted." She pinned the next name, Carla Dawes.

Simon's jaw tightened, just a fraction. "Family makes things messy."

Olivia nodded. "Yeah. I'm learning that." And then the last card, Marvin Pike. She added a notation beneath it: not yet encountered.

Walt jabbed a ghost finger at the name. "Bet he's trouble."

"Wonderful," Olivia muttered. "I'm collecting trouble like it's a hobby." Now motives.

Under MOTIVES, she pinned them one at a time, trying to keep her mind clear.

Bramble: Wanting the property

Hazel: Unknown falling-out with Izzy

Carla: Lake access dispute

Marvin: Fired by Izzy last year, rumored grudge

Unknown: Embezzlement from the B and B accounts

Sir Alistair stood tall, hands behind his back, surveying the board like a general inspecting troops. "Very orderly, Miss March," he said. "A fine military mind."

Olivia snorted. "I'm a pastry chef. My mind is mostly butter and sugar."

Bertie trotted around the base of the board, tail raised, looking pleased with himself as if he had contributed personally.

"And now," Olivia said, voice lowering, "the clues." This was the part that made her chest tighten. One by one, she pinned them under CLUES:

Threatening note: Let the dead rest.

Threatening note #2: You're next

Forced solarium window

Garden tin with photograph

Torn photo piece: 1989–the night she confessed

Empty hiding compartment in gazebo

Parchment scrap with partial word "... March"

Forged will using Izzy's old signature

Handprint in dirt on the solarium glass

Footprint in gazebo

She stepped back when it was done. Seeing it all in one place made it impossible to dismiss. It wasn't just bad luck. It wasn't just grief. It was a pattern.

Lark whistled softly. "That's a lot of universe pointing fingers at you."

Olivia crossed her arms. "The universe can point all it wants. I'm still not thrilled about being the one who has to follow it."

Her eyes flicked to the staircase, the place Izzy had died. The place Flossie hovered near, pale and anxious.

A quiet fury sparked in Olivia's chest. The coroner said accident. The sheriff said, unfortunate. Mistwood said nothing. But the house. The house kept whispering.

Olivia turned to the ghosts, who were staring at her with a strange mix of expectation and eagerness.

"I need help," she said. "And you're all … here."

Walt straightened. "You want recon? I can recon."

JJ lifted his cornet. "I provide mood music. And ambiance."

Monique smiled, slow and sharp. "I do glamor and intimidation."

Simon nodded once. "I will guard the perimeter. Constantly."

Flossie raised her hand timidly. "I … can watch staircases?"

Daisy whispered. "I'll keep an eye on the garden."

Alistair inclined his head. "I will provide strategic insight."

Olivia felt something loosen in her chest. Not because this was normal, because it absolutely was not. But because for the first time since she'd arrived, she was not alone in the madness.

"Don't forget to include me in the effort as well." Lark held up her hand.

"You're always included." Olivia's mouth curved into a smile despite herself. "Then I'll assign tasks."

She pointed, counting them off like she was running a kitchen shift. "Simon and Snowball. Perimeter patrol."

Simon's face brightened with purpose.

Snowball, who had padded into the room with silent feline authority, stiffened beside Olivia and arched her back to show she approved. The tarnished Union service medal on her collar glinted in the morning light.

"Daisy. Garden alerts."

Daisy nodded once, solemnly.

"Walt. Check for structural tampering. Anything weird. Anything changed."

Walt grunted. "Finally. A job with dignity."

"Monique. Watch the street from the solarium. Suspicious visitors."

Monique smiled. "I was born for this."

"JJ. Audio alerts. If danger approaches, play literally anything except an off-key Charleston."

JJ put a hand to his chest as if she'd wounded him. "Ma'am."

Olivia narrowed her eyes. "I'm serious."

"Yes, ma'am," JJ said, but his grin was pure trouble.

"Flossie," Olivia said gently, "main staircase. I need eyes there."

Flossie nodded quickly, relief and fear tangled together.

"And Sir Alistair," Olivia finished, "overall coordination. You're Ghost-in-Chief."

Alistair's expression softened with pride. "An honor."

Bertie barked once, tail wagging hard, as if demanding a title.

Olivia stared at him. "You are … morale support."

Bertie sat and lifted a paw.

Lark, who had quietly set a kettle on the stove, added, "Don't forget me. I'll keep an eye on the living folks."

Olivia turned and hugged her, the scent of rosemary and lemon oil grounding her more than any tea.

"Thank you," Olivia murmured.

Lark squeezed back. "Of course. Also, I made clarity tea."

Olivia pulled away. "Does it taste like clarity?"

"It tastes like herbs," Lark said happily. "Clarity is an attitude."

Olivia's phone buzzed.

She checked it and felt her pulse jump. Luke sent her a text.

"Need to meet. Found something at Hazel's. You're going to want to see this."

Olivia's fingers hovered, then she typed quickly.

"At March House. Come by."

JJ immediately played a jazzy, flirtatious little *ooh-la-la* on the cornet.

Olivia looked over. "Do not."

JJ's grin widened. "I am merely providing ambiance."

"You are providing harassment." She glanced at her clothes. "I'd better get changed. I don't want to greet the deputy dressed in my pajamas."

Luke arrived shortly after, parking along the street and stepping onto the porch with dust on his boots, looking like he'd come straight from the shoulder of a road. He didn't knock so much as rap once and then enter; a man who had decided politeness was optional when murder was involved.

Lark met him in the foyer with a mug.

"For grounding and emotional stability," she said.

Luke blinked at the mug as if it had offered him a horoscope. "Uh, thanks." He took it anyway. For all his gruffness, he didn't dismiss people outright. He listened first. Even though he looked like he wanted to argue.

Olivia came down the stairs. "Let's sit at the table."

He stepped into the dining room and stopped dead. His gaze locked onto the board. "You built a murder wall."

Olivia lifted her chin. "The term is 'investigation board.'"

Luke's eyes tracked across the columns. Suspects. Motives. Clues.

He squinted. "That's … a lot of suspects."

"And I'm not done," Olivia said.

Luke exhaled slowly, he hadn't expected competence to greet him in the dining room of a bed-and-breakfast. Then his expression shifted. The irritation eased into something steadier.

"This is good," he said, voice quieter. "Really good."

Olivia met his eyes.

There was something in that look. Not romance. Not yet. But recognition. He was beginning to see her as more than a nuisance with a spatula.

A partnership.

It warmed her in a way she refused to examine too closely.

Luke set a folded piece of paper on the table. "This was in Hazel's recycling bin," he said. "Looks recent."

Olivia unfolded it carefully, as if the paper might bite.

Hazel's tidy script stared back at her.

"Meeting tonight. Usual place. No more mistakes."

The room seemed to tighten. Even the light through the solarium felt sharper, seemingly holding its breath.

Alistair murmured, "The enemy gathers."

JJ played an ominous chord that made Olivia's skin prickle.

Lark whispered, "The plot thickens … like good gravy."

Olivia pinned the note under a new heading: New Lead.

Her voice was steady when she spoke, steadier than she felt.

"Let's find out where Hazel's meeting is," she said, eyes on Luke, "and who she's meeting."

Luke's jaw flexed, a familiar sign of irritation turning into focus. "Yeah," he said. "We will."

Behind them, the ghosts watched in silence for once, even they understood the moment.

The board stood in the center of the dining room, sunlight catching the pushpins like tiny points of promise.

Olivia stared at it and felt something shift inside her. She was done with being pushed around. Now she was pushing back.

CHAPTER SIXTEEN

Town Secrets Begin Cracking

The kitchen smelled of blueberries, butter, and the faint metallic tang of nerves.

Olivia stood at the counter, sliding a final tray of muffins out of the oven with practiced efficiency. Golden domes rose proudly from their paper liners, studded with berries that had burst and caramelized just enough to promise guests happiness and possibly forgiveness for past dietary sins.

Baking was grounding. Predictable. You followed the rules, respected temperatures, trusted your instincts, and something good came out the other side. Murder investigations did not follow recipes.

She set the muffin tin on the cooling rack and reached for a clean towel just as Lark wandered in, mug in hand, humming a tune that sounded suspiciously like it had once been played on vinyl.

Lark was wrapped in one of her flowy linen sweaters, hair half-tied with a scarf that had seen several decades of service. Steam rose from her rosemary tea, trailing through the kitchen like a gentle ghost of its own. She leaned against the counter, took a sip, and said casually, "Honey, I've been thinking … Hazel and Izzy used to be as close as sisters."

The muffin tin slipped.

Olivia caught it against the counter by pure reflex, metal

clanging sharply enough to make JJ pause mid-hum in the dining room.

"Sisters?" Olivia said. "Hazel told me they were barely acquaintances."

Lark snorted, entirely unconcerned with Hazel's version of events or Olivia's rapidly escalating heart rate.

"Oh, Hazel Finch lies the way other people breathe. Those two were thick as thieves in the late eighties."

Olivia set the tin down carefully.

The phrase *thick as thieves* lodged itself in her chest.

"What happened?" she asked.

Lark shrugged, drying her hands on a sunflower-print towel that had definitely survived at least one questionable decade. "Something big. A fight. I remember Izzy crying for days. Wouldn't let anyone near the solarium. Said Hazel, 'Betrayed the house.'"

The words hit like a dropped plate.

"Betrayed the house?" Olivia repeated.

JJ drifted into the doorway and played a soft, low detective riff that felt like punctuation.

Lark sipped her tea. "Izzy loved this house like a person. Maybe more than some people."

Olivia's mind raced. Hazel had downplayed everything. The history. The closeness. The falling out. And Izzy had never been one for exaggeration.

After breakfast, Olivia climbed the stairs with an armful of linens, the house quieting around her in that attentive way it had when something important was about to surface.

Halfway down the hall, Daisy appeared. She didn't speak. She rarely did when it mattered most. Instead, she reached out and tugged gently at Olivia's sleeve, then drifted toward the old linen closet at the top of the stairs.

That closet had been there forever. Narrow. Crammed. Forgotten.

Olivia followed.

The shelves were stacked with folded sheets, pillowcases embroidered with tiny blue flowers, and towels yellowed just enough to show their age. Daisy floated toward the bottom shelf, hovering insistently.

Olivia kneeled and moved the stack aside.

Behind it sat a dusty shoebox tied with a faded ribbon. The label in Izzy's handwriting:

Hazel–1989.

Olivia's breath caught.

She gently lifted the box, afraid it might dissolve in her hands, and carried it downstairs. The ghosts clustered behind her like curious hens who absolutely intended to see what was inside. They gathered around the dining room table as Olivia untied the ribbon. Inside were pieces of a life that had refused to stay buried. Newspaper clippings, yellowed at the edges. A torn community newsletter. A folded note in Izzy's looping script. A black-and-white photograph of Hazel and Izzy standing stiffly on the March House porch, shoulders angled away from each other, mouths tight. And a manila envelope stamped in red - Historical Society: Restricted Records.

Olivia unfolded Izzy's note first.

Hazel knows what she did. If she doesn't confess, the house will speak for me.

Monique fanned herself dramatically. "Well. That sounds deliciously ominous."

Walt squinted at the photograph. "They're fighting. Look at their eyes."

JJ played a low, suspenseful chord that hummed through the room.

Sir Alistair bowed his head once. "This argument … it scarred them both."

Olivia's fingers trembled as she picked up the first newspaper clipping. LOCAL GIRL MISSING–LAST SEEN NEAR MARCH HOUSE.

Daisy pressed her hands over her mouth.

Simon flickered sharply, posture snapping rigid, eyes distant as if the word *missing* had pulled him somewhere he didn't want to go.

The girl's name stared back at Olivia. Trina Bell–Age 17. Her chest tightened. "Why was Izzy keeping this?" she whispered.

She checked the date. 1989. The same year that was on the shoebox. The same year that was on the torn photo fragment. In the same year, Hazel and Izzy had fallen apart.

The room felt colder.

Lark wandered in, took one look at the table, and sat heavily. "Oh, sweetheart," she whispered. "Trina Bell. Poor kid. Disappeared during a lake party. Hazel organized the search group. Izzy never believed the official story."

Olivia leaned forward. "What official story?"

Lark sighed. "That Trina ran away. Izzy said she knew something. Something Hazel wouldn't admit."

Even the ghosts went still.

Olivia reached for the manila envelope and slid out its contents. A key dropped into her palm. Old-fashioned brass. Heavy. Etched with a single number. 7.

"What is this for?" Olivia asked.

Sir Alistair's brows rose. "Miss March … the historical society archives are numbered. Room Seven was Hazel's private archive room."

Daisy shivered.

"Locked for a reason," Walt muttered.

Monique scoffed. "And Hazel said she barely knew Izzy. Please."

JJ played a mocking riff.

Olivia gathered the items and carried them to the investigation board. She pinned each piece carefully. Then she wrote a new heading. THE 1989 CONNECTION.

The ghosts gathered close.

Alistair nodded. "Your aunt left you more than a house. She left you with the unfinished business of the dead."

Olivia straightened. "Then we finish it."

March House hummed in agreement.

CHAPTER SEVENTEEN

The Music Box Message

Olivia woke with a start, bolt upright in bed, heart hammering as if she'd just run the length of Mistwood Lake in winter boots. For a split second, her brain reached for the usual suspects. A branch scraping a window? A pipe clanking in protest? Snowball launching herself off the dresser because she'd seen a dust mote and decided it was war?

No, this sound was worse. Tinny. Warped. Unmistakable.

The off-key, slightly too-slow strains of "The Charleston" drifted through the dark. Monique's music box.

Olivia sat perfectly still, eyes wide, listening. The melody stuttered in odd places, dragging. A heartbeat pulled underwater. It wasn't playful. It wasn't background noise. It was deliberate.

The music box was supposed to be in the sitting room, perched neatly beside the fireplace like an expensive decoration that screamed, *I have taste and possibly a curse.*

It should not be playing by itself at midnight.

Olivia swung her legs over the side of the bed, pulled on her robe, and shoved her feet into slippers without bothering to turn on a light. She didn't want to wake the entire house. She didn't want to wake herself any more than necessary, either.

The hallway was dark. The old wooden floors cool beneath her feet. The air tasted of winter. The house was holding its breath.

The music drifted stronger as she moved down the hall, guiding her like a crooked lullaby.

Then she saw it. A thin line of light glowed from beneath the sitting-room door. She stopped.

March House had plenty of quirks, but it did not leave lights on without permission. It was a Victorian mansion, not a teenager with a phone charger addiction.

She reached for the knob, paused, and muttered under her breath, "If this is another ghost council meeting, I'm charging rent."

Then she opened the door.

The sitting room was softly lit, not by lamps, but by the faint golden glow coming from the music box itself. It sat on the little table beside the fireplace, lid open, its tiny metal cylinder turning with stubborn persistence as the distorted Charleston spilled out into the room. And standing beside it, shimmering in full flapper glory, was Monique Delacroix.

She looked stunning, as always. Black beaded dress. Feathered headband. Ghost lipstick perfect. Even at midnight, she appeared ready to step into a jazz club and ruin someone's marriage. But her expression was all irritation, chin lifted, eyes narrowed, like Olivia had shown up late to her own funeral. "Well, darling," Monique said, voice silky and sharp, "you certainly took your time."

Olivia blinked at her. "It's after midnight."

Monique waved a hand. "Time is a social construct." The music box stuttered, the tune dragging, too slow, too wrong. It sounded less like a dance and more like a warning.

Olivia stepped closer, the hairs along her arms rising. "Why is it playing?"

Monique's eyes flicked to the box, and something in her gaze softened. Not fondness. Not amusement. Something weightier. "That," Monique said quietly, "is not me, sweetheart."

Olivia's throat tightened. "Then what is it?"

Monique straightened, beads shimmering as her form flickered in the glow. "That is a message."

The temperature dropped. Not the normal chill of an old house at night. This was deeper, heavier. The air thickened as if the room had been filled with invisible water. Olivia's breath fogged faintly in front of her face.

The room didn't feel haunted. It felt purposeful.

Olivia approached the table, and the music box continued to play, its warped Charleston stuttering like a wounded thing. She flipped on the table lamp.

She knelt and gently picked it up. The moment her fingers closed around it, the music stopped abruptly, cutting off mid-note so sharply that Olivia flinched.

The sudden silence felt as if someone had slapped the room. Behind her, JJ appeared in the doorway, half-shimmering, fedora tipped at an angle.

"Spooky," he whispered in a low jazz drawl.

Olivia shot him a look over her shoulder. "Not helping."

JJ lifted both hands. "Just narratin' the mood, ma'am."

Olivia turned the music box over in her hands.

It felt heavier than it should have. Not by a lot. Just enough to make her instincts prickle, the same way they did when she lifted a baking dish and knew, without looking, that the batter was too thick.

She ran her fingers along the bottom panel.

One corner shifted slightly.

Loose.

Someone had opened it before and hadn't bothered to align the screws properly afterward.

Olivia's pulse spiked.

Monique leaned in, her face close, eyes bright with that sharp, theatrical satisfaction she wore like perfume. "Your aunt had impeccable dramatic timing."

Olivia swallowed hard and set the music box gently on her lap. She found a small screwdriver in the side table drawer. Izzy kept everything. Buttons. Twine. Rubber bands. Apparently, tools for future midnight revelations.

Of course, she did.

Olivia unscrewed the bottom panel carefully, each tiny turn loud in the quiet room. The wood creaked faintly as the panel loosened. When it finally lifted away, something pale and folded rested inside the hollow. A piece of paper. Old. Slightly brittle. Edges worn soft as if it had been handled more than once.

Olivia's hands shook as she drew it out.

The handwriting was Izzy's. Not her old, crisp script from postcards and recipes. This was looping and slightly uneven. Post-surgery handwriting, the kind that carried fatigue in every curve.

Olivia's throat tightened painfully.

Monique's voice softened. "She saved this for you, darling."

Olivia didn't trust herself to answer. She smoothed the paper carefully and read it.

Livvy,

If you're reading this, then I have failed to convince Hazel to tell the truth.

She will not, and the town protects her. The missing girl was not a runaway.

Look in the archives. Room Seven. The truth is waiting, but it is dangerous.

Take care of the house. It chose you.

And trust the dead – they see what the living hide.

– Izzy

Olivia's breath caught hard, like she'd been punched gently in the lungs. The words blurred for a moment, and she blinked rapidly, hating the sting in her eyes.

Daisy appeared near the hearth, hands clasped tight to her chest, her gentle face pale with emotion.

Flossie peeked from behind a chair, eyes wide, as if the note might leap up and accuse her of something.

Walt manifested near the edge of the rug, gaze locked on the paper. "Well," he muttered.

Simon shifted closer, protective. He would put himself between Olivia and a piece of ink if necessary.

Monique stood still, and for once, her expression wasn't amused, or dramatic, or sharp. It was sad. "She loved you very much, darling," Monique whispered. "She saved this for you."

Olivia swallowed hard and read the note again. Slower this time. Hazel. The town protects her. The missing girl was not a runaway.

Archives. Room Seven. Dangerous. The house chose you. Trust the dead.

The pieces slammed together in Olivia's mind with the brutal clarity of a puzzle finally clicking into place.

Hazel and Izzy argued in 1989. Trina Bell went missing in the same year. Hazel refused to discuss that night. Izzy believed Trina hadn't run away. Hazel tried to bury the records.

Someone stole the will. Someone attacked Olivia. Someone was still scrambling to destroy evidence decades later.

Olivia lowered the paper and looked at Monique.

"Hazel knows what happened to Trina Bell," she said, voice flat with certainty.

Monique nodded, slow and solemn. "And she is terrified you will find out."

A chill crawled down Olivia's spine, cold and steady. She stared at the note in her hands. At Izzy's looping words. At the warning. Dangerous.

Olivia's gaze flicked toward the side table where the shoebox from the linen closet sat, still open, its contents scattered like history had spilled out and refused to be packed away again. She crossed the room and retrieved the brass key marked **7** from inside, closing her fingers around it. It was heavy. Real. The metal felt cold against her skin. "I have to go into the historical society archives," she whispered.

As if summoned by the word *archives*, Sir Alistair materialized beside her, posture dignified, his expression thoughtful."May I suggest doing so with Deputy Thatcher?" he said. "Breaking and entering is frowned upon in most centuries."

From the doorway, JJ added a mournful little "wah-wah" flourish that sounded like a horn mocking her life choices.

Olivia pinched the bridge of her nose. "I wasn't going to break in. I was going to inquire."

Monique lifted a brow. "With a skeleton key to a restricted room?"

Olivia sighed, long and defeated. "Fine. I'll tell Luke."

She tucked Izzy's note into her robe pocket, her fingers lingering on the paper as if she could hold on to her aunt through the ink.

Then she looked up.

All of them were there now. Her assembled household of ghosts. Watching her with a mix of hope, fear, and loyalty that made her chest ache in a way she didn't have a word for.

A found family she never asked for. A strange army of dead people tethered to objects, bound to this house, and somehow bound to her. Olivia squared her shoulders. "We're going to finish what Izzy started," she said.

Monique smiled proudly.

Daisy glowed faintly. Relief warmed her from the inside.

Walt crossed his arms and gave a single, firm nod.

Simon lifted his hand in a salute, solemn and unwavering.

Flossie's shoulders loosened, her anxious expression easing as if someone had finally promised her the thing she'd needed to hear.

Alistair stood like a sentry beside Olivia, watch chain gleaming.

JJ raised his cornet and played a soft, sweet jazz chord, gentle as a hand on a shoulder.

The house seemed to breathe around them, a long, warm exhale that felt like agreement.

Like acceptance. Like it had been waiting. Finally.

And in the quiet after the note, after the music, after the weight of decades cracking open, Olivia stood in her robe in the middle of the sitting room and realized something with a cold certainty: This was never just about a will. This was about a missing girl. And Mistwood had been hiding her story for thirty-six years.

CHAPTER EIGHTEEN

Olivia Confronts Bramble

Morning sunlight poured into the solarium in long, unapologetic stripes, catching on the glass and turning the space into something bright enough to feel dangerous.

Olivia sat at the small table near the window with a mug of coffee so dark and bitter it could have stripped paint. This was not comfort coffee. This was plotting coffee. The kind you drank when sleep becomes optional and resolve hardens overnight into something sharp.

Spread out in front of her like an accusation were the pieces of the truth. Izzy's note from the music box, folded and unfolded enough times to soften the creases. The brass key, stamped with the number seven, cool and heavy even in the sun's warmth. The newspaper clipping about Trina Bell, its edges yellowed, the headline still capable of quickening her pulse. Hazel's torn photo fragment. The parchment scrap pulled from the gazebo. The forged will, with its false familiarity, now impossible to ignore.

She stared at them, one hand wrapped around the mug, steam curling up past her face.

She was done with being intimidated.

Behind her, Sir Alistair stood straight-backed and solemn, his presence filling the solarium with quiet authority. His silver pocket watch rested neatly against his waistcoat, chain glinting faintly in the light.

At Olivia's feet, Bertie lay stretched out in a patch of sun, paws twitching as he chased something heroic in his ghostly dreams.

Monique reclined elegantly against a chair, basking in the warmth like a cat who knew she was admired. She stretched one arm over her head, beads catching the light.

Walt leaned against the solarium doorway, arms crossed, expression carved from old anger and newer memories. He stared out toward the yard as if he were seeing something no one else could.

Simon stood near the threshold, posture alert, Snowball seated beside him with her tail wrapped neatly around her paws.

Flossie hovered near the far wall, hands clasped tight, eyes flicking between Olivia and the door.

Daisy sat quietly at the edge of the room, waiting. She always waited. Patient. Steady.

Olivia took a slow breath and set the mug down. "I'm going to talk to Bramble."

The air shifted.

It wasn't dramatic. No sudden gusts or rattling windows. Just a ripple, like the house itself had drawn in a careful breath.

Walt straightened. "Take backup."

Olivia reached into her pocket and tapped the small velvet box she'd tucked there, the pocket watch safely inside.

"I am."

Sir Alistair inclined his head approvingly.

Olivia pushed back her chair and stood. She didn't have far to go.

As she stepped onto the wrap-around porch, the crunch of tires on gravel made her stop short.

A sleek black SUV rolled to a smooth halt at the curb in front of March House, its engine purring with expensive confidence. The driver's door opened, and Theodore Bramble stepped out like he owned the street, the town, and possibly the weather.

Tailored jacket. Perfectly pressed slacks. Loafers that had never seen mud in their lives.

And a smile polished to a salesman's shine.

"Miss March!" he called as he adjusted his cuffs. "Just the woman I hoped to see."

From somewhere inside the house, JJ's cornet let out a snarky little *oh boy* riff.

Olivia stayed exactly where she was, at the top of the porch steps. Higher ground. Better sightlines. The house solid at her back.

"I have questions," she said.

Bramble's smile widened, practiced and smooth. "Of course. Always happy to help the new proprietor."

"You threatened me," Olivia said evenly. "You forced your way into my house. You tried to scare me off. And now you're back. Why?"

He lifted both hands in a mild, placating gesture. "I simply want to make sure you're making wise decisions."

For just a flicker of a second, something cold lit behind his eyes. Anger. Fear. Calculation.

Behind Olivia, Sir Alistair appeared, tall and imposing, his presence looming like a silent warning.

Bertie rose to his feet, hackles lifting, a low growl rumbling in his chest.

Bramble couldn't see them. But he felt something.

He hesitated, then took a subtle step back.

Olivia folded her arms. "What do you know about Izzy's will?"

Bramble stiffened. Barely. But it was there. "Nothing," he blurted. "Not a thing."

"Funny," Olivia said. "You told me the house would 'swallow me the way it swallowed her.' How would you know that? Unless you knew she'd found something before she died."

He hesitated. Just a fraction.

But Olivia saw it.

Alistair's voice murmured at her shoulder. "He falters."

Bertie growled louder.

Bramble cleared his throat. "I merely meant the house has … a history."

"You stole something from the gazebo," Olivia said.

He froze. Only for a heartbeat. Only long enough for the truth to flash across his face before he could hide it.

"I don't know what you're talking about," he said.

"You do," Olivia replied calmly. "Because only someone who knew what Izzy hid would go looking for it." His jaw tightened.

Olivia stepped closer, her voice lowering, sharpening.

"You went to the archives, too. Didn't you?"

This time, he flinched. A real, unmistakable flinch. He covered it poorly, shifting his weight, adjusting his jacket as if it could shield him.

"Miss March," he said, voice tightening, "I don't think you realize how dangerous it is to—"

"To what?" Olivia cut in. "Ask questions? Follow the truth? Your threats don't scare me anymore."

His eyes narrowed. "You have no idea what you're bringing back. Some things should stay buried."

Before Olivia could answer, another engine approached.

The deputy's SUV pulled up behind Bramble's, gravel crunching as it slowed to a stop.

Luke stepped out, boots hitting the ground with solid finality. He took in the scene at a single glance. Olivia stood tall at the top of the porch. Bramble was at the bottom of the steps. Tension stretched tight enough to snap. "Everything okay here?" Luke asked.

Bramble forced a smile that didn't reach his eyes. "Deputy. Just a neighborly conversation."

Luke's gaze flicked to Olivia, then back to Bramble. "You're not her neighbor."

Olivia bit back a smile.

Behind her, Alistair stood proud. Bertie sniffed the air near Bramble's shoes with deep disapproval.

Bramble took another step back, recalculating. "Be careful what stones you overturn, Miss March," he said.

"Funny," Olivia replied. "I was about to say that to you."

Luke moved closer to her side, presence solid and grounding.

Bramble retreated to his SUV, got in, and drove off without another word.

Luke turned to Olivia. "What did he say to you?"

She told him everything. Every hesitation. Every flinch. Every sentence that didn't quite add up.

Luke listened, jaw tightening. "He knows more than he's saying," he said.

"And he knew Izzy was hiding something," Olivia added. "He's trying to shut me down."

Luke nodded. "Then we hit Hazel next. And we do it with evidence."

Alistair murmured approvingly, "A sound strategy."

JJ played a triumphant riff from inside the house.

Olivia looked out over the lake, the house warm behind her.

"We're close," she said. "Too close for him to hide anything for much longer."

Luke nodded. "Then let's keep pushing."

As Luke left, the ghosts gathered behind Olivia like a shimmering army.

The wind stirred the lake.

The house creaked softly.

CHAPTER NINETEEN

The Restricted Room

Luke picked Olivia up just after sunset, when the sky over Mistwood Lake had gone that uncertain blue-gray that made everything feel slightly unreal. He parked, with the headlights off, a half block from the Mistwood Historical Society, letting the engine idle only long enough to settle before turning it off completely. The sudden quiet rang in Olivia's ears.

She stayed seated for a moment, hands folded in her lap, feeling the weight of what she carried. Inside her jacket pocket was Izzy's brass key, stamped with the number seven. It pressed hard against her palm, cool and solid, a physical reminder that whatever waited inside that building had been hidden deliberately. That it had been waiting.

The historical society loomed ahead. It was an old brick structure, dignified in the stubborn way of buildings that had outlasted several generations of secrets. White columns framed the entrance, their paint chipped and flaking like the edges of old bones. Above them, a weathervane shaped like a trout creaked softly as it turned, metal squealing in protest at the evening breeze.

The place looked harmless. Educational. The building that smelled like dust and lemonade and hosted talks no one attended. Which meant it was perfect.

"You still good?" Luke asked quietly.

Olivia nodded. "If I stop now, I won't start again."

Luke studied her for a beat, then opened his door. Olivia followed, the gravel crunching softly beneath her boots. Behind her, unseen but unmistakable, Sir Alistair Pruitt materialized with quiet dignity. His silver pocket watch ticked faintly, steady as a heartbeat. Bertie padded along at his heels, nose twitching, tail lifted with investigative interest.

JJ had protested not being allowed to come.

"I am not explaining a jazz cornet to a judge," Olivia had told him.

Snowball remained at March House, which meant Simon stayed behind as well, guarding the property with military seriousness and a white cat who took perimeter patrol personally.

Luke climbed the steps and reached for the door. "Historical records are public," he said as he slid his department key into the lock. "Just … not all rooms. So whatever we do, we didn't break in."

Olivia arched an eyebrow. "That's the legal reassurance I needed."

The door opened with a low, tired creak. They slipped inside.

The smell hit Olivia immediately. Old paper. Lemon polish. Dust that had settled into corners decades ago and never left. And beneath it all, something else. Something closed-in. Secrets that had been stacked, boxed, filed, and forgotten, but never erased.

The door closed softly behind them. The building felt different at night. Smaller. Like it had drawn its shoulders in.

Alistair glided behind Olivia, silent and severe, his presence a comforting weight at her back. Bertie immediately began sniffing along the baseboards, tail wagging, as if the building itself had offended him.

They moved down the main hall. Black-and-white photographs lined the walls. Founders. Lumber barons. Early settlers posed stiffly in Sunday clothes, eyes flat with the confidence that came from believing history would remember them kindly. Display cases held antique tools and fishing gear. Rusted hooks. Hand-carved oars. Ledgers with thick spines and thinner truths.

A framed map of Mistwood Lake from 1901 hung near the far

wall. The shoreline looked raw and unfamiliar. The town barely more than a suggestion.

Then Olivia saw the bulletin board. It was crowded with yellowed clippings, thumbtacked in uneven rows. Names. Dates. Faces staring out with the blank hope of people who did not know they were about to disappear.

She stopped. Her chest tightened as she stepped closer. There it was. TRINA BELL–MISSING. LAST SEEN: June 15, 1989. The same headline. The same photograph. The same hollow ache that had followed her since she opened Izzy's shoebox.

Luke slowed beside her.

"I wasn't born yet," he mumbled. "But everybody in Mistwood knows about Trina Bell. The file was still in the sheriff's archives when I came on. My uncle talked around it sometimes. I always got the feeling it was … unfinished."

Olivia didn't look away from the clipping. "Clay talked about it?"

Luke shook his head. "Not directly. But every time he went through old boxes, he'd get quiet around that era. Like there was something he hoped would stay buried."

The building seemed to lean in, listening.

They moved on. Room Seven sat at the end of a narrow corridor, separated from the rest of the archives like an afterthought. The overhead lights flickered faintly as they passed beneath them. A heavy metal plate above the door read: RESTRICTED ARCHIVES — AUTHORIZED STAFF ONLY.

Olivia stopped. This was it. Her fingers trembled just slightly as she pulled Izzy's brass key from her pocket. The number seven gleamed dully in the low light.

Luke stood back, giving her space. "Whenever you're ready."

She slid the key into the lock.

For one long, awful second, nothing happened. Then—Click. The sound echoed far too loudly in the narrow hall. The door swung open.

Luke exhaled slowly.

Olivia stepped inside. Room Seven was small and windowless. The air was stale and close. Filing cabinets lined the walls, their metal surfaces dulled with age. Cardboard boxes sat stacked neatly by decade. Microfiche drawers bore careful labels in neat handwriting. A single reading desk stood beneath a broken lamp. A dusty rotary phone sat beside it, its cord coiled like something asleep.

And then Olivia saw the mess. One filing cabinet gaped open. Files were scattered across the floor, papers fanned out in chaotic disarray. A box lay on its side, its contents spilled. The entire back shelf stood bare, empty wood where something had clearly once been stored.

Her blood ran cold. "Someone trashed this room," Olivia whispered.

Luke crouched beside the fallen box, brushing his fingers across the papers. "And recently. These aren't dusty."

Bertie growled from the corner, the sound low and sharp, vibrating with warning.

Alistair stiffened beside Olivia, his presence sharpening like a blade drawn halfway.

Luke reached into the scattered pile and lifted a torn folder. The label was faded, but still readable. BELL, TRINA (1989)

Olivia's heart slammed against her ribs. She moved toward the back of the room and saw photographs scattered across the carpet, some face-up, some trampled, all discarded without care.

She crouched, gathering them gently. Trina Bell with friends at the lake, sunburned and laughing. Trina at a school dance, hair curled, hands folded awkwardly at her waist.

Trina inside the historical society, smiling uncertainly as if she didn't quite belong. Trina standing in front of March House, the porch behind her unmistakable. Alive. Present. Real.

"Izzy was right," Olivia whispered. "This girl didn't run away."

Luke studied the photos grimly. "These should've been in that missing box."

"They were," Olivia whispered. Something crunched under her knee. She shifted and spotted a torn envelope beneath the desk. Carefully, she picked it up. The handwriting on the front was neat and familiar. Hazel Finch, President, Mistwood Historical Society, June 16, 1989

One day after Trina vanished.

Inside was a single note.

Hazel,
Destroy the file.
You know why.
– I. M.

Olivia's stomach dropped.

"Izzy told Hazel to destroy the file?" she said. "Why?"

Luke shook his head. "I don't think Izzy meant what Hazel thought she meant. And Hazel didn't destroy it. She hid it."

Alistair leaned over her shoulder. "This room held truths Hazel wanted buried … but someone else wanted them more."

Olivia stared at the empty shelf. The box labeled BELL, TRINA (1989) was gone.

"The entire file is missing," Olivia said.

Luke nodded. "They knew exactly what they were looking for."

"They stole everything Hazel hid."

"And they did it before we even got here."

Alistair's voice dropped to a warning murmur. "You must be cautious, Miss March. The enemy anticipates your moves."

They stepped back into the corridor.

And Olivia froze. A shadow moved at the far end of the hall. Tall. Still. Watching.

Luke's hand went to his sidearm. "Who's there?"

The shadow vanished around the corner.

Bertie barked furiously, sound echoing off the walls.

Luke took off down the hall, Olivia right behind him, pulse roaring in her ears. They reached the turn together.

Nothing.

Empty hallway.

Stillness pressing in on all sides.

Luke scanned the corridor, jaw tight. "Someone knew we'd come looking."

Olivia pressed her fingers around Alistair's watch in her pocket, grounding herself in its weight.

"They're trying to erase the past," she said. "Izzy tried to protect it. Hazel hid it. Now someone is cleaning house."

Luke nodded grimly. "We're not stopping. Not now."

Olivia closed her eyes for a heartbeat. March House. The ghosts. Izzy's voice. "We keep going."

CHAPTER TWENTY

The Hidden Room

It started with Snowball. Which, in Olivia's experience, was how most of the truly alarming things started at March House. Not with a scream or a crash or a dramatic lightning strike over the lake. No, her life had decided that the harbinger of doom would be a white cat with Fancy Feast looks and the moral superiority of a Victorian schoolmarm.

Olivia stood in the dining room with her investigation board, staring at the heading she'd pinned there like a dare. THE 1989 CONNECTION.

The words looked too clean for what they meant. Too tidy for a missing girl and decades of silence, and a town that smiled politely while it buried its own history in the backyard.

The ghosts hovered in their usual haunts, a messy constellation of personalities and opinions. The house itself felt quieter than normal, as if it were listening. Waiting.

Olivia was adjusting the angle of the Trina Bell clipping when Snowball's ears twitched.

The cat lifted her head sharply, the way she did when a can opened three rooms away. Only this time, there was no comforting rattle of food. Her eyes narrowed, and her whole posture shifted from lazy domestic royalty to alert predator.

"What is it?" Olivia asked automatically.

Snowball hopped down from her chair and trotted toward the

back hallway without hesitation, tail held straight like an exclamation point.

Simon appeared instantly behind her, posture protective, his gaze sweeping the hallway as if expecting an enemy charge.

Olivia followed, heart rate picking up speed in that unpleasant way it did when she knew something was about to happen and couldn't stop it.

"Snowball," she called softly. "If you found a mouse, I'm letting Walt handle it."

Snowball ignored her, as cats do when they believe you are beneath their current mission.

She stopped beside the wall near the old servants' bell panel. Then she meowed sharply and pawed at the plaster like she was trying to dig through it.

Alistair materialized beside Olivia, tall and composed even in the narrow hallway. "It seems the feline wishes to show us something," he said, as if this were a perfectly normal sentence to say on a perfectly normal morning.

Bertie bounded in behind them and barked at the wall, because apparently ghost dogs also had opinions about architecture.

From somewhere farther back in the house, JJ's cornet drifted out a suspicious jazz riff, the musical equivalent of *uh-oh.*

Olivia stared at the wall. "It's … a wall," she said.

Snowball pawed again, more insistently.

Simon's gaze sharpened. "Ma'am," he said quietly, "the cat appears agitated."

"Yes," Olivia muttered. "That's because she lives here."

Then Lark swept into view, carrying a basket of clean towels and looking entirely unbothered by the fact that Olivia was currently being directed by a cat.

"Oh!" Lark said, spotting Snowball's focus. "That wall."

Olivia turned. "That wall."

Lark nodded, as if Olivia had simply asked about a spice rack. "Izzy always said it made funny echoes."

Before Olivia could respond, Lark tapped the wall with her knuckles. The sound that came back wasn't solid plaster. It was hollow.

Olivia froze so completely she felt her pulse in her throat.

Lark tapped again, more firmly. Hollow.

Olivia crouched, pressed her palm flat against the wall, and held her breath. The surface was cool beneath her hand. Normal. Innocent. But the sound .... "There's space behind this," Olivia whispered.

Flossie flickered into view, wide-eyed and anxious, nodding so vigorously that Olivia half expected her to give herself ghost whiplash.

Walt appeared next, scowling like he'd been summoned by the word *structural.* "What now?" he grumbled, then leaned in and eyed the wall. "Huh."

Snowball pawed at the servants' bell panel again, a sharp, impatient motion.

Olivia looked up.

The old bell system was mounted on the same wall. Dusty brass plates. Little labels for rooms that didn't exist anymore. It looked like something meant to summon staff in 1901, back when people believed ringing bells would solve their problems.

Lark called it the ghost intercom.

Olivia had always assumed it was decorative. Another historic quirk. Another piece of March family theater. Now she leaned in closer, eyes narrowing. Most of the bell pulls were dusty, dull with age. But one … one was newer. Slightly shinier. Not dusty like the others.

Olivia stared at it.

The house felt like it was holding its breath again.

"Well," Olivia said slowly, "that's not suspicious at all."

Walt leaned closer, squinting. "That one's been touched."

Monique materialized behind them with a soft shimmer, taking in the bell panel with immediate interest. "Oh," she murmured, voice delighted. "Izzy, you sneaky minx."

Olivia reached out and wrapped her fingers around the shiny pull. It felt slightly warmer than the others, as if it had been handled recently. She tugged.

Click.

Not loud. Not dramatic. A barely audible internal shift inside the wall, like gears engaging or a latch releasing.

Olivia went completely still.

Walt's mouth fell open a fraction. "Well, I'll be," he said, awed despite himself. "She hid a door."

Alistair's brows rose. "Remarkably concealed."

Bertie barked once, triumphant, as if he'd personally discovered it.

Snowball meowed sharply, clearly pleased with herself.

Olivia ran her fingertips along the baseboard beneath the bell panel, moving carefully, searching. Her nails caught on something. A recessed notch. Her pulse jumped. She pressed it.

A thin seam appeared in the wall. Dust sifted out as if disturbed for the first time in years.

And then the panel swung inward. The movement was so smooth that it made Olivia's stomach drop. This wasn't a loose board. This wasn't an accident. This had been built. Deliberately.

Dust billowed out in a soft cloud, catching the hallway light in swirling particles.

Lark gasped, hand flying to her mouth. "Izzy," she whispered, reverently. "You clever girl …"

Beyond the panel was a narrow passage, tight enough that Olivia had to turn sideways to look into it. It led into the darkness. Into a completely hidden room inside her house. Her house.

The place where she slept. The place where she cooked. The place where she had believed foolishly that it was safe enough to breathe.

JJ's cornet floated out from the dining room, playing a single awe-filled chord like the soundtrack to a terrible discovery.

Olivia pulled out her phone and turned on the flashlight. The beam stabbed into the passage, revealing dust, old wood, and the faint outline of a doorway at the end.

She swallowed. Then she stepped inside.

Alistair glided at her shoulder like a stern guardian.

Bertie padded in close behind her, body tense.

Daisy trailed after them, quiet but present.

Flossie hovered near the entrance, wringing her hands, clearly regretting every choice

that had brought her into this century.

Simon remained in the hallway with Snowball, posture rigid, guarding the opening like a soldier at a trench.

The hidden room was small and windowless. The air inside was stale, thick with disuse. It had been sealed away along with everything it contained. And it contained a lot. Boxes labeled with years were stacked along one wall. Three crates of old receipts sat in the corner like abandoned evidence. A locked metal file drawer waited beneath a shelf. A stack of ledgers leaned against a wooden support beam. A milk crate full of newspaper clippings sat beside a dusty table with an oil lamp. And on the far side of the room, half hidden behind boxes, was a small safe.

Olivia's heart lodged in her throat. "This," she whispered, voice barely there, "this is where Izzy hid everything."

Monique clasped her hands together, eyes shining. "Very glamorous for a secret archive."

Walt stared at the crates. "Receipts," he said with reverence. "Now that's my kind of treasure."

Olivia set her phone on the dusty table to throw light across the room. The beam illuminated the ledgers, the crates, and the safe. It made the space feel even smaller. Claustrophobic. Like the walls were inching closer, curious. She reached for the top ledger. Leather-bound, worn from handling. The label on the front made her breath catch. March House Accounts – Restricted.

Olivia flipped it open. Inside were notes written in Izzy's hand. Missing funds. Expenses Izzy never authorized. Transfers that matched the embezzlement she'd suspected earlier, now confirmed in ink. Her stomach tightened as she turned pages. Then she found it. A list of names:

Hazel Finch. Carla Dawes. Theodore Bramble.

Olivia's skin went cold. She turned another page and stopped dead.

A handwritten note dated 1990.

Hazel knows the truth about what happened that night.
I begged her to go to the sheriff.
She refused.
Signed: Izzy.

Daisy made a soft, sorrowful sound, so small Olivia almost missed it.

Alistair's expression darkened. "Grim," he murmured.

Walt shook his head slowly.

Olivia's fingers curled around the edge of the page. She wanted to rip it out. She wanted to shove it under Hazel's nose. She wanted to march straight into the historical society and pin it to the door of Room Seven like a public accusation. Instead, she forced herself to breathe.

"This was never just about money," she whispered. "This was about Trina." She turned toward the safe. The metal looked old but sturdy, the sort of thing built to outlast the people who thought they owned what was inside.

Olivia knelt in front of it. Combination lock. She tried Izzy's birthday. Nothing.

She tried Hiram March's birth year. After all, he was the ancestor who built March House.

Nothing. She exhaled sharply, frustration rising.

From the doorway, Lark leaned in, her eyes bright with that particular brand of helpfulness that always came with chaos.

"You know," Lark said, "Izzy always used the same combination for everything else."

Olivia blinked. "What combination?"

Lark smirked. "The year disco died."

Olivia stared at her.

Lark's expression was absolutely innocent. Absolutely smug.

Olivia hesitated, then dialed 1979. Click. The safe opened.

Olivia let out a breath she didn't realize she'd been holding.

Inside were a velvet pouch, a stack of envelopes, a jewelry box, an empty manila file, and a single index card.

The card was written in Izzy's looping hand.

If you're reading this, Livvy, then someone beat you to it.

Olivia's mouth went dry.

She stared at the empty manila file. The will had been here.

Izzy hid it. And someone stole it anyway.

Alistair's face darkened, his dignified calm sharpening into something colder. "They slipped into this room," he whispered. "While you were in the house."

Flossie let out a small whimper, hands flying to her mouth.

Bertie growled low and long, a sound that made Olivia's skin prickle.

Olivia's pulse thundered. This wasn't a break-in from the outside. Not necessarily. This was someone who could move through the house. Someone who had access. Someone who could slip in and out while she slept, while she cooked, while she stood in the dining room pretending she was only haunted by the dead.

Her gaze snapped to the velvet pouch. Her hands shook as she opened it. Inside was a key, a tiny folded note, a locket, and another torn piece of parchment. Another fragment.

It matched the one from the gazebo. Her breath hitched. Olivia unfolded the tiny note.

Livvy—The house will show you the truth. Follow the pieces. They all lead to Trina.

Olivia's heart pounded so hard it hurt. Confirmation. Izzy had been investigating the disappearance. Izzy knew Hazel lied. Izzy hid evidence here. Someone stole part of it — but not all. And whoever had taken the will had missed this pouch. Or hadn't had time. Or hadn't realized what it was.

Olivia stood slowly, locket pressed in her palm, Izzy's note burning against her skin.

Then, her phone chirped. DING.

A new-message alert.

The sound snapped through the house like a gunshot.

Olivia backed out of the hidden room, breath shallow, and stepped into the hallway. Simon stood rigid with Snowball beside him, both of them watching the corridor like they expected someone to emerge from the walls.

Olivia grabbed her phone.

A text from Luke.

"We need to talk. I'm on my way."

Olivia stared at the screen, heart racing.

Because the horrifying truth had finally settled into place with cold certainty. The intruder who broke into the archives also broke into March House. Into Izzy's hidden room.

Into her home. Into the one place she had believed, despite everything, she could let her guard down.

Olivia pressed the locket to her chest.

"Izzy," she whispered, voice breaking on the name, "what were you trying to tell me?"

The ghosts gathered around her in a silent, protective circle.

And March House suddenly felt smaller. And more dangerous.

CHAPTER TWENTY-ONE

The Worst Thing

Olivia retreated to the dining room because the dining room was the only place in March House that still pretended to be a normal room in a normal house. The kitchen had turned into a crime scene with appliances. The back hall felt like a throat that might close. The hidden room inside the wall felt like a secret artery she'd accidentally cut open. Even the solarium, usually bright and smug with sunlight, now seemed too exposed, too glassy, too visible from outside.

So she sat at the dining table. She planted both hands flat on the wood as if anchoring herself to something solid could convince her body it was not currently in free fall.

The investigation board stood nearby, a fortress of pushpins and paper, and the new heading Olivia had written earlier stared back at her like an accusation.

THE 1989 CONNECTION A missing girl. A town that protected someone. A hidden archive box that had already been stolen. And now, a secret room inside her own house with an empty file that should have held the missing will. Someone had been inside March House.

Not years ago. Not in Izzy's time. Recently. Recently enough that the thought still had sharp edges.

Lark came in without asking, because Lark did everything

without asking, and Olivia did not have the energy to argue. She set a mug down in front of Olivia with a solemnity usually reserved for funerals and football games.

"Emergency lavender courage tea," Lark announced. "Smells like anxiety wearing perfume."

Olivia managed a small, strangled laugh that didn't quite make it to her eyes. She curled her trembling hands around the mug. The warmth sank into her palms. The steam rose in pale ribbons. The scent was floral and soothing and slightly insulting, as if the tea itself was trying too hard.

"You're rattled, sweetheart," Lark said gently, as if speaking too loudly might shatter her. "Anybody would be."

Olivia nodded because she didn't trust her voice. She could still feel the hidden room pressing around her, the stale air, the safe door swinging open like a mouth revealing it had been bitten into already. She could still see that index card, Izzy's looping handwriting delivering a message she never meant to receive this way. *Someone beat you to it.* She swallowed hard, throat tight.

Behind her, Sir Alistair stood sentinel, perfectly still, late-Georgian posture immaculate, expression controlled, but his eyes sharp. He didn't pace. He didn't fidget. He simply watched the room as if it were a battlefield and Olivia the only person worth guarding.

At her feet, Bertie curled into a tight little ghost-dog coil. Every so often, he let out a low growl, rumbling deep in his chest, as if growling could physically keep danger away.

Daisy sat at the far end of the table, wringing her hands over and over. She didn't speak. Her presence was a soft, steady thread trying to hold the room together.

Monique leaned against the sideboard with her chin lifted and her expression set in practiced disdain. "This stress is terrible for my complexion," she announced, as if she might sue the universe for emotional damages. But she kept flickering, her form shifting an inch here, an inch there, like she couldn't settle.

Simon had stationed himself by the front door. He didn't sit. He didn't lean. He stood with a soldier's rigid focus, eyes trained on the glass panes, listening for anything that didn't belong.

JJ hovered near the piano, cornet lowered. He wasn't playing a song, not exactly. Just a quiet, steady rhythm, soft enough to be more vibration than sound. A heartbeat. A nervous one.

Flossie clung to the banister at the base of the staircase, pale, hands gripping the wood as if she might fall through it. Her eyes kept darting toward the back hall, then back to Olivia.

The entire house felt alert. Not creaky. Not eccentric. Not haunted in the whimsical, antique-store way Izzy had romanticized. Alert. Like a hunting dog listening for footsteps in the brush.

Olivia lifted the mug and tried to drink. The tea did taste like lavender and courage, and Lark's insistence on believing that herbs could solve anything, including attempted murder.

She took another sip anyway. The back hallway creaked. Olivia froze mid-swallow.

It was small. Subtle. It could have been wood settling. A pipe complaining. The normal groans of an old Victorian being asked to exist.

But it wasn't one of those familiar sounds. Olivia had been cataloging the house's noises since she arrived. She knew which floorboard squealed by the pantry, which stair made a sigh at the third step, which hallway plank protested in damp weather.

This creak was wrong. Then came a footstep. Soft, but deliberate. Then the faint scrape of something against the floorboards, a slow drag like someone shifting weight carefully.

Olivia set the mug down with exaggerated gentleness, as if noise might summon whatever was making that sound.

The ghosts went still.

JJ's cornet cut off mid-beat.

Monique stopped flickering.

Daisy's hands froze in mid-wring.

Snowball, who had been lounging on a dining chair like a queen observing her subjects, snapped her head toward the back hall. Her fur puffed up instantly, tail shooting straight up like a flag of alarm.

Simon appeared beside her in a blink, posture rigid, ready.

Olivia's voice came out as a whisper. "Lark?"

Lark, who had been folding towels at the sideboard, looked up slowly. Her face drained of color.

"That wasn't me," she said.

The temperature dropped. Not the normal drafty chill of March House. This was sudden, sharp, as if the air itself had recoiled.

Alistair's voice was low, calm, and terrifying in its precision. "Miss March, step back."

Olivia's muscles locked for a heartbeat. Then she forced herself to obey, sliding her chair back an inch, eyes fixed on the hallway opening.

A faint shadow moved there.

Then the kitchen light flickered.

Once.

Twice.

And went out.

Darkness swallowed the back of the house, thick and complete. The dining room light didn't reach far into the hallway now. It turned the doorway into a mouth.

A shape moved in the dark. Fast. Purposeful.

Olivia's instincts screamed at her to run, to put distance between herself and whatever that was, to get to the solarium where there was space and light and glass, even if glass suddenly felt like a terrible idea.

She bolted.

Her slippers slid on the floor. Her heart slammed against her ribs.

She was halfway to the solarium door when something seized her arm from behind.

Hard.

Fingers dug into her sleeve and skin with brutal strength. Olivia screamed. Olivia gasped and twisted, trying to yank free. Pain flared where the grip tightened. She stumbled, catching herself on the edge of the table.

A voice hissed close to her ear, low and furious. "Stop digging."

The words shot straight through her like ice water.

Olivia cried out, trying to wrench away, trying to see the face in the darkness, but the figure stayed behind her, an outline of solid menace. The grip tightened until her fingers went numb.

And then the ghosts hit back.

Simon lunged first, barreling through the intruder like a cold shockwave. The only thing a living person felt when a ghost passed through them was chill and discomfort, but Simon made it count. The intruder jerked, shuddering violently as if a winter wind had slammed straight through their bones.

Walt appeared next, roaring, swinging his wrench through the shadow. The intruder flinched again, stumbling, their breath catching in surprise at the strange sensation of something heavy and cold passing through them.

JJ blasted a blaring, discordant cornet note that rattled the windows and vibrated through the house. It wasn't music. It was a shock wave.

Alistair stepped closer to Olivia.

Bertie launched at the intruder with a furious bark, leaping through their legs, circling back, barking again, a relentless storm of ghost-dog outrage.

The intruder backed up, startled, unable to understand what was happening. They couldn't see the ghosts. They felt only the sudden chill. The disorientation. The pressure of an unseen force. And for the first time, they hesitated.

Olivia wrenched her arm free as the grip loosened, stumbling forward, breath tearing in her lungs.

The intruder bolted. Boots pounded across the kitchen. The back door flew open. It slammed shut so hard the frame rattled. Silence crashed down, heavy and shocked.

Olivia's legs gave out. She hit her knees, shaking violently, palms pressed to the floorboards, trying to convince her body she was still in one piece.

Lark dropped everything and rushed to her, skirts swishing, hands steady despite the terror in her eyes. "Oh, honey — honey, breathe! You're okay, you're okay—"

She wrapped Olivia in a fierce hug, muttering grounding chants under her breath. The chant didn't matter. The sound of Lark's voice did. The fact that someone warm and alive was holding her did.

Olivia sobbed once, sharp and shocked, then forced air back into her lungs. "They were in the house," she gasped. "They grabbed me. They—"

Lark tightened her hold. "You're safe. We're here. We're all here."

The ghosts gathered around like a protective ring, hovering close, radiating anger and fear, and loyalty.

Lark helped Olivia stand, one arm braced around her waist. Olivia's knees wobbled. Her arm throbbed where she'd been grabbed.

CHAPTER TWENTY-TWO

The Real Motive Emerges

The knock on the front door came like a gunshot. Hard. Urgent. Then Luke's voice, too loud, sliced through the house. "Olivia! Open the door!" Luke Thatcher hit the door of March House like it personally owed him money. The cold air rolled in behind him, biting and sharp, like Mistwood itself had decided to crawl indoors and supervise the fallout. His boots thudded on the kitchen floor. Denim. Buckskin. Frustration. The full package.

Olivia stood near the doorway to the dining room, arms folded tight across her chest, physically holding her ribs together through sheer stubbornness. Her skin still had that washed-out adrenaline look, the kind that made her feel both too hot and too cold at the same time. She could taste fear in the back of her throat, metallic and stubborn, and every time her gaze flicked to the broken door, her heart tried to sprint ahead of her.

Luke's eyes cut straight to the damage. The splintered wood. The scuffs on the floor. The faint smear of mud that should not be inside her house. Then, his gaze snapped to her.

He stopped so fast his jacket swung forward and then settled. The muscles in his jaw flexed like a warning. "You're not okay," he said, voice low and harsh. "Don't tell me you're okay."

Olivia's brain attempted to supply a calm, responsible answer. Something adult. Something composed. Her mouth did not cooperate. "I'm …" She cleared her throat. Tried again. "I'm alive, so—"

"That's not okay." Two words would have been easier. That sentence was not easy. It landed like a hand on her shoulder, steady and unyielding. Luke's expression was a careful kind of fury, the type that had been shoved into a tight box and taped shut, but the box was shaking.

He inhaled visibly, forcing himself not to explode.

Olivia watched him do it, watched him choose control, and that choice made something in her chest ache in a way she had no plans to examine tonight.

Luke pointed at a chair as if he were issuing a lawful order, and the furniture itself had better comply. "Sit. Talk. Tell me everything."

Olivia opened her mouth again, but her legs decided for her. They were done. They lowered her into the nearest dining room chair with the exhausted obedience of someone who had reached the end of her daily allotment of terror.

Lark stood beside her, arms crossed, wild gray hair falling out of a loose braid, sage tucked behind her ear like a pencil she used to take notes on the living. Her expression said she was one wrong word away from smacking someone with a wooden spoon. Possibly Luke. Possibly Olivia. Possibly the universe. "I'm staying for this," Lark said.

Luke nodded once. No argument. No hesitation. He was not, Olivia noted, stupid.

"Good," Luke said. "Because I'm not doing this twice."

From the hallway, a cluster of unseen witnesses gathered. The ghosts filled the edges of the room like a silent storm front.

JJ hovered near the archway, cornet in his hands, expression serious. He gave a low, dramatic jazz note.

Monique drifted closer to the table, fanning herself, the entire scene terribly stressful and also deeply under-accessorized.

Walt appeared half-faded near the baseboard heater, scowling. "This is why you install better locks," he muttered. "Nobody listens."

Flossie hovered near Olivia's shoulder, clutching her pearl-handled comb like it was both a comfort and a weapon.

Daisy stayed near the window, wringing her hands, eyes wide and glimmering.

Simon positioned himself by the broken back door, standing guard with the grim focus of a man who had seen worse and refused to see it again.

Sir Alistair stepped into the dining room with his usual composed grace, hands folded behind his back, expression grave.

Bertie sat at his feet, tail wagging, clearly delighted that Luke had arrived. Bertie loved dramatic entrances. It was among his many flaws.

Olivia felt them all, the way the air shifted when they gathered. Luke could not see them, could not hear them, but he paused for half a second, sensing something. As if the house itself had inhaled.

Olivia cleared her throat. "Ignore the … vibes," she said.

Luke's eyes narrowed slightly. "What vibes?"

Olivia waved a hand vaguely. "The house has vibes. It's old. It's haunted by debt and questionable woodwork. Lots of vibes."

Walt snorted. "Tell him it's haunted by common sense and he still won't take the hint."

"Walt," Olivia hissed under her breath.

Luke stared at her. "Who are you talking to?"

"My trauma," Olivia said immediately. "It's extremely talkative."

Luke studied her for a moment, then nodded, deciding that this was not the strangest thing he would hear tonight. "Fine. Your trauma can take a number." He moved into the dining room and looked down at the table as if expecting a neat little stack of evidence and a bow. What he got was chaos arranged with the care of someone trying to keep her sanity from spilling off the edges.

"All right," Luke said, voice steadier now. "Show me."

Olivia spread everything out across the dining room table; it could have been a cooking demonstration titled: *How to Ruin Your Life in Twelve Simple Clues.*

Izzy's ledger sat open in the center, its pages worn, the ink dark and deliberate. Next to it lay the note from the music box, a small scrap of paper that had cost Olivia about three heart palpitations and one full nervous breakdown.

The torn parchment scrap from the gazebo rested near the ledger like a missing tooth, jagged edge and all. The forged will sat to the side, smug in its falsehood, practically radiating fraud.

Room Seven's files formed a careful stack, because Olivia could handle murder evidence but not disorder. The newspaper clipping of Trina Bell lay beside them, the photo grainy and old, the headline screaming decades later.

Izzy's note to Hazel, the one that said '*destroy the file*', sat in the corner, giving a warning.

The missing safe contents were represented by an empty space that felt far louder than any object on the table. Absence had weight. Olivia hated that.

Luke's additions were clinical and solid: the scrap of fabric sealed in a bag, the muddy footprint photo, the key to Room Seven, and two handwritten threatening notes that made Olivia's stomach clench every time she looked at them.

The entire spread looked like an entire season of a detective show condensed into one horrifying centerpiece.

JJ gave another low note; a soundtrack cue.

Monique fanned herself. "So dramatic," she whispered. "I adore it. I hate it. Continue."

Luke leaned over the table, both hands planted on the wood. He scanned each item, eyes sharp and focused, his face tightening as the story took shape in front of him. "This is bigger than Izzy's death," he said. His voice went quieter, but not softer. "Bigger than the will." He looked up at Olivia, anger and worry tangled together in his eyes. "This is a whole cover-up."

Walt snorted. "Finally. Someone says it out loud."

Olivia swallowed. Her hands were still trembling, so she curled them into fists under the edge of the table, nails pressing into her palms until the sensation anchored her. "I think it starts with money," she said, and reached for the ledger.

Luke's gaze snapped back down.

Olivia flipped to the section Izzy had marked. The pages were full of carefully recorded numbers, dates, and notations that looked dull until you realized dullness was the perfect disguise.

"Look," Olivia said. "Money went missing from March House accounts … starting in nineteen eighty-eight."

Luke's brows drew together. "Nineteen eighty-eight."

"Yes," Olivia said, and tried to keep her voice steady. "Small amounts. Quiet. Hard to trace. But consistent."

Luke lifted his head. "That's the year before Trina Bell disappeared."

The air in the room seemed to tighten. Even the house felt like it had leaned closer.

"A correlation," Sir Alistair murmured, voice calm and precise.

"A guilty one," Walt added, because Walt had never met a subtle moment he couldn't punch in the face.

Olivia flipped another page. "It kept happening through the early nineties. Over and over. Not enough to raise immediate alarms, but enough to bleed March House slowly."

Luke's jaw flexed. "So someone was using March House as a piggy bank."

Olivia nodded. "And Izzy figured it out in eighty-nine." She held the ledger up a little, showing Luke the way Izzy's handwriting sharpened around that year. The notes became more urgent. More pointed. Like Izzy had stopped writing numbers and started writing warnings.

"That's why she confronted Hazel," Olivia said.

Lark's hand came down lightly on the edge of the ledger, her fingers resting there with an odd tenderness. "Izzy wasn't angry at Hazel," she whispered. "She was scared for her."

Olivia's breath caught, the implication sliding into place like a puzzle piece that had been waiting for the right angle.

"Hazel wasn't the thief," Olivia whispered.

Luke's gaze sharpened. "What makes you think that?"

Olivia looked at Lark, then back at the ledger. "Because if Hazel was stealing, Izzy would have been furious. Izzy could be kind, but she wasn't a doormat. If Hazel had been the one taking money, Izzy would have confronted her with fire."

Lark nodded, eyes sad. "But she confronted her with fear."

Olivia's hands tightened around the ledger. "Hazel was protecting someone else."

Luke went still for a moment. Then his voice dropped. "Someone who could hurt her."

"Someone who did hurt her," Olivia corrected softly. "Or at least threatened to."

Monique whispered from the edge of the room, voice like perfume and steel. "Fear makes liars of good people."

Daisy nodded, face pale. "And prisoners."

Luke's gaze dropped to the newspaper clipping. He picked it up carefully, as if it could cut him.

"Trina wasn't a runaway," he said. "We know that now."

Olivia's throat tightened. "She saw something. Or found something. Something she shouldn't have."

"Children always see more than adults," Monique whispered again, and this time her voice carried a sorrow that made Olivia's chest ache.

Luke's eyes narrowed as he stared at the clipping. "If Trina saw the embezzlement," he said slowly, "or saw who was doing it … then she wasn't just inconvenient. She was a threat."

Olivia's stomach twisted. "And threats get removed."

Luke looked up at her, his expression hardening. "That's what you think is happening now."

Olivia had not meant to say it out loud, but once it was in the air, it was undeniable. "Yes," she said. "They attacked me. In this house. They broke in as if they owned the place. Punishing me for looking too closely." Her hands were shaking again.

Flossie drifted closer, her presence gentle and protective.

Simon shifted slightly by the broken door. He wanted to step between Olivia and every danger in the world.

Olivia forced herself to breathe.

Luke's voice was quiet, but the anger in it was sharp. "Not again."

Olivia blinked. "What?"

Luke's jaw clenched. "Not again. Not another girl. Not another woman in this town getting silenced because someone wants to keep a secret."

The words hit Olivia hard. Luke was not just angry because she had been attacked. He was angry because he had seen this story before and had lived with its echo.

Olivia swallowed. "Then we're close."

Luke nodded once. "We're close."

Olivia lifted the torn parchment scrap from the gazebo. "The real will is part of the same mystery," she said. "Izzy hid it because she knew the thief would try to destroy it."

Luke's eyes flicked toward the hidden room, the safe that had been breached, the secret archive violated. "And so the thief did. They broke into March House. Into your aunt's secret archive. And they stole the will."

Olivia's pulse quickened. "And the last pieces of the Trina Bell file."

Sir Alistair's voice sharpened, his calm slipping into something colder. "The enemy repeats his crimes across decades."

Walt muttered, "Because nobody ever stops him."

Lark planted her palms on the table, grounding the room with sheer, stubborn presence. "Hazel isn't the villain," she said firmly. "She's terrified."

Olivia nodded slowly. "She's protecting someone. Someone who threatened her. Someone who threatened Izzy."

Luke's eyes narrowed. "Someone who made Trina disappear."

Olivia met his gaze. "Yes."

Luke exhaled, slow and controlled, like he was forcing the anger back down into that box again. "That means Hazel knows who it is."

"She just won't talk," Olivia said.

The silence that followed was heavy.

Even the ghosts seemed quieter, their usual commentary subdued by the weight of what was emerging.

Olivia pushed back from her chair and started pacing because if she stayed still, she might start shaking again, and she was tired of shaking.

"They stole the will," she said, counting on her fingers like she was building a recipe for disaster. "They stole parts of the file. They attacked me. They thought breaking into the archives would stop me. They thought breaking into March House would scare me." She stopped pacing and looked at Luke. "And it worked."

Luke's eyes softened slightly. "It scared you."

Olivia's laugh came out sharp and humorless. "Luke, I screamed so loud I'm pretty sure the lake filed a noise complaint."

JJ gave a tiny, sympathetic riff, offering moral support through music.

Olivia took a breath. "But it also made me mad."

Luke's mouth twitched, the closest thing to a smile he'd offered since arriving. "Good."

Olivia looked at the table again. At the spread of evidence. At the notes. At the gaps.

"They're desperate," she said. "And desperate people make mistakes."

Luke nodded. "And they just made a big one."

Olivia stopped and faced him. "Which one?"

Luke reached down and tapped the evidence bag with the scrap of fabric. "This. This is new. This gives us something concrete. Clothing fabric. Thread type. Color."

Olivia's pulse jumped, hope sparking fast and bright. "We can match it."

"We can try," Luke corrected, because Luke lived in the land of facts, not wishes. But his eyes were sharp with purpose now. "If it's from a jacket or a sleeve, someone in town is walking around with a tear they didn't have yesterday."

Olivia imagined it. Someone is hiding ripped clothing. Someone is making excuses. Someone is suddenly wearing a different coat. A mistake.

"But we need Hazel," Luke said. "She knows the truth. All of it."

Olivia stopped pacing. The bolt slid into place, hard as steel.

"Then we talk to Hazel," she said.

The ghosts reacted as if she'd struck a match.

Sir Alistair bowed his head, solemn approval.

Daisy's glow brightened, courage soft and steady.

JJ played a determined riff that sounded like a promise.

Simon saluted, crisp and fierce.

Flossie hugged her comb.

Monique smirked as if she were ready for drama.

Walt cracked his ghostly knuckles, muttering something about finally getting somewhere. Bertie barked once, sharp and pleased.

Lark reached into her pocket and pressed a small jar into

Olivia's hand. Inside were rosemary sprigs, green and fragrant. "For protection."

Olivia stared at the rosemary. "Is this protection, or is this garnish?"

"Yes," Lark said.

Luke's gaze lifted to Olivia's face, and the intensity there made her chest tighten. Slow burn or not, she was not blind. Not dead. Not immune.

His voice was low, steady, and full of promise. "And this time," he said, "she's going to talk."

Olivia's grip tightened around the jar.

The dining room felt crowded, not just with evidence and ghosts and fear, but with something else. A partner who believed her. A house that had chosen her, even if it expressed affection through creaks and hauntings and occasional attempted murder. Ghosts who adored her in their own chaotic ways. And a truth that had been buried for decades, now clawing its way to the surface.

Olivia lifted her chin. "Then let's go make Hazel talk," she said, voice steady.

March House listened.

And somewhere in Mistwood, the person who thought they could keep the past buried forever probably felt the walls closing in.

CHAPTER TWENTY-THREE

Confronting Hazel Finch

Hazel Finch's house looked like a committee of rules had designed it. Rigid. Symmetrical. Proper to the point of hostility. It sat behind a prim, steel-gray dome of rhododendrons and judgment, the sort of landscaping that didn't whisper *welcome* so much as *wipe your feet and your opinions before entering.* The front walk was too straight. The porch railing too evenly painted. The mailbox stood at attention as if it had once served in the military and still expected daily inspections.

Olivia and Luke parked along the street because getting any closer felt like asking to be arrested by the shrubbery.

Olivia shut her door and stood there for a second, staring at the house, letting her lungs catch up with her heartbeat. The sky was overcast, the air cold enough to make her nose sting, and the silence around Hazel's place felt deliberate. It seemed even the birds had signed a non-disclosure agreement.

Next to her, Luke glanced at the windows. The curtains were drawn, but not fully. There was a tiny gap, just enough for someone inside to watch without being seen. The curtains twitched.

Luke muttered under his breath. "This woman has more locks than a bank."

Olivia's hand went to her coat pocket without thinking. Inside, her fingers closed around Sir Alistair's silver pocket watch, cool and solid. It was ridiculous, having a dead Georgian gentleman's watch as a comfort object, but Olivia had reached the point in her life where she no longer argued with what worked.

Alistair's presence hovered close behind her, steady as a spine.

Bertie trotted at Olivia's side, invisible to Luke, tail wagging, utterly unaware that they were about to walk into the emotional equivalent of a bear trap.

Alistair's voice came quietly, a calm murmur meant only for Olivia. "Proceed with caution, Miss March."

Olivia nodded once. "Always," she whispered back.

Luke looked sideways at her. "What?"

"Nothing," Olivia said quickly. "Just … mentally preparing for the Finch Hospitality Experience."

Luke snorted. "Yeah. I'm sure there'll be complimentary judgment and a gift shop on the way out."

They started up the walk. The house did not look friendlier up close. It looked cleaner. Colder. Warmth had been banned in 1973 and never allowed back.

Olivia knocked before she could overthink it.

Hazel answered the door the instant her knuckles made contact. No delay. No footsteps. No surprise. Just the door swinging open. Hazel had been standing there with her hand on the knob, waiting.

Hazel Finch was stiff and guarded, dressed neatly as always, her gray hair pinned into place as if one loose strand would signal the collapse of civilization. Her eyes flicked from Olivia to Luke, then back.

"Well," Hazel said dryly. "I suppose you're not here for tea."

Olivia held her gaze. "No. I'm here for answers."

Hazel's lips tightened. For a moment, Olivia thought she might slam the door in their faces and pretend they were a hallucination, which honestly would have been consistent with how this town handled problems. Then Hazel hesitated. And stepped aside. "Come in," she said. Her face showed it physically hurt her to offer.

Olivia walked into Hazel Finch's house and immediately felt she'd violated a museum exhibit.

The sitting room was immaculate in a way that went beyond clean. Every doily was crisp. Every framed photo was dust-free. Every antique was painstakingly polished, as if Hazel had been scrubbing away time itself. Every rug was aligned with mathematical precision. Every book spine was straight. Even the air smelled organized. There was no dust. No clutter. No warmth.

Olivia had been in professional kitchens that felt more welcoming.

Luke stood near the door the moment they entered, arms crossed, body angled just slightly toward the exit. Silent. Watchful. Brimming with readiness. He looked like the human version of a guard dog who did not trust your intentions, your furniture, or your throw pillows.

Alistair stood behind Olivia, a dignified shadow. His posture formal, his presence quietly protective. If Hazel noticed any chill, she didn't show it.

Bertie sniffed at Hazel's carpet and sneezed dramatically, offended by the lack of crumbs.

Hazel moved to her chair and sat with stiff control, smoothing her skirt, arranging herself, preparing for an interrogation she had been avoiding for thirty years. Her eyes lifted to Olivia. "Say what you came to say."

Olivia swallowed, then reached into her bag. One by one, she placed the evidence on Hazel's coffee table. The torn photograph of Hazel and Izzy, edges ragged like a friendship ripped in half. The key to Room Seven. The Trina Bell newspaper clipping, yellowed and haunting. Izzy's handwritten note. The ledger page referencing Hazel. The note that said '*destroy the file*'. The parchment scrap. And finally, a photograph of Room Seven trashed, chaos and violation captured in stark clarity.

Hazel's face drained of color.

It was not dramatic at first. It was subtle. A tightening around her mouth. A flicker in her eyes. A tiny tremor in her fingers that she tried to hide by folding her hands together.

Luke watched her like a hawk that had just spotted movement in the grass.

Olivia leaned forward slightly, keeping her voice calm. Controlled. She had learned how to do that in Chicago, where panic was a luxury, and mistakes got served with humiliation. "We know you lied. We know Izzy confronted you. We know Trina didn't run away. We know you hid the file."

Hazel's fingers trembled.

"And someone else stole it," Olivia added, letting the words sit between them like a knife.

Hazel's throat bobbed as she swallowed. "I did what I had to do," she said, voice clipped.

Olivia held her gaze. "Tell us what happened. Izzy wanted the truth out. She left it for me."

Hazel's lips trembled. It was small, but it was the first crack in her armor. The first sign that beneath all that polish and control, something was fraying. Hazel's eyes flicked toward the window, the curtains, and the street beyond. Fear. Old, ingrained fear.

Olivia felt it in her bones.

Luke didn't move, but the tension in his posture shifted. He tightened every muscle in preparation for whatever Hazel might do next.

Hazel stared down at the evidence as if it might bite. Then, without warning, she slammed her cane against the floor.

The sharp crack startled even Luke. Olivia's heart jumped into her throat.

Alistair took one dignified step forward, calm and protective, his presence filling the space behind Olivia like a wall.

Hazel's voice rose, breaking through her control with a rawness that didn't belong in such a pristine room. "You don't understand!" Hazel snapped. "You don't … you weren't there!"

Olivia didn't flinch. She had been yelled at by Michelin-star chefs with egos the size of planets. Hazel Finch's rage was terrifying, but it was also soaked in grief.

"Then tell me. Tell me what Izzy tried to protect."

Hazel's shoulders sagged. And for the first time, she looked older than she had moments before. Smaller. Fragile. Like all the symmetry and rules had been holding her upright, and without them, she might crumble. Her voice broke. "I loved that girl," Hazel whispered. "Trina was like a daughter to me."

Olivia's breath caught. "Trina Bell?"

Hazel nodded. Tears formed in her eyes, bright and unwelcome, as if her body had betrayed her by showing something human. "She volunteered with me at the historical society," Hazel said, voice shaking. "Bright girl. Sweet. Too curious for her own good."

Luke's arms uncrossed slightly, just enough to show he was listening with something deeper than suspicion.

Olivia felt the room tilt. The name Trina Bell had been a headline, a rumor, a ghost story in town gossip. Hearing Hazel say she loved her made Trina real in a way the clipping never could.

Hazel wiped at her eyes with stiff fingers, annoyed at herself for the tears. Her voice dropped to barely a whisper. "It wasn't a runaway," Hazel said. "Of course it wasn't."

Luke leaned forward, careful, calm, his voice gentler than Olivia had heard it in days. "What happened?"

Hazel stared at the carpet, at the perfect alignment of the fibers. It was safer than looking at them.

"She found something," Hazel whispered. "Numbers in the records that didn't add up. Large withdrawals from March House's account."

Olivia felt cold spread through her chest. "Embezzlement."

Hazel nodded once. "She tried to talk to him."

Olivia froze.

Luke went still. His voice was quiet and dangerous. "… him?"

Hazel began to cry, the sound sharp and sudden, like something that had been trapped behind her teeth for decades and finally broke free. "Theodore Bramble."

Alistair's presence surged. His calm sharpened into something colder. His eyes narrowed, fury tightening his features.

Bertie let out a low growl, the sound vibrating through Olivia's awareness like a warning bell.

Luke's expression turned lethal.

Hazel's shoulders shook as she spoke, words stumbling out faster now, the dam breaking.

"He wasn't just a developer," Hazel whispered. "He worked for the bank in nineteen eighty-nine. He approved the loans. He funneled the stolen money."

Olivia felt physically ill. Her stomach turned, bile rising as if the truth had teeth.

"And Trina confronted him," Hazel finished, voice cracking.

Olivia's mouth went dry. "He killed her."

Hazel covered her mouth, shaking her head violently as if she could refuse the idea. "I don't know," she sobbed. "I don't know. She went to meet him by the lake and … and she never came back."

Olivia's hands clenched in her lap.

Luke's face was hard, his eyes dark, but his breathing stayed controlled, measured. Like he was holding back a storm.

Olivia's voice cracked when she spoke again. "Izzy knew."

Hazel's sob turned into a broken sound, half grief, half rage at herself. "Yes," Hazel whispered. "Izzy believed Trina had been murdered. She begged me to go to the sheriff."

Hazel's eyes squeezed shut. "But Sheriff Ray Morton was Bramble's closest friend. He wouldn't have listened."

Luke's face went pale with anger. His gaze dropped to the floor, jaw tight.

Olivia heard him whisper, barely audible. "Or worse … he would have warned him."

Hazel nodded violently. "Yes. Yes. He would have buried the report. He would have buried everything."

Luke's hands clenched, then loosened, then clenched again, like he was trying not to break Hazel's perfectly aligned coffee table in half.

"I was scared," Hazel said, voice shaking. "We all were. Izzy tried to gather proof. She hid it in Room Seven. She hid part of it in her house. She kept digging." Hazel swallowed hard, as if the next words were knives. "And Bramble threatened her."

Olivia's body went cold. She trembled, not from fear now, but from recognition. "He threatened me too," Olivia whispered.

Hazel's eyes opened, glassy with agony. "He won't stop," she whispered. "He never stopped."

Olivia leaned forward, heart pounding. "Hazel … what exactly did Trina find?"

Hazel stared at her hands, then slowly opened them, palms up, trembling. "Proof," Hazel whispered. "Bank papers. Signed forms. A ledger page with Bramble's name. Everything tying him to the stolen money."

Luke went rigid. The words had snapped something into place. "That's why she disappeared," Luke said.

Hazel nodded, tears sliding down her cheeks. "And why Izzy hid the will," Hazel whispered. "The will showed who should inherit March House … and he could be exposed and lose everything."

Olivia's breath came shallow. Her mind raced, pieces connecting into a final, horrifying shape. "Bramble," she whispered.

Hazel nodded again, exhausted and broken. "Yes."

Olivia slowly began gathering the evidence back into her bag, hands shaking so hard she had to pause to steady herself. The room felt smaller now, and the air thicker. The truth had taken up physical space.

Hazel looked years older. Her posture sagging, her control gone. "Child," she whispered, voice thin and desperate, "if you keep digging … you'll end up like Trina."

Her gaze flicked to Olivia's face, then dropped, as if she couldn't bear what she saw there.

"Or Izzy."

Olivia straightened, spine stiffening with something fierce.

Alistair stepped forward, fierce and formal, his voice carrying a weight Hazel could not see but Olivia could feel. "Miss March is not alone," Alistair said.

Olivia swallowed, then met Hazel's gaze. "He already tried, and I'm still here."

Hazel stared at her, awe and fear tangled together. She had spent decades believing survival was impossible, and now she was looking at proof that it wasn't.

Luke nodded solemnly, his voice low and steady. "We're finishing what Izzy started."

Hazel's mouth trembled. The last of her strength seemed to drain out. "Then God help you," she whispered.

Outside, the street remained quiet. Inside, the mystery finally had a face. And Olivia could feel, with sick certainty, that Theodore Bramble would not appreciate being cornered.

CHAPTER TWENTY-FOUR

Preparing for the Confrontation

The walk back to the car felt longer than the walk up. Hazel Finch's house sat behind them; a sealed vault, rigid and spotless and full of ghosts that did not float or flicker. The type of haunting that stayed lodged in the living, in their lungs and bones, in the way fear became routine.

Olivia's body felt wrung out. Emotionally, mentally, spiritually, and, if she was being honest, also physically. Her shoulders were tight. Her throat hurt from holding back everything she wanted to scream in Hazel's sitting room. Her head throbbed in a dull, steady way that suggested her brain had spent the last hour sprinting uphill.

Luke walked beside her, steadying her. He did not talk much. He did not try to fill the silence. He just stayed there, close enough that Olivia could feel his presence, steady and solid. If she tipped sideways, he would catch her before she hit the pavement.

Which was thoughtful. Also inconvenient. The last thing Olivia needed was to be emotionally stabilized by a grumpy deputy with a jawline that belonged in a romance novel.

She opened the passenger door and slid in. Luke circled to the driver's side and got behind the wheel. His hands gripped it for a moment, knuckles whitening, and Olivia watched him take a slow breath.

Reaching into her pocket again, the cool weight of Sir Alistair's pocket watch in her coat pocket reassured her.

As they drove back toward March House, Olivia stared out the window at the gray sky and the bare branches and the lake beyond, steel-blue and calm, as if nothing in Mistwood had ever gone wrong. "I feel like I just got dragged backward through a thicket of secrets," Olivia muttered.

Luke's eyes flicked to her. "Yeah," he said, voice rough. "Me too."

Olivia glanced at his profile. The set of his jaw. The tired lines around his eyes. The way he looked like he'd been holding up this town with duct tape and black coffee for years. He had been angry when they went in. He was still angry now, but it had sharpened into something more dangerous. Focus.

Olivia swallowed. "Hazel's scared."

Luke's grip tightened briefly on the wheel. "Hazel has lived scared for thirty years," he said. "That does things to people."

Olivia nodded. It had done things to Izzy, too. It had made her hide evidence like a squirrel hoarding acorns in winter, except the acorns were proof of murder, financial crimes, and a forged will. No pressure.

When March House finally came into view, Olivia felt a strange surge of relief that surprised her. The Victorian mansion stood on Main Street as it always did, proud and creaky and stubborn. Turrets against the gray sky. Wraparound porch on the right, balustrades flaking like old lace. Solarium on the left, glass catching the weak daylight, reflecting Mistwood Lake beyond. Home, she thought. Which was absurd, considering the house had recently tried to scare her to death with both ghosts and intruders.

Luke pulled into the drive and killed the engine. For a second, neither of them moved.

Olivia forced herself to speak first. "Okay," she said. "We do not spiral."

Luke let out a quick breath. "Too late."

"That's fair," Olivia admitted. "But we can do it in a productive way."

Luke looked at her. "How do you spiral productively?"

Olivia pushed the door open. "With tea," she said. "And evidence boards."

Luke grunted and followed her out.

They stepped onto the porch, and Olivia felt it immediately. The shift in the air. The familiar charged thickness that meant March House was awake and aware and full of personalities that did not pay rent. Inside, the ghosts gathered instantly.

JJ appeared first, hovering near the dining room doorway, cornet in hand. He played a soft, worried riff that sounded like a question: Are you okay? Did you die? Please do not die.

Monique materialized in a swirl of chiffon and attitude, her flapper dress shimmering as she glanced between Olivia and Luke with theatrical concern.

Walt faded into view near the radiator, arms folded, frowning so hard his ghostly brows nearly joined. "Took you long enough," he muttered. "I've been judging the locks."

Daisy hovered near the staircase, hands clasped, face pale with worry.

Flossie hid behind Lark's chair, peeking out like a frightened kitten, comb clutched tight.

Simon stood at the front door with Snowball, posture straight, eyes alert, the Union medal on Snowball's collar glinting as the cat trotted in a tight, purposeful little circle.

Alistair stepped in behind Olivia with his usual measured dignity.

Bertie trotted beside him, tail wagging, then paused to sneeze at the air, as if Hazel Finch's sterile scent had followed them home and offended him personally.

Lark was already in the dining room, sitting at the table with two cups of tea waiting. Knowing Lark, she had been expecting them. She was the type to sense an emotional catastrophe the way some people sensed rain.

She looked up as Olivia and Luke entered. "You both look awful."

Olivia managed a tired half-smile.

Lark patted the chair beside her. "Sit, sweetheart. Drink."

Olivia obeyed. Her body sank into the chair, something it had been longing for all day.

Luke sat too, but he did it as if he was bracing for impact. Tension radiated off him in waves. His shoulders tight, his jaw clenched.

Lark studied him, eyes narrowing in that blunt, spiritually intuitive way that made Olivia suspect Lark had once stared down a bear, and the bear had apologized.

"And you," Lark said to Luke. "Try not to explode until after tea."

Luke huffed, and for a split second it almost sounded like a laugh. Almost. "I'll do my best," he said, then immediately got serious again, because Luke Thatcher did not trust joy to last longer than two seconds.

Olivia wrapped her hands around the teacup, letting the warmth seep into her fingers. The steam smelled faintly herbal, grounding. She took a sip and felt her shoulders loosen a fraction.

Around them, the ghosts lingered in a loose semicircle, watching like a committee of highly opinionated relatives.

Monique leaned toward JJ. "If he explodes, I will say I told you so."

JJ played a tiny, worried note.

Walt muttered, "If he explodes, I'm charging him for repairs."

Olivia exhaled slowly and pulled her evidence bag onto the table.

"All right," she said. "Full picture. No denial. No avoidance. No pretending Mistwood is just a quaint tourist town with artisanal soap."

Luke leaned forward.

Olivia began laying everything out again, but this time with Hazel's confession fresh in her mind, every piece heavier.

Luke leaned forward, eyes scanning each item. His voice came low and hard. "This is everything," he said. "Thirty years of secrets tied to one man."

Monique flicked her fingers at Bramble's photo pinned to the board on the wall. "He always had the aura of a villain."

Walt growled, the sound rough. "Coward."

Olivia nodded, throat tight. "Bramble stole money directly from March House's business accounts."

Luke's expression darkened. "Hazel said Trina found altered statements. Withdrawals. Loan documents rewritten." He tapped the ledger with one finger, careful, controlled. "All tied back to Bramble."

Olivia traced a line in Izzy's ledger, her finger sliding over the ink as if she could feel the past in it.

"Trina Bell found the missing funds," Olivia whispered. "She confronted him." Her voice cracked on the last part. "And she disappeared."

Daisy trembled softly.

JJ played a low, mournful chord that made Olivia's chest ache.

Luke's jaw flexed. "He silenced her."

Olivia swallowed hard and pulled the forged will to the center of the table. The paper looked harmless, like any legal document. Like it wasn't the type of thing people murdered over.

"Bramble forged the will to get control of March House." Her fingers curled around the edge of the paper, anger hot beneath her skin. "If he controls March House, he can bury every trace of his embezzlement."

Luke nodded grimly. "And avoid being exposed for Trina's disappearance."

Olivia's gaze lifted to Luke's face. "He's terrified the truth will come out."

Luke's eyes narrowed. "Which means he's dangerous."

The ghosts pressed closer, their forms flickering with protective intent.

Simon shifted subtly, standing straighter. He was ready to defend the house with nothing but principle and a bad attitude.

Snowball padded onto the table because cats believed themselves above evidence rules. Her blue eyes narrowed at the forged will, then she sniffed it and looked offended.

"Even the cat hates it," Olivia said.

Luke's mouth twitched. "Smart cat."

Olivia pulled her hand back before Snowball could knock anything off the table, because cats cannot be trusted with fragile, decades-long conspiracies.

Luke reached into his jacket and pulled out his notebook, flipping it open with practiced ease. "We need three things to bring him down," Luke said, pen poised. He wrote as he spoke. "One. The remaining parchment pieces."

Olivia nodded.

"Two. Proof of the embezzlement."

She nodded again.

"Three. A confession or corroboration."

Olivia's stomach tightened. "Hazel might give a statement."

Luke's expression remained grim. "She's scared."

"She will," Olivia insisted. "If we protect her."

Luke's pen paused. He looked at Olivia, the look sharp and assessing, but also something else. Respect. Trust. The kind that built slowly, brick by brick, not the kind that flared and burned out. "Yeah," Luke said finally. "If we protect her."

Alistair placed a hand on Olivia's shoulder. The pressure light but firm. A steadying presence. "You must tread carefully, Miss March," Alistair said. "Cornered men are unpredictable."

Olivia let out a shaky breath. "Tell me about it."

Walt muttered, "Cornered men do stupid things."

Monique sighed. "And dramatic things."

JJ played a small, suspenseful note, like a warning.

Lark, who had been quietly watching the evidence and the tension like she was reading an emotional weather report, pointed at one of Izzy's envelopes.

"Izzy mentioned the house choosing you," Lark said.

Olivia frowned. "What does that mean?"

Lark shrugged, but there was something knowing in her eyes. "Places remember things," she said. "Izzy always said the house held her secrets safely. If she wanted something hidden, she'd put it somewhere this house wouldn't give up easily."

Olivia sat up straighter, a spark of energy cutting through her exhaustion. "You think the house has another hiding place," Olivia said slowly.

Lark smiled as if she had been waiting for Olivia to catch up. "I think you haven't searched everywhere."

Alistair inclined his head. "It would be wise to follow the intuition of those attuned to the home."

JJ played a little suspenseful flourish, like a soundtrack cue: *ding ding ding, clue.*

Olivia pushed back from the table, standing so fast her chair scraped the floor. She stared at the evidence spread, at the notes, keys, scraps, documents, and the empty space where the safe contents should have been.

"Izzy left clues everywhere," Olivia said, the words coming quicker now. "Notes. Keys. Documents. But she would leave the most important thing somewhere only I would find."

Luke stood as well, moving with her, eyes narrowed. "Where?"

Olivia's gaze lifted to the ceiling, past the second floor, past the third. Her throat tightened with the memory. "Izzy's private attic," Olivia said. A beat. "Where she used to hide Christmas presents from me."

Lark made a sound of realization, half gasp, half delighted horror. "Oh! Oh, honey … yes."

Olivia's eyes flicked to Lark. "She never let anyone up there."

Lark nodded. "Never. Not even me. And I have been in every room of this house with a mop and a mild sense of trespassing."

Olivia's stomach flipped. "Then that's where the real will is."

Every ghost flickered with anticipation.

Simon's posture stiffened further. He was ready for battle.

Flossie drifted closer, eyes wide.

Daisy's hands clasped tighter.

Monique leaned forward as if she had front-row seats to the finale.

Walt muttered, "About time."

JJ played a determined riff.

Alistair's voice was formal and urgent. "Then we must go. At once."

Olivia turned toward the staircase, heart pounding, and started toward it.

Luke followed immediately, footsteps heavy behind her.

Olivia paused at the bottom step and looked back over her shoulder.

"You're coming with me?" she asked, because part of her still could not quite believe Luke Thatcher was choosing this madness willingly.

Luke met her gaze, expression steady. "I'm not letting you go up to a dark attic full of secrets alone," he said.

Bertie barked in agreement, tail wagging like he'd been waiting his whole afterlife for an attic adventure.

JJ played another determined riff.

Snowball trotted toward the stairs, tail high. She owned them. Simon followed close behind, vigilant.

Olivia took a breath, feeling the weight of the watch in her pocket, the warmth of tea in her stomach, ghosts at her back, and Luke beside her like a solid wall.

The fear was still there. The danger was real. Theodore Bramble was cornered, and cornered men did not play fair. But she was not alone.

Olivia's voice came quiet, steady. "Then let's end this." She stepped onto the staircase. And March House, old and watchful, seemed to hold its breath as they climbed.

CHAPTER TWENTY-FIVE

The Attic Revelation

The third floor of March House had always felt different. Not haunted differently. The entire house was haunted differently depending on the weather, the hour, and whether Walt was in a bad mood about the plumbing. But the third floor carried a weight the rest of the house did not. It was quieter. Heavier. The walls held their breath up here. Izzy's absence echoed louder in this hallway.

Olivia stood at the top of the narrow staircase, staring at the attic door at the end of the corridor. It was smaller than she remembered, the sort of door designed for storage and secrets and not much else. The paint on it had yellowed with age, and the knob was old iron, dull and cold. It had never warmed to the touch of a human hand.

Luke stood beside her with a flashlight, the beam cutting a pale wedge through the dimness. The light caught dust motes floating in the air, drifting lazily. The dust had slowed down out of respect for the silence.

Olivia could hear her own breathing. She could also hear Luke's steady and controlled, trying to hold the entire situation in place with sheer willpower.

Behind her, Sir Alistair stood at her back, posture noble and still. He looked as if he belonged in a portrait, not in an Idaho bed-and-breakfast hallway, but that was basically the story of Olivia's life now.

Bertie flickered in and out beside Alistair, tail wagging

nervously. For a dog who had been dead since 1802, he conveyed anxiety in a very living, very dramatic way.

Olivia swallowed and whispered, because speaking loudly up here felt like it might crack the ceiling. "Izzy never let anyone up here."

Luke's gaze stayed on the door. His voice was low. "Then she meant for you to find this."

The words landed in Olivia's chest, heavy and strange and comforting, all at once. She slid her hand into her pocket and pulled out the old iron key. It was cold enough to make her fingertips ache. The metal looked like it had been forged in a time when keys were designed to be dramatic and slightly threatening. She fitted it into the lock. Her pulse hammered. It clicked.

The sound was soft, but in the silence of the third floor, it felt loud, like the house had just cleared its throat.

Olivia turned the key slowly.The door swung open with a long, deep groan. Walt, somewhere below, would probably have called it a structural complaint. Olivia thought the past was waking up.

Luke raised the flashlight, angling it into the attic. Dust floated through the beam, swirling like tiny ghosts. The air that drifted out was cooler than the hallway, stale and faintly scented with old fabric, paper, and time.

Olivia stepped forward.

The attic was part storage room, part time capsule.

Luke's flashlight swept across stacks of old hatboxes, their lids slightly warped with age, each one labeled in Izzy's handwriting. Dress racks stood along one wall, draped with decades of fashion protected by plastic covers that rustled softly when the air moved. Christmas decor sat in carefully labeled bins, each box stacked neatly as if Izzy had been organizing holiday magic into manageable portions.

A rocking chair sat near the center, covered in a crocheted blanket. It looked like it had been waiting for someone to sit down and pick up a story where it left off. Beside it was a horsehair trunk, battered but sturdy, the type of luggage that had traveled when travel meant trunks and steam and goodbyes. There were boxes of photos stacked near the far wall. Next to them, a pile of newspaper bundles tied with twine sat like a tower of old secrets. It should have felt cluttered. It didn't. It felt curated. Like Izzy had arranged the attic with the same care she used to arrange her antiques downstairs. Not chaotic storage. Deliberate preservation.

Luke's flashlight swept farther, toward the back corner.

And Olivia's breath stuttered.

There, half-hidden behind a dress rack, sat a trunk covered in a quilt. The quilt was faded but lovingly folded, its stitching careful, its colors softened with age. On the trunk was a single label. Written in Izzy's unmistakable script. For Olivia.

Olivia went still. Her throat tightened so fast she could barely swallow.

Alistair's voice murmured softly behind her. "Your aunt loved you very much."

Olivia managed a brittle little sound that might have been a laugh if it hadn't been so close to a sob. "She was also terrifyingly organized," Olivia whispered. "This is like emotional blackmail, but with better handwriting."

Luke glanced at her, expression softening just slightly. "You ready?"

No, Olivia thought. Absolutely not. "Yes," she said anyway, because being ready had never been a requirement in Mistwood. She crossed the attic and kneeled beside the trunk. The quilt shifted as she moved it aside. The latch was old brass, tarnished but intact. Her fingers trembled as she lifted it. The latch opened with a quiet snap. She took one breath. Then lifted the lid.

Inside the trunk was not random storage. Stacked carefully inside were envelopes tied with ribbon. A legal folder, thick and official. A cloth-bound journal. A thick, sealed manila file, heavier than it looked. A small tin box. A velvet pouch. And resting on top, like the first card in a deck, was a letter addressed to her.

Livvy,

If you're reading this, trust your instincts.

Olivia pressed her fingers to her mouth. Her vision blurred instantly. Her eyes had decided they were done pretending to be tough.

Luke lowered himself beside her, careful and gentle, the way you approach something fragile and important. "Go ahead," he whispered. "We're here."

The simple steadiness of that sentence made Olivia's chest ache. She nodded once, then reached past the letter and picked up the legal folder first, because if she opened the letter right now, she might collapse into a puddle on Izzy's attic floor and become one of the house's permanent features. She opened the folder. Inside was a document, neatly organized and crisp despite its age. The Last Will and Testament of Isadora March. Handwritten. Signed in Izzy's post-surgery signature, the one that always looked slightly shaky but stubborn. Properly witnessed. Properly dated. Three years before her death.

Olivia's breath caught. She scanned the lines, her heart pounding as if the words might change if she didn't read fast enough. And then she hit the last line. *March House and all assets are left to my niece, Olivia March, to protect, preserve, and restore as she sees fit.*

The sentence hit Olivia like a blow to the chest. Her vision blurred completely. Her hands tightened around the folder. For a second, she couldn't breathe. Izzy meant this. Izzy chose this.

Izzy chose her.

Luke's hand came down gently on her shoulder, grounding her without taking over. The pressure was light, steady, a reminder that she was not alone in an attic full of ghosts and history.

"Well," Luke said softly, "that settles that."

Olivia let out a shaky breath that sounded more like a broken laugh.

Alistair smiled, faint but proud.

Even Bertie wagged his tail harder. He personally approved of legal clarity.

Olivia wiped at her eyes with the back of her hand, annoyed with herself for crying, then immediately annoyed with herself for being annoyed. Grief did not care about her pride. She set the will carefully back into the folder, then placed it in her lap as if it were the most precious thing she had ever held. Then she reached for the thick, sealed manila file. Her fingers hesitated.

Luke's flashlight beam held steady on the trunk, illuminating her hands. "Do it," Luke whispered.

Olivia swallowed and opened the file. Inside was everything they feared and everything they needed. The original altered loan documents, pages marked and annotated, signatures, and numbers that did not belong together. Copies of early withdrawal slips signed under Bramble's authorization, the ink dark and damning. Bank statements showing missing funds tied to March House, numbers aligned into a pattern so clear it made Olivia's skin prickle.

Izzy's notes were clipped to the pages, comparisons and observations written in her sharp, quick handwriting. She had circled discrepancies, underlined names, and drawn arrows between accounts; a general mapping a battlefield. There was a photocopy of Trina Bell's handwritten journal entry from the night she disappeared.

Olivia's breath hitched. She stared at it for a moment, feeling the weight of that handwriting. The reality of a teenage girl writing what she saw, not knowing those words might be all she left behind. Then Olivia found a slip of paper tucked between two documents.

Hazel, he threatened her. Please talk to me.

Izzy.

Olivia choked, the sound sharp and ugly. "She trusted Hazel," Olivia whispered, voice breaking. "Hazel was terrified."

Luke's expression was grim, his eyes dark with anger and sorrow. He nodded slowly. "And Izzy kept digging."

Olivia's hands shook as she slid the file back into the trunk. She couldn't bear to hold it for too long. It felt like holding a live wire.

The attic seemed colder. Even the dust motes in the flashlight beam looked heavier.

She reached for the small tin box next. Its lid snug, it had kept whatever was inside safe from time. She opened it and found a broken friendship bracelet. The beads cracked and faded. A tiny gold earring shaped like a star. A Polaroid photo. And a typed report addressed to:

Sheriff Ray Morton.

Luke inhaled sharply, the sound cutting through the silence.

"That's the original missing-person report," Luke said, voice tight. "The one Hazel couldn't find."

Olivia stared at the typed pages, the official header, the stark language that tried to reduce a missing girl to paperwork. Her fingers brushed the Polaroid. She turned it over. The back read:

Trina, taken on the day she found the bank papers.

Olivia's throat tightened. She flipped the photo around. Trina Bell smiled nervously beside March House's garden gate, her expression caught between pride and worry. The gate behind her looked familiar. The same gate Olivia had walked past a hundred times since arriving. The same gate that now felt like the boundary between the past and the present. Izzy had assembled everything Trina saw. Everything she tried to say. Everything her killer tried to erase.

Olivia's hands trembled so hard she had to set the photo down before she crushed it.

Monique's whisper drifted through the attic, voice soft. "Poor darling."

JJ played a low, aching note that sounded like mourning.

Daisy hovered closer, her face pale, her eyes shimmering with tears she couldn't quite shed.

Olivia swallowed and reached for the cloth-bound journal. It was heavy. Not in weight, but in meaning. She opened it carefully. Izzy's handwriting filled the pages, looping and familiar. It was like hearing her voice again.

Olivia flipped toward the end, her pulse pounding. The last dated entry stopped her cold.

If anything happens to me, it will be Bramble. Livvy must find this. She must finish it. The house will guide her. The dead will protect her.

Olivia's breath caught, sharp and painful. Izzy left a roadmap. Not for Hazel. Not for the town. For her.

Luke's hand came over hers, covering it gently, anchoring her trembling fingers against the page. "She trusted you with the truth," Luke whispered. "And she knew you'd be brave enough to face it."

Olivia blinked hard, wiping at her eyes again. “I’m not brave,” she whispered.

Luke’s gaze held hers. “Yeah, you are.”

Olivia looked down at Izzy’s handwriting, at the certainty in it. The love. The warning. The faith. She swallowed. “I’m not afraid anymore.”

The words surprised her with their steadiness. She expected her voice to shake. It didn’t.

Fear was still there. It existed. But it no longer owned her.

Luke nodded once, slow and approving. Then he began sorting through the documents again, more carefully this time, as if he expected the trunk to contain yet another hidden layer.

His fingers paused. He pulled out a folded sheet of fresh paper from the bottom of the trunk.

His brow furrowed. “This isn’t Izzy’s paper. Or her handwriting.”

Olivia’s pulse stuttered. She reached for it and unfolded it. A recent bank withdrawal slip.

Clean. Crisp. Modern. And the signature at the bottom made Olivia’s stomach drop. Carla Dawes.

Luke stared, his expression going flat with shock. “That’s my aunt,” he said.

Olivia’s breath came shallow. “She accessed the old accounts? Why would she …?”

Luke finished grimly, his voice hardening. “Because Clay and Carla owe Bramble a lot of money. They might be helping him. Or hiding something.”

Olivia felt March House tilt around her, the attic suddenly too small, the air too thin.

“This isn’t just Bramble,” Olivia whispered. “This is a whole rotten circle.”

Alistair’s eyes sharpened, fury tightening his dignified features. “The enemy stands revealed,” he said softly. “And they fear you now, Miss March.”

Olivia stared at the withdrawal slip, at the signature, at the confirmation that Mistwood’s rot went deeper than one man.

Luke’s jaw flexed. “We don’t have much time.”

Olivia nodded, numb and fierce at once. She gathered everything with shaking hands.

The real will. Trina's evidence. Izzy's journal. The missing-person report. The bank documents.

Carla's recent withdrawal slip. She stacked them carefully because chaos would not be allowed to steal this from her now.

Luke stood, adjusting his grip on the flashlight, eyes scanning the attic as if he expected Bramble to leap out of a hatbox.

Olivia rose to her feet, arms full, heart pounding. She looked at Luke. "We take all of this," Olivia said, voice steady. "We confront Bramble. We finish this."

Luke nodded, his expression unwavering. "I'm with you," he said. "All the way."

The words landed in Olivia's chest like a vow. Not romantic. Not sweeping. Just solid, genuine commitment, the kind that mattered.

At the attic door, Olivia paused. Behind her, her ghosts gathered, flickering with determination.

JJ's eyes were serious.

Monique's expression was sharp.

Walt looked ready to haunt someone into the ground.

Daisy hovered close, trembling but brave.

Flossie clutched her comb.

Simon stood tall, Snowball at his feet, ready to follow.

Alistair's presence was strong and steady.

Bertie stood alert, tail wagging, a tiny four-footed soldier.

Olivia turned her face slightly, as if Izzy might be listening in the walls, in the dust, in the quiet breath of the house itself. "Izzy," Olivia whispered. "I found it."

The house creaked softly, almost in reply.

Olivia stepped out of the attic. And the path toward the last confrontation snapped into focus, sharp and unavoidable.

CHAPTER TWENTY-SIX

Closing In

By the time Olivia and Luke made it back down from the attic, March House had fully shifted into crisis mode. Not the fun kind of crisis mode where Lark forgot to take the bread out of the oven and the entire house smelled like charcoal. This was the other kind. The kind that made the air feel sharp. The kind that turned every creak of the floorboards into a warning and every shadow into a question.

Olivia carried Izzy's old leather satchel pressed tight against her ribs like a life vest. It smelled faintly of paper, lavender, and the particular stubbornness of an aunt who had never done anything the easy way. The satchel was heavier than it should have been, not because of the documents, but because of what they meant. Truth. Proof. A way out.

Luke walked beside her, shoulders squared, head up, eyes scanning as if expecting Theodore Bramble to be waiting behind the coat rack with a smile and a shovel.

The ghosts gathered around the house. A silent group of witnesses.

Olivia walked into the dining room and stopped. The table already looked like a paperwork tornado had hit it, but now it was worse. Now it was the war room. She set the satchel down carefully, then opened it and began laying the attic evidence. Carefully placing it where it fit in with the other clues.

The real will, inside its folder, was placed dead center like a crown. Izzy's cloth-bound journal sat beside it. Trina's Polaroid, face up, with that nervous smile staring into the present.

The missing-person report addressed to Sheriff Ray Morton. Its official header cold and impersonal. The embezzlement documents stacked, annotated, condemning. Bank withdrawal slips, the paper edges crisp, the numbers ugly. Carla Dawes' recent transaction sheet, the signature was a slap. In the *destroy the file* note, Izzy's handwriting sharp and urgent. The parchment scraps, jagged pieces of truth. When she finished, the table looked less like a place for breakfast and more like a battlefield of paper.

Lark stood at one end, arms crossed, sage still tucked behind her ear like a pencil. She stared at the spread, eyes narrowed, then let out a long breath. "This," Lark said, "is enough to bury Bramble and the Dawes under a mountain of karma."

JJ played a triumphant few notes.

Monique fanned herself dramatically. "Finally."

Walt muttered from near the radiator, voice rough. "At last."

Daisy hovered anxiously, glancing toward the windows as if she expected shadows to move.

Flossie wrung her hands.

Simon remained at the door with Snowball, who sat like a sentry cat, tail twitching, her furry face fixed in a look of permanent disapproval.

Luke leaned over the table, brow creased, eyes scanning every document with a focus that made Olivia's skin prickle. He looked like a man doing math in his head and finding it deeply offensive. "This is everything," Luke said. "But we need to be strategic."

Olivia let out a breath she did not realize she was holding. "Strategic is good. Strategic means we don't die."

Luke's eyes flicked to her. "That's the goal."

Olivia pointed at the papers as if presenting evidence in court, except their audience was a housekeeper, eight ghosts, and a cat who had already decided everyone involved was an idiot.

"Okay," Olivia said. "Who do we take this to? Clay is compromised."

Luke nodded firmly. No hesitation. "He can't see any of this. We go above him."

He flipped open his notebook, pen already in hand because Luke Thatcher was the type of man who carried a notebook like it was an extra limb. "Idaho State Police," Luke said. "They take over the case since Clay is implicated."

Olivia's adrenaline rose, sharp and bright. She nodded quickly. "We can go tomorrow morning."

Luke's pen paused. He looked up. "We are going tonight."

Olivia blinked at him. "Tonight? Why?"

Luke snapped his notebook shut with a sharp sound that made JJ jump, and Snowball to flick her tail in annoyance.

"Because Bramble knows you probably found the will. And he's not going to wait until dawn."

A cold prickle passed through the room, so tangible that Olivia felt it crawl down her spine.

The ghosts flickered uneasily.

Monique's eyes widened.

Daisy clutched her journal tighter.

Flossie drifted closer to Lark's chair as if she wanted to hide behind it again.

Alistair's expression sharpened, icy and controlled.

Olivia forced herself to swallow. "You think he knows already?"

Luke's gaze dropped to the satchel, then to the will, then to the window. "I think the minute you walked up those attic stairs," Luke said, voice low, "something in this town shifted. Bramble has been controlling this narrative for decades. He does not let go easily."

Olivia stared at the papers, at Trina's photo, at Izzy's handwriting. "He's not going to let go at all," she whispered.

Luke's jaw flexed. "Exactly."

Preparing the evidence felt like packing up explosives. Olivia gathered everything back into Izzy's leather satchel with careful hands. When she zipped the satchel, Lark stepped forward with something small in her hand. A charm tied with twine and a tiny bundle of herbs. She looped it onto the zipper pull with brisk efficiency.

"For warding off creeps," Lark said.

Olivia stared at it. "Is this charm legally binding?"

Lark gave her a look. "Sweetheart, at this point, I'll staple rosemary to your forehead if it keeps you alive."

JJ played a snarky little flourish that translated clearly to: *you will need it.*

Alistair leaned in slightly, inspecting the satchel with solemn approval, like he was the ghost expert of document transport. "Your aunt would be proud, Miss March," Alistair said.

Olivia breathed in, steadying herself. The scent of tea and herbs and old paper filled her lungs. "I hope so," Olivia whispered.

Luke adjusted his stance, checking his weapon at his hip, then grabbing his keys from the counter. The movement was calm and practiced, but Olivia saw the tension beneath it, the readiness. "We drive separately," Luke said. "Less chance of being intercepted."

Olivia's stomach clenched. "Intercepted. Love that word. Hate what it implies."

Luke's gaze met hers. "You're not wrong."

Olivia tightened her grip on the satchel strap, heart beating hard enough to shake her ribs.

Then Snowball darted toward the front window. Not a casual cat trot. A full-body, fur-puffed sprint, claws skittering on the hardwood.

Olivia's blood went cold.

Simon materialized instantly behind her, posture rigid, soldier-still, eyes locked on the street.

Walt's voice rumbled from near the radiator. "Someone's out there."

JJ let out a low warning note, like a siren muted by concern.

Alistair stepped forward, expression turning sharp and icy. "Miss March," he said quietly, "we have unwanted company."

Luke moved to the window, careful, peering out between the curtains. His shoulders tightened. "A dark sedan," Luke said. "Just down the block."

Olivia moved closer, but Luke held up a hand, silently stopping her.

"Engine running. No lights. A silhouette inside." Luke's voice lowered to a growl. "That's not a neighbor."

Olivia's pulse spiked so fast she felt dizzy. "He's watching the house," she whispered.

Luke nodded grimly. "He knows we're close."

Olivia clutched the satchel tighter, the leather creaking under her grip. "Closer than Izzy ever got." The words came out before she could stop them, and the grief from them was sharp. Izzy had built all of this, hidden it, protected it, and still died before she could see it finished.

Luke's jaw clenched, his gaze still fixed on the sedan. "Yeah," he mumbled. "And he's scared."

Lark stepped closer, moving behind Olivia in that protective way that made Olivia feel like she had an emotional bodyguard. "You're not going out there alone," Lark said firmly.

Luke turned from the window to Olivia, his eyes intense. "Listen to me. Change of plans. Once we leave this house, we don't separate. Not for a second."

Olivia nodded, throat tight. "I trust you."

Luke's expression softened for the briefest moment. The words had hit something human inside him. Then it hardened again, because danger did not allow softness to linger.

"Good. Then let's move."

The ghosts apparently agreed that moving was an excellent idea, but they also had opinions on how.

They assembled like a spectral task force, lining up as if March House had become their command center.

Simon took perimeter guard duty near the front door, posture straight, eyes sharp, like he was about to defend the house from a siege with nothing but principle and anger.

Walt moved through the rooms, checking locks with a grumbling intensity. "If anybody dies because of a loose latch, I'm haunting everyone involved," he muttered.

Daisy drifted toward the solarium, hovering near the glass panes, watching the street through the warped reflection like a nervous scout.

Monique vanished upstairs, reappearing near the landing window, her flapper silhouette poised as she watched the street with the dramatic intensity of a woman who had lived for scandal and now had one worth dying for.

Flossie stationed herself near the staircase, comb clutched tight, eyes wide, determined to monitor who went up and down.

JJ hovered near the dining room, cornet lifted slightly. He was ready to sound alarms via musical threats.

Alistair remained closest to Olivia, the lead ghost guardian, calm and dignified, his presence steadying her racing heart. He bowed slightly. "We shall defend the home in your absence."

Olivia pressed her hand to her chest, feeling the pounding there. "Thank you," she whispered.

Bertie gave two sharp ghost-barks, as if volunteering to bite ankles.

"You are a dog." Olivia nodded to him. "Your entire job is biting ankles."

Bertie wagged his tail, proud.

Luke watched Olivia's face, clearly confused by half the conversation, and Olivia tried very hard to look like she was simply thinking deep, normal thoughts. Deep, normal thoughts about not dying.

Luke pocketed his keys, turning back to Olivia. "There's one thing we need before we go," he said.

Olivia blinked. "What?"

Luke's eyes darkened. "To make sure Clay doesn't stop us before we reach someone."

Olivia stared at him. "You think Clay would help Bramble?"

Luke did not answer immediately. His gaze flicked back to the sedan. Then to the evidence satchel. Then to Olivia.

"I think Clay likes his job more than justice," Luke hissed. "And if Bramble leans on him …" He didn't finish. He didn't have to.

Olivia felt sick. "So we can't trust the sheriff. The sheriff's wife is on bank slips. And there is a suspicious sedan outside my house, like we're in a budget thriller."

Lark nodded solemnly. "Welcome to Mistwood, sweetheart. Try the scones."

Olivia let out a strained laugh that sounded more like a cough. "This town really commits to the theme."

Luke's expression did not soften. "We move fast," he said. "We keep the evidence on you. We get the State Police involved."

Olivia nodded, fingers tightening on the satchel strap. Then she reached for her phone, because if she was going to be hunted, she was at least going to be hunted with good communication.

"I'll text Hazel," Olivia said. "Tell her to stay inside and lock her doors."

Luke nodded. "Good. And copy me on the message."

Olivia unlocked her phone.

Before she could type, it buzzed. A new message. Unknown number.

Olivia froze. The screen glowed in her palm, bright and ominous.

Luke stepped closer, his voice low. "What is it?"

Olivia stared at the text, her heart pounding so hard she could hear it in her ears. Her throat went dry. She read it aloud, voice barely above a whisper. "Stop. Turn over the will. You have one chance." The words sat on the screen like a threat pressed into her skin.

Before Olivia could even breathe, a second message arrived instantly. "Or you're next."

Olivia's blood turned to ice.

The ghosts flickered violently around her, their forms pulsing with agitation.

JJ's cornet let out a sharp, discordant note.

Daisy gasped.

Flossie's eyes went wide.

Monique swore in French.

Walt muttered something unprintable about cowards.

Lark gasped, one hand flying to her mouth.

Luke's expression went flat. Deadly. Unshakeable. "They know you found it," Luke said.

Olivia's voice shook. "And they're not going to let me walk out of this house tonight."

Luke's jaw tightened. His eyes cut toward the front window, toward that dark sedan, toward the silhouette inside.

"Then we don't walk out," Luke said.

Olivia stared at him, stunned.

Luke stepped closer and took her hand.

His grip was steady. Strong. Warm.

For a split second, Olivia felt the jolt, the way her skin reacted to his touch like her body had been waiting for reassurance in exactly that form. Slow burn or not, her nerves had opinions.

Luke's voice stayed low. "We run."

Olivia swallowed hard, fingers tightening around his.

Outside, the sedan's engine continued to idle.

Inside, March House held its breath.

And Olivia realized, with horrible clarity, that the climax was not waiting politely for morning.

CHAPTER TWENTY-SEVEN

The Trap Springs

The air inside March House didn't just feel tense. It felt electrified, like the house had plugged itself into a storm cloud and was waiting for someone to touch the wrong doorknob.

Olivia stood in the dining room with Izzy's satchel clutched to her chest, and she could swear the walls were listening harder than usual. The floorboards creaked under her feet as if they were testing their own nerves. Even the stained glass seemed darker, the colors muted by the night pressing against the windows.

Every ghost in the house was on edge.

Simon stalked between windows like a haunted guard dog. He moved with military precision, pausing at each pane as if he could see through the night itself.

Snowball trotted after him, tail puffed, her face fixed in judgment so severe it could have been used as a weapon.

Alistair stood tall and unwavering behind Olivia, posture noble and still. He looked carved from stone, calm in a way that made Olivia feel both safer and more nervous, because when Alistair went full ghost-general, things were usually about to get unpleasant.

Bertie, tethered to Alistair like a tiny afterlife satellite, growled softly with each exhale. It was a ridiculous sound coming from a whippet, even a dead one, but Bertie made it work through sheer conviction.

Lark swept into the room holding two tiny vials like she was about to perform a witchy shot service. She pressed them into Olivia's hand. "Protection. Emotional and … otherwise."

Olivia stared at the vials. One looked like rosemary. One looked like salt. Both looked like Lark's idea of a security system.

"I feel like this is either going to save my life or season my corpse," Olivia muttered.

Lark gave her a look. "Both can be true."

Olivia tucked the vials into Izzy's satchel between the evidence folders, because at this point, she was not turning down any help, including herbal. She grabbed her coat and put it on. Alistair's watch was still in her pocket.

Luke checked the broken back door one last time, jaw clenched, gun holstered but ready. His whole body radiated controlled violence. He was holding himself in place with sheer willpower. "We go out the front," Luke said. "Lights off. Stay behind me. Once we hit Highway 55, we don't stop."

Olivia nodded, her throat tight. "Let's go."

Alistair's voice came quietly behind Olivia. "Courage, Miss March."

Olivia tightened her grip on the satchel strap. "I'm doing my best," she whispered, not sure if she was speaking to him, herself, or the house.

Luke moved first, crossing the dining room and stepping into the front hall. Olivia followed, staying just behind his shoulder the way he told her to.

The ghosts drifted with them, filling the edges of the space, an invisible escort.

They reached the front door.

Luke's hand paused on the knob. He took one breath. Then he opened it.

The night slapped Olivia in the face with cold so sharp it stung. The air smelled of pine and lake water and that metallic bite that came right before snow. Streetlights cast long shadows across the gravel and the porch railing, distorting everything. She stepped onto the porch and immediately felt exposed, like she'd walked onto a stage with the spotlight aimed directly at her fear.

The dark sedan they'd seen earlier had moved. It was no longer just down the block. It was parked directly across from March

House. Engine running. No lights. A heavy presence on the street, a predator lying low.

Luke noticed instantly. His shoulders tightened. His gaze locked on the sedan. "Driver's alone," Luke said, voice low. "But someone else might be nearby."

Olivia clutched the satchel tighter. The leather creaked under her grip. At her side, Alistair appeared, expression carved from stone, his ghostly form crisp in Olivia's vision but invisible to everyone else. His eyes were sharp. His jaw set. "Courage, Miss March."

Olivia swallowed hard. "Oh, I'm full of courage," she whispered. "It's spilling out of my ears."

Luke shot her a glance. "What?"

"Nothing," Olivia said quickly. "Just … cold."

Luke's eyes flicked back to the sedan. "Stay behind me." They moved off the porch and down the steps, keeping to the shadows.

Olivia's boots hit the gravel. The sound felt too loud. Every crunch made her flinch. Her whole body vibrated with adrenaline.

Luke led her toward his truck parked near the curb. He reached the truck first and opened the passenger door for her.

Olivia stepped toward it. Just as her boot hit the curb, she heard it. Another car rolled up behind them. Lights off. Silent. Her stomach dropped.

Luke turned sharply, his hand lifting instinctively toward his weapon. "Get in the truck," he snapped. "Now."

Olivia lunged for the open door.

Luke's hand went to his weapon.

"Olivia, move!" he shouted.

A figure stepped out of the shadows behind the dark sedan. Another person emerged from the second car. And a third stepped out from the hedge on the side of March House. They'd been waiting there the whole time, blending into the yard's darkness.

They were surrounded.

Olivia's breath caught in her chest, the air freezing in her lungs.

"No," she whispered. "No. No. No—"

One figure lifted a flashlight. The beam snapped on, bright and harsh, cutting through the dark. It hit Luke first, then slid to Olivia, blinding her.

Olivia squinted, trying to see past the glare. And then she saw the face behind the light.

Sheriff Clay Dawes.

Olivia's stomach went hollow.

Clay looked exhausted, anxious, and furious all at once. His uniform was neat as always, because Clay did not do messy appearances, but his eyes were bloodshot, and his smile was gone.

"Luke." Clay's voice sounded strained. Then his gaze shifted to Olivia. "Olivia." His voice tightened, as if he were trying to keep control of a situation that was slipping through his fingers. "We need to talk."

Luke's stance shifted, his whole body angling between Clay and Olivia like a shield. Outraged betrayal and grim resolve mingled on his face, and Olivia's chest tightened at the look.

"Clay," Luke said, voice low and dangerous. "What did you do?"

Clay lifted a shaky hand, palm out, trying to calm a wild animal. "You have something that belongs to Theodore Bramble. I need you to hand it over."

Olivia felt the bottom drop out of her stomach. The text messages. The threats. The sudden urgency. It all snapped into place.

"You forged the text messages," Olivia said, voice shaking. She did not sound brave. She sounded like someone staring into the face of betrayal and trying not to vomit.

Clay winced. "Just give me the satchel," he said. "After that, nobody has to get hurt."

Luke stepped fully in front of Olivia, blocking her from Clay's line of sight. His voice was a cold growl. "I'm not letting you take her. Or the evidence."

Clay's deputies inched closer, shifting. They were preparing to grab Olivia, not arrest her. This was a takedown.

Olivia's heart hammered so hard she could feel it in her throat. Behind her, March House loomed, silent and watching. Inside, something moved.

JJ sensed it first. The danger outside, the tightening tension around Olivia, the way the night had shifted into a trap. He blew a sharp, brassy cornet blast that rattled the windows.

Olivia heard it as if it was inside her bones. The sound did not reach Luke or Clay as music, but the vibration made the house itself tremble.

Olivia flinched, her focus snapping sharply.

The ghosts were warning her. She put the satchel's strap over her head and onto her shoulder.

On the porch behind her, ghost-light flickered at the edge of her vision.

Monique, Daisy, and Walt gathered, visible only to Olivia. Not to anyone else.

Clay's deputies felt nothing but a strange, sudden chill at their backs.

One deputy shivered, rubbing his arms. "Cold outta nowhere …" he muttered.

Walt moved through him. The man jolted as if he'd walked through an icy spiderweb, eyes going wide.

Another deputy stepped forward, then hesitated, frowning at the sudden drop in temperature over the walkway. "Anyone else feel that?" Deputy #2 asked, voice uneasy.

Daisy hovered near Olivia, wringing her hands. Her anxiety pulsed through the air like faint static, raising goosebumps on Olivia's arms.

Monique flickered close to Olivia's shoulder, her face sharp with urgency, visible only to Olivia. "Run, darling. RUN!"

Simon appeared beside Olivia, the ghost of a young Civil War soldier with a torn coat and hollow, determined eyes. No fur. No cat posture. Just solemn protection. He passed through a deputy. The man gasped, clutching his ribs as a freezing punch of cold tore through him.

"What the …something just … did you feel that?!" Deputy #3 yelped.

But there was nothing to see. Only the night and the sudden fear.

Alistair stepped in front of Olivia, towering and severe. His ghostly form blocked her view of Clay for a moment, a protective psychological barrier only she perceived.

Bertie darted around Olivia's legs, stirring dust and dead leaves into swirling patterns that made the deputies glance around nervously.

They could not see him. They felt only the odd breeze.

Alistair's voice came quietly but commanding, meant only for Olivia. "Miss March," he said. "Now. RUN."

Olivia's grip tightened on the satchel strap.

Luke could not see the ghosts, but he felt the shift in Olivia, the sudden sharpness, the urgency that made her posture change.

"Olivia," Luke shouted. "Go! GO!"

Olivia hesitated for half a heartbeat, fear locking her knees.

Clay stepped forward, voice cracking. "Luke ... please. Don't make me do this."

Luke's voice was a cold growl. "You already did." The look on Luke's face broke something in Olivia's chest. Betrayal. Rage. Hurt. The grief of realizing the one person who should have protected the town had chosen the wrong side. Olivia's heart felt like it might tear in half.

The ghosts gathered behind her like a shimmering battalion.

"Run," Alistair commanded.

"Run," Walt growled.

"Run, darling!" Monique hissed.

JJ blasted another sharp warning trumpet note.

Daisy whispered, frantic. "Hurry!"

Simon hissed, eyes burning.

Flossie cried, hovering near the porch like she wanted to clutch Olivia and never let go.

Luke locked eyes with Olivia.

And Olivia whispered, mostly to herself, "Okay. Okay. I can do this."

She tightened her grip on the satchel. A ghost wind swirled around her ankles, cold and urgent. And she bolted.

Chaos erupted instantly.

Clay yelled, voice panicked. "Stop her!"

Luke shouted with pure fury. "Don't touch her!"

A deputy lunged at Olivia.

Bertie leaped with a furious bark. The chill went through the deputy, causing him to stumble.

Another deputy grabbed Olivia's arm.

The sudden frigid blast of Walt running through his extended arm caused him to lose his grip.

The sedan revved. Doors flew open.

Olivia sprinted down the street toward the side path that led to the beach, heart in her throat, lungs burning. The satchel slapped against her hip with each step, heavy and precious.

Luke barreled after her, shouting, “Olivia, keep going! Don’t stop!”

Olivia didn’t. She couldn’t.

Behind her, she heard Clay yelling, voice breaking. “If she gets away with that evidence, Bramble’s going to bury us all!”

Luke roared back in rage. “You did that yourselves!”

Olivia’s legs pumped. Her mind screamed. Her breath came sharp and ragged. The path was ahead, dark and narrow between two thick hedges, like a tunnel cut into the night.

She reached it and kept running. Behind her in the distance was the sound of several people arguing. The only voices she recognized were Luke’s and Clay’s. It wouldn’t be long before they would be after her again. The trap was snapping shut.

CHAPTER TWENTY-EIGHT

The Call That Changes Everything

Olivia had never been good at standing still. In Chicago, standing still meant you got elbowed out of the way, burned by a hot pan, or verbally filleted by a chef who believed screaming was a love language. In Mistwood, standing still meant something far worse. It meant you got caught.

Olivia ran along the beach until she came to the path behind the private residences and businesses that back up to the lake. The lake path was narrow and dark, packed dirt threading between reeds and private docks. The moon painted a pale stripe on Mistwood Lake to the right, turning the water into black glass with a silver scar. The air smelled of wet earth and cold water and fear.

Olivia was heading toward the marina. When she was a child, this path was one of her favorite walks. Now it could be her only way of escape.

Olivia ran as if the lake itself was trying to catch her. The narrow path whipped past in a blur of reeds and dock shadows, her breath burning in her throat, her lungs screaming, her legs already protesting and filing a grievance with management. The satchel slammed against her side with every stride, the strap biting into her shoulder, the evidence inside feeling heavier with every second.

Behind her, the pursuers were louder than the wind. Branches snapped. Men shouted her name, some with fury, some with panic.

Flashlights flickered through the trees, harsh beams slicing across the dark, searchlights hunting prey.

Bramble's crisp voice carried over the lake, deep and commanding. The world still belonged to him.

Clay sounded panicked and ragged behind him, a man who had lost control of his own choices and was now chasing the consequences on foot.

Olivia's heart hammered so hard she could feel it in her teeth. At her side, Alistair kept pace effortlessly, booted feet not touching the ground, his ghostly form crisp and steady even in motion. He looked like he'd been born to march into danger, which was mildly infuriating when Olivia was one bad step away from face-planting into reeds.

"They are closing in," Alistair said, voice calm and sharp. "We must act now."

Olivia's mind raced, frantic and hot. She couldn't outrun them. She couldn't hide. They would sweep the shoreline. They had flashlights and radios and the authority to turn every passerby into a reluctant accomplice.

She couldn't rely on the ghosts, not out here. Only Alistair and Bertie remained tethered to her beyond March House, and Bertie, for all his brave little dead-dog heart, could not take down three grown men.

She needed help from the living. Actual help. Official help. And then it hit her, a spark snapping into place. Her hand dove into her coat pocket. Her fingers closed around her phone.

She yanked it out, thumb trembling, screen glaring bright for a split second in the dark. She almost fumbled it because her hands were slick with cold sweat and adrenaline.

"Come on," she gasped under her breath. "Come on, come on."

Bertie sprinted ahead, a pale blur, then darted back, barking sharply as if he could tell her phone was about to betray her out of spite.

Alistair's gaze flicked to the device. He did not ask what she was doing. He did not question. He simply adjusted his position beside her, protective and steady.

Olivia yelled into the phone, call 911. The phone rang once.

Then connected. A calm voice came through, steady and professional. "Mistwood County 911, what's your emergency?"

Olivia nearly sobbed with relief. The calmness was absurdly comforting, like being handed a blanket while your house was on fire.

She gasped into the phone, whispering fast, words tumbling over each other. "I'm being chased. Deputies. Sheriff Clay Dawes. Theodore Bramble. I have evidence. I need help."

The dispatcher's voice sharpened instantly. "Ma'am, I need your location—"

Olivia didn't answer. Not because she didn't know. Because if she paused to explain where she was, she would lose distance, and distance was the only thing keeping her from being tackled into the lake.

Instead, she did something that felt both brilliant and insane. She shoved the phone back into her coat pocket. The call remained connected. Still recording. Still live. Still listening.

Alistair's mouth twitched in something like approval. "Well played," he murmured.

Olivia's brain screamed, yes, yes, yes.

Dispatch would hear everything. Bramble's orders. Clay begging her to stop. Deputies shouting. Threats. Incriminating statements. All of it. Every word carried over the lake. Every breathless command. Every panicked confession. Open-mic surveillance, whether they realized it or not.

Olivia did not need to outrun them forever. She just needed them to talk long enough to bury themselves.

The path curved, with reeds thickening on one side, docks looming on the other. Olivia's shoes hit packed dirt and then a softer patch where sand had drifted in, her foot slipping slightly.

She caught herself, almost stumbling, and her satchel swung forward, slamming into her ribs as if it were punishing her for poor balance. She kept running.

Flashlight beams swept closer behind her, and the voices got louder. Then, like the universe enjoyed dramatic timing, Carla appeared.

Carla stepped into the path ahead, blocking Olivia's escape. Not rushing. Not chasing.

Blocking.

Her face was blotchy and streaked with tears. Her hair was disheveled. Her hands shook violently, and the small metal key in her fist glinted faintly in the moonlight.

Olivia skidded to a stop, panting, chest heaving.

Carla's voice was small, terrified. "Olivia, just give it to me. Please. I can't let you go to the State Police."

Olivia's heart twisted. She could see the desperation all over Carla, the way fear had wrapped around her like barbed wire.

"Carla," Olivia said, voice shaking, trying to keep it steady, "listen to me …"

Carla cut her off, panic sharp. "If Bramble doesn't get that evidence tonight, he'll kill Clay. He'll kill me. Do you understand that?"

In Olivia's pocket, the phone was still connected. 911 heard Carla's trembling voice. The fear and, most importantly, the names. Clay. Bramble. Evidence. State police.

Olivia's mind sparked with grim satisfaction. Keep talking, Carla. Keep talking.

Behind Olivia, branches snapped. Boots pounded the dirt. Men shouted.

Bramble's voice was the closest, barking through the night like a whip crack. "Carla? Do NOT let her leave!"

911 heard that too.

Olivia stepped forward, voice low and urgent. "Carla," she said, "look at me. What you're doing right now … this is what he did to Trina."

Carla recoiled as if slapped, tears spilling.

"I didn't know!" she sobbed. "I didn't know what he was capable of!"

"You know now," Olivia said.

Carla shook harder. "If you publish what's in that will, Clay loses everything. His job, his reputation, he'll be arrested ..."

"He should be," Olivia said, the truth sharp. "He covered for a murderer."

Carla's breath hitched. "He did it to save me …"

911 heard that. Clay did it to save her. Not justice. Not the town. Her.

Olivia kept her voice pleading, pushing through Carla's fear. "Saving each other by protecting a killer isn't saving," she said. "It's drowning."

Carla's shoulders shook.

Then the men arrived, crashing into the path behind Olivia.

Clay first, red-faced, sweating, breath ragged. "Carla! Honey! Get away from her!"

Bramble behind him, calm in the way only predators were calm.

Carla flinched, torn.

Clay reached toward her.

Bramble grabbed Clay's arm and yanked him back.

911 heard Bramble's voice, cold and controlling. "Leave her. She's finally thinking straight."

Clay's voice broke, furious and scared. "This wasn't the deal."

Bramble's reply was a growl. "Life changes deals."

Clay backed up, words spilling out like panic. "We were supposed to contain her, not kill anybody …"

"You do what you're told," Bramble snapped.

911 heard every word.

Olivia could practically feel the dispatcher on the other end sitting up straighter, typing, recording, and logging.

Carla looked at Clay. Trembling, guilt-stricken.

Carla looked at Bramble. Cold, furious, controlling.

Carla looked at Olivia. Shaking, brave, clutching Izzy's satchel like a shield.

"I'm so tired of all this," Carla whispered.

Olivia held out her hand. "Then end it," she said.

Carla stepped forward, arm shaking.

"Take it," Carla whispered, pressing a key into Olivia's palm. "Please. Get this away from him. It's the key to a safe deposit box."

911 heard that, too. A safe-deposit box. Proof. Key.

Bramble roared, the calm finally gone. "Carla, NO!"

Clay shouted, voice cracking. "She's right! Stop this!"

Bramble's voice cut through like a knife. "Shut up and grab her!"

Olivia bolted. And the phone in her pocket kept recording

Behind them, Clay lunged at Bramble, shoving him back.

Deputies surged. Carla screamed. Men cursed. Flashlights swung wildly, beams bouncing off reeds, dock posts, and lake water.

Olivia ran.

She ran toward the public beach, legs pumping, nearly slipping as the path gave way to sand again. Wet sand this time, slick and uneven, a cruel joke under her feet.

Bertie raced ahead, barking ghostly warnings, darting back to urge her on.

Alistair stayed beside her, his voice sharp now, commanding. "Faster, Miss March!"

Olivia wanted to snap that she was moving as fast as her very alive legs allowed, thank you, but she didn't have breath for sarcasm. She'd save it for later, if she survived.

The biggest deputy caught her.

One second Olivia was running. Next, powerful arms wrapped around her waist and hauled her backward as if she weighed nothing.

Olivia screamed, a raw sound torn from her throat.

The satchel jerked. The key dug into her palm. She kicked and thrashed, panic making her limbs wild. In her pocket, the phone was still connected.

911 heard her scream, the scuffle, and the deputy grunting.

Clay's voice rose, frantic. "STOP! Don't hurt her! DON'T!"

Olivia kicked harder, heel slamming into something solid.

The deputy tightened his grip.

Alistair surged.

Olivia felt it like a sudden plunge into ice. The air turned sharp and cold.

Alistair passed through the deputy's chest.

The man gasped, his arms loosening as shock hit him like winter punching through his ribs.

He dropped Olivia.

She staggered forward, lungs heaving, half falling.

And then Bramble reached her.

Of course, he did.

He grabbed her coat collar and yanked her upright so hard her teeth clicked. His grip was powerful, fingers digging in, his face close enough that Olivia could smell his cologne and the bitter edge of control.

"You're done, girl," Bramble hissed. "You're done."

Olivia sobbed, breathless, fear and fury tangled together. She clawed at his hand, trying to break free, her voice cracking.

"Help," she gasped. "Someone, please—"

In her pocket, the phone captured every word.

Bramble's threat.

Olivia's plea.

Clay's frantic shouting behind.

The deputies' cursing.

All of it.

Bramble's eyes were hard, triumphant, sure he could still take what he wanted.

Then the night changed. Multiple sirens, loud, fast, and growing louder, carried on the night air.

They came from across the lake road, from town, from behind the cabins, converging on the shoreline like a net closing around them.

Clay's head snapped up.

The deputies froze, eyes widening, hands hesitating mid-motion.

Carla gasped and backed away, her face white with horror and relief.

Bramble snarled, his grip tightening on Olivia's collar. "What the …," he barked. "Who called them?!"

Olivia's chest heaved. Her hands shook. She looked up at Alistair, who stood tall beside her like a ghostly wall.

She whispered, voice barely audible, "I did. I left 911 open."

Alistair straightened, proud as any ghostly father figure could be.

Then Luke's voice erupted through the trees, furious and breathless, cutting through the sirens like a command. "BRAMBLE! LET HER GO!"

Olivia's heart jolted at the sound. Luke. Here. Close.

"State police are en route!" Luke roared. "DO NOT TOUCH HER!"

Bramble's eyes went wide.

For the first time all night, the man looked genuinely startled.

He realized too late that he had been caught. Caught by a clever, persistent pastry chef and a cell phone.

Olivia stared him down, shaking with fury, her collar still clenched in his fist, her knuckles white around the satchel strap and the tiny key that could destroy him.

"It's over," Olivia said. Her voice trembled, but the words landed like a verdict.

And the sirens kept coming.

CHAPTER TWENTY-NINE

The Standoff on the Beach

Sirens did not belong in Mistwood. Mistwood's soundtrack was supposed to be lake water lapping against old docks, wind threading through pine branches, and the occasional sound of the local wildlife.

Sirens belonged to cities. To highways. To places where danger was expected. Not here.

Not on this quiet stretch of wet sand where March House sat down the beach, its tall silhouette visible under the moon like a watchful old guardian. The house looked calm from here, lights dark, windows blank, as if it had no idea its newest owner was being held by the throat fifty yards away.

Olivia stood trembling on the wet sand, feet half sinking with each shaky breath.

Theodore Bramble's fist gripped her coat collar, knuckles white, hard enough to bruise. His other hand hovered near her satchel, hungry for it, as if he could rip truth right out of leather.

The sirens drew closer, louder, splitting the night into sharp wails. Red and blue reflections rippled across Mistwood Lake, dancing over the black surface like frantic fireworks. The narrow road that hugged the beach lit up in pulses as vehicles approached, one after another. A fire engine. An ambulance. Two Idaho State Police cruisers.

Olivia's stomach lurched at the sight, relief and terror colliding in her chest. Help was coming. The cavalry was here. Help was also the thing Bramble feared most, which meant he might do something truly stupid.

Bramble's fingers tightened painfully around her collar. "What did you do?" he hissed, low and furious.

Olivia's breath came ragged, her voice shaking, but she forced herself to meet his eyes. "I called for help," she said.

It was not a clever line. It was not snarky. It was simply the truth.

Beside her, Alistair stood tall in ghostly form, a spectral Georgian gentleman with excellent tailoring. His face was grave, his outline shining faintly in the moonlight that did not quite belong to him. He could not touch her. He could not shove Bramble away. He could not wrench Bramble's hand off her coat. But he could stand there, calm and unbreakable, like a pillar in a storm. "Take heart, Miss March," Alistair murmured, voice soft as a vow. "The tide has turned."

Olivia swallowed hard. She believed him. She had to.

Bertie hovered close to her feet, flickering like pale smoke, whimpering ghost-soft. The sound made Olivia's throat tighten. Even dead dogs understood fear.

The cruisers screeched to a stop on the road above the beach. Doors flew open. Floodlights snapped on, bright beams slashing across the sand. Trooper #1's voice boomed across the night. "IDAHO STATE POLICE! EVERYONE STAY WHERE YOU ARE!"

The welcome sound of a direct commandment.

Bramble jerked Olivia closer, his body tensing, panic flashing behind his rage.

"Back off!" Bramble shouted. "BACK OFF!"

The troopers stopped, but they did not retreat. They stayed focused, hands near their holsters, shoulders squared, their floodlights fixed on Bramble's grip on Olivia as if it was the center of the universe.

Behind them, the fire engine blocked the road. Firefighters spilled out, scanning the scene, alert and ready. The sort of men and women who ran toward danger because they were built differently than the rest of humanity.

The ambulance lights pulsed too, a reminder that this might not end cleanly.

Olivia's knees wobbled.

Bramble's grip kept her upright.

Clay stumbled onto the beach seconds later, breathless, frantic, sweating through his uniform like he had run from his own soul and lost. His face was red. His eyes wild. His breath came in harsh bursts.

He saw Olivia in Bramble's grip, and something in him cracked. "Let her go, Theo!" Clay's voice broke on the last word. "This wasn't … this wasn't the plan!"

Bramble snarled, his face twisting with rage. "There IS no plan anymore!"

Clay looked like he might collapse.

Olivia's heart hammered. Bramble was cornered. Clay was panicking. Troopers were watching. Firefighters were watching. The whole town might as well have been watching, because Mistwood loved a spectacle almost as much as it loved secrets.

And in the middle of it, Olivia was stuck in Bramble's fist, her satchel pressed between them like a hostage.

Then Carla appeared. Carla ran down the slope toward the beach, still shaking, clutching her arms as if she could hold herself together by sheer force. Her hair was wind-tangled. Her face streaked with tears. She looked like someone who had been dragged through a nightmare and finally stopped running inside her own head. Her voice ripped through the night, loud and raw.

"He murdered Trina Bell!"

Bertie whined beside her, flickering harder, his ghostly form trembling in sympathy.

Carla sobbed harder, words tumbling out. "There's proof in the safe deposit box!" Carla cried. "Bramble killed her! He threatened us. He threatened my husband. He—"

Bramble whipped his head toward Carla, his face contorting, eyes burning with rage.

"You STUPID woman …" he barked.

Clay stepped between them, shaking violently, his hands raised as if he could block Bramble with his own body. "Don't you touch my wife." His voice was a gravel scrape of fear and fury. Something shifted. It was not redemption. Not yet. But it was the first time Clay sounded like he might choose Carla over Bramble.

Bramble's grip tightened around Olivia's collar again, dragging her focus back to him.

Trooper #2 stepped forward cautiously, voice controlled. "Sir, put your hands where we can see them—"

Bramble did not. He moved. Fast. He yanked Olivia closer, his arm hooking around her like a leash, and reached toward her satchel with his free hand, fingers clawing for the zipper like he could tear the evidence out in one violent motion.

Olivia's heart seized. This was it. This was the stupid move. This was the moment when he decided that if he could not own the truth, he would destroy it.

And then Luke appeared behind him. No shouting. No warning. Just speed and fury. Luke slammed into Bramble from behind with a football tackle hard enough to knock the wind out of both men.

Bramble went down like a tree cut at the base. He hit the sand face-first with a dull thud.

Olivia staggered free, her coat collar yanked loose, her body stumbling forward as the pressure vanished. Her knees buckled. She fell to the sand, catching herself with shaking hands.

Her satchel stayed strapped across her body. Thank God. She clutched it to her chest, desperate, protective, like it was her own heart.

Luke rolled with Bramble, pinning him down. Still no shouting. Just grim efficiency. Luke's whole body moved with trained precision and rage held in tight control.

Alistair stood beside Olivia, unable to touch, but his presence radiated relief like warmth.

"Bravo, young man," Alistair murmured.

Bertie darted frantic circles around Olivia, a pale blur of panic and loyalty.

The troopers sprinted in immediately.

Trooper #1 barked, "Hands behind your back! NOW!"

Bramble sputtered sand, twisting like a trapped animal. "You can't arrest me! You don't know what's—"

Click. Handcuffs snapped shut.

Trooper #2 dragged Bramble upright while he thrashed and spat, sand spraying. "You are under arrest for assault, attempted kidnapping, obstruction," Trooper #2 said, voice flat and unimpressed, "and anything else that falls out of this mess."

Bramble roared, veins standing out in his neck. "YOU'RE ALL DEAD! YOU HEAR ME? DEAD!"

Trooper #1 gave him a look that could have frozen the lake. "Great, making threats while in custody. That'll help."

They shoved Bramble into a cruiser. The door slammed. The sound was final.

For a single beat, silence fell like a blanket. Even the sirens seemed to fade behind the moment.

Olivia stared at the cruiser door, her whole body shaking, her breath coming in ragged bursts. It was over. He was locked in metal and glass. He could not touch her. He could not take the satchel. He could not erase what Izzy had hidden.

Olivia's vision blurred. Then Luke was there. Luke did not check in with anyone else. He did not look at Clay, or Carla, or any of the other people present. He ran straight to Olivia and dropped to his knees in the sand in front of her, breathless, hands open like he was afraid to touch her without permission. His eyes were wide, frantic, and focused entirely on her face. "Olivia," he said, voice thick. "Olivia, are you hurt?"

She shook her head. The motion made her dizzy. Then she collapsed forward into his arms, shaking so hard she could barely breathe. Her forehead hit his shoulder. Her hands clutched his jacket as if it was the only solid thing left in the world.

"I thought," she sobbed, words breaking apart, "I thought he was going to kill me ..."

Luke wrapped his arms around her, holding her tight. A steady comfort and a safe harbor in the storm. His voice was low, fierce, steady. "I've got you. I've got you, Livvy. You're safe."

The nickname hit Olivia's chest like warmth. Safe. She clung to him, shaking, feeling his heartbeat under his jacket, solid and real.

Luke did not flinch. He did not let go. He just held her, breathing with her until her lungs remembered how to work.

Luke did not see Alistair watching them with quiet pride. He did not see Bertie curling ghostlike at Olivia's feet, the little whippet's form flickering softer now, comfort instead of panic.

But Olivia did. And it steadied her, like her ghosts were bracing her from one side while Luke braced her from the other.

March House stood down the beach, visible in the moonlight, its silhouette calm and tall, watching as if it had been waiting for this moment for a very long time.

~

Clay broke. It did not happen in a dramatic, cinematic collapse. It happened in small pieces, like his spine had been holding up a lie for too long and finally cracked under the weight.

Carla sank into the sand, sobbing, her shoulders convulsing. Her hands clutched at her sleeves, trying to hold herself together.

Clay stumbled toward her and dropped to his knees beside her, completely undone. His face crumpled. His eyes shone with tears he did not bother to hide. "I should've stopped him," Clay choked. "I should've protected you."

Carla let out a sound that was half sob, half laugh, half something broken. "You protected me," she cried. "You protected me, and you let him … you let him …" Her words collapsed into sobs again.

A trooper stepped closer, watching, listening, assessing. The air around Clay and Carla felt thick and heavy with consequences.

Carla's eyes flicked toward Olivia, toward the satchel strapped across her body, toward the key clenched in Olivia's fist. Her face twisted with shame. "Trina didn't run away," Carla whispered, voice raw. "She didn't. He … he killed her."

Olivia's stomach clenched all over again. Now there was only the cold, hard truth settling into place.

Luke's arms tightened around Olivia for a second, as if he felt the tremor in her body.

Olivia swallowed, forcing herself to breathe. Evidence preserved. Bramble arrested. She lifted her head slightly from

Luke's shoulder, eyes stinging, voice hoarse. "It's going to be okay," she whispered, not sure who she was saying it to.

Alistair's voice murmured beside her, gentle and grave. "Justice arrives slowly, Miss March. But it arrives."

Olivia closed her eyes. For the first time since she inherited a haunted bed-and-breakfast in this cursed town, she believed it.

CHAPTER THIRTY

The Morning After

Dawn over Mistwood Lake looked like the world was trying to apologize. The light came in soft and gold, spilling across the water in gentle bands, turning the lake into something almost harmless. The ripples glittered as if the surface had never held secrets. As if it had never been the edge of a nightmare. As if it had never reflected headlights and flashlights and the furious, frightened faces of men who thought they could keep the truth buried forever.

Olivia woke up to the light. She woke up to the smell of old wood and faint lavender. To the quiet creak of March House settling around her like a living thing exhaling. To warmth and weight on her feet.

Snowball. The cat was curled against her ankles like a fluffy ankle monitor, her purr vibrating faintly into Olivia's sore bones. Olivia sat up slowly on the couch in the front parlor, blinking into the morning, her body aching in places she did not remember owning. She had not meant to fall asleep here. She had only intended to sit for a moment after the longest night of her life, to let her heart stop trying to escape her chest, to let her brain reboot from "kidnapping attempt" to "basic human function."

But Lark had wrapped her in a blanket. And Snowball had decided Olivia was not allowed to move without permission.

Olivia's body, finally realizing she was not actively being attacked, had shut down like a phone at one percent battery.

Olivia pushed herself upright, wincing. Everything hurt. Even her dignity. She rubbed her face with both hands and stared at the lake through the parlor window. The morning sun made the water look calm enough to swim in. Which was rude. The lake, she decided, owed her at least a decade of calm. Then she noticed she was not alone.

Alistair stood near the window, translucent in the morning light, his form faintly gilded by the sun. He looked as composed as ever, walking stick tucked under one arm, posture noble, expression grave. He bowed lightly. "Good morning, Miss March. The house is quite relieved to have you still in one piece."

Bertie lifted his ghostly head from where he hovered near the rug, his tail giving a soft, silent wag. He looked sleepy and proud at the same time, which was a deeply unfair combination.

Olivia managed a small smile, the kind that felt like it had to travel a long distance to reach her face. "I'm relieved too," she said.

Snowball opened one eye, blinked slowly, and then closed it again, clearly satisfied that Olivia had not died overnight, then stretched and hopped onto the floor.

Olivia swung her legs off the couch and immediately regretted it. Her muscles protested.

Her ribs protested. The area where the coat collar had rubbed viciously protested loudly. She took a breath. "Okay," she muttered. "We are going to stand up like normal people. We are going to walk. We are not going to fall on our face in front of the ghost aristocrat."

Alistair's mouth twitched, as if he were politely pretending not to hear her coaching herself like a toddler.

Olivia stood up carefully. She did not fall. She counted that as a victory worthy of a medal. The blanket slipped from her shoulders. The air felt cool, but not threatening. March House felt quieter than it had in days, as if the walls themselves had finally unclenched.

Last night had been chaos. This morning felt like the first calm breath after a storm.

Then footsteps sounded in the hallway, and the scent of tea drifted toward her.

Lark entered carrying two steaming mugs, her hair piled in a messy knot, her eyes bright with exhaustion and triumph.

"You're up," Lark said. "Good. Drink. Now."

Olivia took the mug with shaking hands. The heat seeped into her fingers like life returning. "What is it?" Olivia asked, voice hoarse, "And will it make me forget I was almost kidnapped on a beach?"

Lark's smile was sharp. "It's tea. And no. But it will keep you from turning into a haunted raisin."

Olivia sipped. The tea tasted of herbs and warmth, and someone trying very hard to keep her upright.

Lark sank into a chair, then immediately stood up again, as if sitting still offended her. She paced two steps, then leaned against the doorway, mug in hand.

"The state troopers went through everything until about four a.m.," Lark said. "Everything. The satchel, the will, the journal, the bank papers, the missing person report. If Izzy wrote it down, they photographed it."

Olivia's chest tightened at the mention of the satchel. She glanced instinctively toward the side table where it sat. Izzy's old leather satchel looked ordinary now, like it wasn't the reason a developer was wearing handcuffs.

Lark continued, voice steady. "Clay resigned on the spot."

Olivia blinked. "He did?"

Lark nodded. "In front of everybody. Troopers. Firefighters. Carla. The entire lakefront. His face looked like it had aged ten years in ten seconds."

Olivia swallowed hard. Clay stepping down did not undo what he had done, but it meant the town could finally stop pretending he was a lawman.

Lark took a sip of her tea, then shrugged. "Carla's cooperating."

Olivia's shoulders sagged with relief. "Good."

"And Bramble," Lark said, making a little dismissive flick with her fingers, "well."

She shrugged again. "He was still screaming about conspiracies when they drove him off."

Olivia let out a slow exhale. It's over. Not everything, but the worst of it.

Lark lifted her mug and pointed it at Olivia like a wand. "Oh, and your 911 call? Dispatch said it's the cleanest evidence they've ever heard from a civilian."

Olivia stared. "Seriously?"

Lark nodded solemnly. "Apparently, you provided a full audio documentary of corruption, attempted kidnapping, and one furious developer losing his mind on a beach."

Olivia laughed. It surprised her. The sound bubbled up as if it had been trapped in her throat since last night. It came out shaky but real. "I guess pastry chefs can do sleuthing in a pinch," Olivia said.

Lark snorted. "You've got the weirdest resume."

Olivia took another sip of tea, warmth spreading through her chest. "At least I'm versatile."

Alistair's voice murmured from the window, dry as dust. "Versatile is one word for it."

Olivia glanced at him. "Do not judge me, sir. I'm doing my best."

Alistair bowed slightly, as if granting her permission to continue existing.

Snowball yawned and stretched as if she had personally defeated Bramble.

Then there was a knock at the front door.

Olivia's whole body stiffened. Her pulse jumped. The night's fear was still close enough to taste.

Lark's eyes sharpened, and she set her mug down with deliberate calm. "I'll get it."

Olivia shook her head quickly. "No." She forced herself to breathe, to uncoil her fingers, to let the morning in. "I'll get it," Olivia said. She walked to the door, each step careful, as if the house might suddenly turn into a battlefield again. She opened it.

Luke Thatcher stood on the porch. He looked beaten-up, exhausted, and somehow still annoyingly handsome in that grumpy-deputy way that made Olivia's stomach do a small, inconvenient flip.

His hair was slightly mussed. His eyes were shadowed. There was a bruise blooming along one jawline, and his knuckles looked scraped, like sand had tried to fight him and lost.

He held his hat in his hands, posture respectful, shoulders tense but contained. His voice was soft when he spoke. "Morning. Wanted to check on you."

Olivia blinked at him, warmth spreading through her chest that had nothing to do with tea.

"Luke," she said, voice gentler than she intended, "are you okay?"

He gave her a crooked smile and a small shrug. His body currently suffered from the memory of last night's tackle in every joint. "I'll live," Luke said. "That tackle of Bramble felt good, though."

Olivia smiled despite herself. "You tackled him like you've been waiting your whole life."

Luke's eyes flicked to her face, a brief flash of something like relief. "I might have been."

Olivia stepped aside to let him in.

Luke crossed the threshold, boots quiet on the hardwood. The air between them held that strange mix of comfort and awkwardness that came after surviving something together.

He glanced around the parlor, then at Olivia, as if confirming she was truly upright and breathing.

Lark appeared behind Olivia, arms crossed, watching Luke as if she was trying to decide if he deserved to be indoors.

Luke's gaze shifted to Lark, then back to Olivia. "But," Luke said, voice turning serious, "I thought you should know. The real will? The county clerk already ran the signature. It's legit."

Olivia's throat tightened so fast she almost choked.She stared at him, her brain trying to process the words. Legit. Real. Valid. "So March House …" she whispered.

Luke nodded, voice quiet. "Is yours."

Olivia's hand drifted to her chest, fingers pressing over her heart like she could hold herself together that way. Emotion surged up, hot and sudden, not just relief but grief and gratitude and a deep ache. Izzy had chosen her, protected her, and left her a future.

Luke's voice softened, and his expression gentled in a way that made Olivia's knees want to betray her. "It always was," Luke said.

Olivia swallowed hard. Her eyes stung. She did not cry. Not yet. She'd done enough of that last night. But the tears hovered.

Luke stepped closer, voice gentler still. "State Police have officially reopened Trina Bell's case," Luke said. "They think Bramble buried her out by the old resort development. Ground-penetrating radar is coming in today."

Olivia's stomach twisted. The words were ugly, but they were real. They were official. They were the beginning of justice.

Luke continued, listing facts as if he were building a ladder out of the horror. "The deputies involved have been suspended. Clay has agreed to a full statement."

Olivia swallowed hard. Carla's words echoed in her head. Proof that Trina Bell was murdered.

"Izzy tried to tell them," Olivia whispered.

Luke nodded. "And now they'll listen."

Something loosened inside Olivia's chest, a knot finally untying after years of being pulled tight. Hope. Relief. Peace, fragile but real.

Luke shifted, looking awkward for the first time since Olivia had met him. It was almost endearing. He had been built for tackling villains, but not for emotional conversations. "I just …" Luke cleared his throat. "I'm glad you're safe, Olivia."

Olivia's chest warmed in a way that startled her. "Because you got to me in time," she whispered.

Luke's ears went slightly red, which was, frankly, rude. How was he allowed to be both grumpy and blushy? He cleared his throat again, like it was a stubborn engine. "I'll let you rest," he said. "You've had … a night."

Olivia huffed a tiny laugh. "That's one way to put it."

Luke paused at the doorway, hand on the frame.

"And Olivia," Luke said, voice low, "if you ever need me. Day or night. Just call."

Olivia nodded, throat tight. "I will."

Luke held her gaze for one long beat, then stepped out onto the porch and down the steps, heading to his car.

Olivia watched him go until he drove away. Only then did she finally exhale.

The instant Luke was gone, Olivia felt the shift. A gentle dip in temperature. The softest ripple in the air. Like the house itself had been holding its breath while Luke was inside, and finally released it once he left. Her ghosts returned. Not in a dramatic burst. Not in a chaotic swirl. In quiet. They gathered in a cluster like a family returning after a long, hard night.

JJ appeared at the hall archway, silent but shimmering, cornet resting at his side.

Walt leaned against a coat hook, arms crossed, his expression set in grumpy satisfaction.

Flossie fluttered near the stair rail, eyes bright with emotion.

Daisy stood close, hands clasped, giving Olivia a relieved, brief nod.

Monique draped herself dramatically over a chair, as if exhaustion were an accessory.

Simon stood straight near the doorway, hand at his ghostly cap.

Bertie curled near Olivia's feet, tail wagging softly.

Alistair stood tall and dignified, walking stick tucked under his arm, his face grave and proud.

They gathered without words. Just presence. Just relief. Olivia's eyes stung. The emotion she'd held back threatened to spill now that she was surrounded by the only witnesses who fully understood what last night had cost.

"We did it," Olivia said softly. "All of us."

JJ gave a single celebratory toot, quiet but triumphant.

Flossie dabbed her eyes.

Monique sighed theatrically. Even justice was exhausting.

Walt muttered something that sounded suspiciously like approval. "Took long enough."

Daisy glowed faintly.

Simon gave a solemn nod.

Bertie wagged his ghost-tail harder.

Alistair bowed, his voice quiet and certain. "Your aunt would be proud, Miss March."

Olivia pressed her hand to her heart. "I hope so."

The house felt alive again. Not haunted. Not threatening. Alive! It had been waiting for someone to finally fight for it.

Lark leaned against the doorway, arms crossed, watching Olivia with that soft, fierce look she got when she cared too much. "So," Lark said. "Boss lady. You staying?"

Olivia looked out over March House's lawn, at the light shining through the stained-glass windows in the morning sun. The world looked calmer, but she knew better now. She knew what lived beneath calm surfaces. And still. Her decision was clear. "I'm staying," Olivia said.

Lark's eyebrows lifted slightly. She'd known, but still needed to hear it.

"And I'm opening that coffee shop," Olivia added, voice firm.

From the hallway, Walt muttered, "'Bout time."

Olivia laughed, the sound lighter this time.

The house felt hopeful. Ready. So was she.

Olivia stepped onto the porch, the morning air cool against her cheeks. She looked toward the lake, toward the gold light on the water, toward the quiet stretch of beach where last night had tried to break her. She whispered into the breeze, voice soft and sure. "I'm home, Izzy."

A soft, warm pulse of air brushed her cheek, like a gentle hand that could not touch but could still comfort. Olivia closed her eyes. Her life had a new beginning. With an old bed-and-breakfast full of ghosts and a woman who had finally decided to stay.

Olivia March wants nothing more than a quiet escape for a few days from her haunted bed-and-breakfast and coffee shop, so when she's invited to NorthStar Summit ski lodge for a business networking meeting, she jumps at the chance. But peace is short-lived. A beloved teacher turns up dead, and Olivia's discovery of a ghostly skier tied to a decades-old disappearance proves Mistwood's past is far from buried. Coming May 26, 2026. It is currently available for pre-order.

Join my newsletter and stay up-to-date on upcoming releases and sales. You will also learn fun and interesting things about Mistwood, along with sneak peeks of future stories, background information, and special insights into my unique characters.

Newsletter: https://augustinavanhoven.com/join-newsletter/

www.ingramcontent.com/pod-product-compliance
Lightning Source LLC
LaVergne TN
LVHW010055110826
845155LV00028B/351

9781951534387